He clutched the towel closer to his body. "I have to put some clothes on."

"You're fine, but if *you* would be more comfortable…" Mischief danced in her eyes.

He'd thought no woman could stomach what had happened to his body, the scars left by remnants of a rocket. But then Jenny had experienced combat herself even if she'd been an observer rather than participant. Maybe the wound *made* her a participant.

Still, he couldn't believe that any woman would actually be comfortable with the scars.

As if reading his thoughts, Jenny touched his chest and ran a finger down it, arousing all sorts of reactions. "You have great muscles and all the important stuff," she said as she continued to study him. "I like your face a lot, too," she added with a grin.

Damn, but she knew how to get inside his head. "Are you finished with your survey?"

"I'm getting there," she said. "I have a few scars of my own, you know."

Dear Reader,

I usually start a book by living with the hero and heroine for a month or more before starting a manuscript. After that, the story is up to them, and it rarely turns out the way I first envisioned. Any resemblance to the original idea is purely coincidental.

So it was with this book. The characters just didn't want to do what I originally thought they would do. Travis, a Special Forces major, objected to being wounded in spirit as well as body. Jenny, a war correspondent who was wounded while covering a story, turned out to be equally stubborn. I never knew what she was going to do or say next.

The book has a special place in my heart. In the past, I've tried not to put myself in a book, but I failed this time. Jenny has a lot of me in her. She is a reporter (which was my original career), and I know the type well. Unbridled curiosity is the reporter's—and writer's—most valuable asset. Jenny takes this quality to the extreme. She wants to know everything about everyone, which can be quite annoying. And then the story she's chasing is always more important than anything else, including relationships.

In *The Soldier's Homecoming*, I turned her loose on an unsuspecting cast of characters and watched her change others as well as herself. I hope you like her as much as I enjoyed bringing her to life.

And this time I'm also sharing my newly adopted elderly citizen rescue dog, Anna, with you. Like Anna in the book, it was love at first sight.

Patricia Potter

PATRICIA POTTER

The Soldier's Homecoming

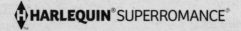

HARLEQUIN® SUPERROMANCE®

Recycling programs
for this product may
not exist in your area.

ISBN-13: 978-1-335-44921-4

The Soldier's Homecoming

Printed in U.S.A.

USA TODAY bestselling author **Patricia Potter** has been telling stories since the second grade when she wrote a short story about wild horses, although she knew nothing at all about them. She has since received numerous writing awards, including *RT Book Reviews'* Storyteller of the Year, its Career Achievement Award for Western Historical Romance and Best Hero of the Year. She is a seven-time RITA® Award finalist for RWA and a three-time Maggie Award winner, as well as a past president of Romance Writers of America. Character motivation is what intrigues her most in creating a book, and she sits back and allows those characters to write their own stories.

Books by Patricia Potter

**HARLEQUIN
SUPERROMANCE**

Home to Covenant Falls
The Soldier's Promise
Tempted by the Soldier
A Soldier's Journey
The SEAL's Return

HARLEQUIN BLAZE

The Lawman

**HARLEQUIN
HISTORICAL**

Swampfire
Between the Thunder
Samara
Seize the Fire
Chase the Thunder
Dragonfire
The Silver Link
The Abduction

Visit the Author Profile page at Harlequin.com for more titles.

This book is dedicated to the men and women who better the lives of veterans through many Horses for Heroes programs throughout the country.

PROLOGUE

Aleppo, Syria

JENNY TALBOT KNEW she was in trouble the moment she heard the sound of approaching aircraft.

The sound grew thunderous as four planes appeared in the sky over Aleppo, leaving a trail of explosions in their wake. They were heading straight at her.

A cease-fire was supposed to have been declared while volunteer medical personnel tended the wounded in one of the few remaining makeshift hospitals in the doomed Syrian city.

The volunteer doctors and nurses, who had just arrived in a marked medical convoy, scattered, seeking cover. She and Rick Cowan, also a freelance journalist, were accompanying them. Although they worked for different news services, they had been together when they heard about the medical mission to Aleppo. It hadn't been easy to get permission from the supporting agency, but the promise of alerting the world to conditions in a city caught in the cross fire of three ruthless armies finally won them approval. It was emphasized that it was at their own risk.

So much for cease-fires.

As explosions grew louder, Jenny and Rick ran for cover with Ali, their driver and translator. All three ducked behind a pile of rubble that had once been a house.

Jenny instinctively grabbed the camera that hung around her neck and under the hijab she wore to cover her flaming red hair. Out of habit, she took several rapid shots of people fleeing among burning buildings and vehicles. She wanted proof of the violation of the cease fire.

Ali turned to them. "I go get jeep," he shouted over the noise, then sprinted around the rubble. Jenny regretted now that he'd hid the jeep several blocks down to avoid thieves.

A little girl suddenly ran into the road, screaming as another explosion threw rocks and flaming shrapnel in every direction. The girl fell, her arms reaching out as if for help. Jenny saw bright red blood flow from the child's leg.

A doctor turned back toward her but he was too far away. Jenny instinctively rose from her position and started to climb over the rubble to go after the child. Rick pulled her down. "Stay here, dammit," he said. "I'll go."

As he started to scramble over the rubble, she

followed. Another group of planes roared over them, raining more fire on the street. Explosions deafened her. Chunks of flaming metal flew through the air. Two cars and an ambulance used by the doctors burst into flames. She struggled to the top of the debris. Dust and smoke was everywhere. She couldn't see the child.

"We've got to find her," she said to Rick. A trailing plane came in low and dropped its munitions. The building across the street sustained a direct hit and started to crumple.

"I have to find the girl," she shouted to Rick.

"You'll be killed out there," Rick shouted and pushed her down. "Nothing can survive out there right now. They're pounding that street."

She huddled against the rubble as heat seared her, gluing her tan T-shirt to her body. She wore a flak vest over the T-shirt and BDU pants, which she had selected for the additional pockets. The pockets were filled with everything she needed to do her job, from cell phone, notebooks and pens to a small recorder.

"The hospital?" she asked Rick, just as another explosion tore up the wreckage, only a few yards from them. The heat burned her arm, and the impact threw her back against a pile of debris. Her shoulder felt on fire, the skin burning. She looked down at her shoulder to see metal protruding from a jagged wound. She stared at it for a moment, and then the pain hit.

Rick uttered a curse as he scooted over to her to study the wound. "I'm afraid if I remove it, you'll bleed out," he said. "I'll try to get one of the doctors. Ali should be back here with the jeep."

He bolted over what was now a wall of broken cement, and she clenched her teeth to stop from moving, from crying out. The pain grew worse. She could smell her own burned skin.

She couldn't tell how large the piece of shrapnel was inside, but she knew that the medical people, if they were still alive, were going to be busy with wounds worse than this.

She also knew they couldn't stay here. Syrian troops or ISIS fighters often followed the planes, killing those the planes missed.

She didn't know how long Rick was gone. It seemed like hours before he appeared over the wall. "They can't come," he said. "Three of them are wounded, and the others are busy trying to keep all the civilians alive. They're afraid soldiers will follow the bombs."

"The little girl?"

"I don't know. I didn't see her on the street and it was too crowded in the hospital. Right now, we have to get you out of here."

He didn't have to explain more. She knew what might await her as an American woman.

"They gave me some pills, burn salve and pressure bandages," he said. "I was told to get you to a refugee camp as fast as possible. I found Ali. He and the jeep are pretty close." He hesitated, and then he added, "I have to pull that piece of metal out. The jolting in the jeep could do even more damage."

Jenny understood. She'd been under fire before. She knew the risks.

"Do you think you can walk if I help? I can take out that shrapnel when we get to the jeep."

She nodded. She had to. There was no way Rick could carry her any distance. He didn't weigh much more than she did.

He handed her a canteen and several pills. Painkillers and antibiotics, she assumed. After she swallowed them, he helped her to her feet. She barely made it. The rocks and ruined buildings were going in and out of focus. One step, and then another. *You have to do this.*

No one paid attention to them as they stumbled through debris toward the jeep. It took every ounce of Jenny's strength to put one foot ahead of the other as pain coursed through her, growing stronger by the minute. Only Rick's steady arm kept her upright.

She was beyond grateful when she saw Ali

and the jeep. But she didn't say anything. She couldn't. It was all she could do to stay upright. A few more steps. Gunshots. Behind them.

Everything dimmed…

CHAPTER ONE

Walter Reed Hospital Rehabilitation Unit

LIFE WILL NEVER *be the same.*

Major Travis Hammond leaned on his crutches and watched a young corporal take halting steps on a new prosthesis that substituted for a right leg. Danny Ware's face was contorted with determination as he tried to walk without hanging onto the bars.

In the months they'd shared these rehab facilities, along with other wounded soldiers, Travis had grown fond of Danny. Maybe because of the kid's unfailing optimism despite getting a really bad deal. He reminded Travis of his brother.

Danny was a foster kid, and the army had been one of the few options he'd had after finishing high school. But now that option was gone. Danny hadn't been able to save much money on an enlisted man's pay, and Travis knew it would take months before his disability pay arrived. Travis had seen the fear and uncertainty when the kid thought no one was watching, but a "what the hell" grin would usually spread across his face if he caught eyes on him.

The military rehab facility was, as usual, full, with both new patients and those returning for additional surgeries. It had become a second home to Travis after two years and multiple surgeries. But now there were only a few days left before he was released.

He would miss the other soldiers. They shared the pain. And the fear, though it was unspoken. Always unspoken. The future, which had been so clear before, was now a fog. He felt lost, and he knew that others felt the same uncertainty.

For most of them, life as they knew it would never be the same. There were the nightmares. The survivor's guilt. The loss of a tight-knit family. Those were things that could never be understood by someone who hadn't experienced them.

He turned his attention back to Danny Ware. He'd admired the kid's grit as he had strengthened his arms and walked on one leg and crutches, while a prosthesis was still being constructed. Now it had finally arrived, and Danny was taking his first awkward steps.

It was difficult to cheer anything at the moment, but the grin on the younger man's face as, on his third attempt, he took twenty steps without touching the bars, helped him forget his own problems. If Danny could conquer his demons, then certainly Travis could, as well. Or should.

The simple fact was inertia had overtaken him. Having undergone five operations—three on his right leg and foot and two on his hand— he was left with a leg that would never work right and a hand missing two fingers, not to mention numerous scars across his body. It meant the end of his career as an active member in the Special Forces. Desk job? Possibly. But it wasn't a sure thing, and it was not particularly appealing.

And his love life. Nonexistent since his fiancé had taken one look at him and blanched. It hadn't helped that she was a television reporter in Georgia, and he was in Washington. Dinah had tried, but her visits to the military hospital grew less frequent over time, and he understood that he was no longer what she wanted as a husband. He was the one who ended the engagement. Her protest was feeble at best, and he knew he'd made the right decision…

Still, it had hurt. But he couldn't blame her. He turned his attention back to Danny, who made a victory sign with his fingers. Then the kid started to fall.

The physical therapist caught him and eased him into a wheelchair. Tears of frustration leaked from his eyes.

Travis knew that frustration. He'd never again be the athlete he once was, but at least he had resources. Danny didn't. He ached for the boy.

"I want to try again," Danny said.

"Not today," Kate, the physical therapist, said. "You did great, but you don't want to overdo it."

She confirmed the next appointment, and then she turned to Travis. "Ready, Major Hammond?"

He hesitated, and then he limped over to Danny. "You did damn good," he said.

"Thanks, Major," Danny said, his face brightening.

Travis wanted to continue, but anything more might be construed as pity. He turned to the therapist. "Only a few sessions to go," he responded. After the last of his surgeries, he'd finally succeeded in wiggling his toes on his right foot. He'd never thought wiggling a toe could be a major achievement.

After the last operation, his surgeon urged him to do just that with toes peeking out from a cast. Some patients were never able to move their foot, he explained. Travis had spent days and nights staring at his damn toes, willing them to move. It was momentous when they did. It meant he wouldn't have to walk with a brace.

"I'm hurt when my patients are so anxious to leave me," Kate said with a grin.

"I doubt that," he said. "We're a motley lot."

The smile widened. "I *will* miss you—and Danny, too." Kate replied. "You've been good for him. He really looks up to you."

"I like him," he said simply.

"Well, today is *your* big day," she said. "We walk without the brace." It was always *we*, not *you*. He was amazed at her ability to remain cheerful. She had coaxed, badgered and cajoled him when he got frustrated. She had celebrated with him at hearing about the great toe awakening. She was his tormentor and savior.

She helped him take off the brace and watched him as he stood.

"You don't want to put too much weight on it yet," she said, studying him as he took several steps.

"You've practiced," she accused him.

"How can you tell?" For the past several nights, he had taken off the brace and walked with the crutches only.

"Too much confidence. What if you'd fallen and twisted it?"

"I didn't."

Kate just shook her head. "Okay, cowboy. Let's see you climb the stairs."

As the doctor warned, his foot had limited up-and-down movement, but it was still part of his body, and for that he was thankful. The stairs were just six steps up, with railings on both sides and a platform at the top. He walked haltingly to the bottom. Then she took the crutches, and he grabbed the railings.

"Good," she said. "The main thing now is not to get overconfident and overdo it. Until you get used to how much movement you have in that ankle and foot, you could trip."

They spent the rest of the hour on exercises, first for his leg and then for his hand. When they finished, he wanted to throw away the brace for good.

"Don't get ahead of yourself, Major. Keep your walks short for now. Use the crutches until you feel comfortable." Kate reached into the pocket of her uniform and pulled out an envelope. "I was asked to give this to you," she said.

He took it gingerly and opened it. There was one sheet of paper enclosed, and it contained only a name and phone number.

The name stopped him. Memories flooded back. He looked up. "Where did this come from?"

"My boss gave it to me. He said it came from a psychologist at Fort Hood. An admirer, perhaps?" Kate, a lean, attractive woman in her forties, grinned at him. It was no come-on. She openly talked of her husband in a way that left no doubt she was madly in love with him.

"Doubt that, since he was my best staff sergeant."

"Well, it must be important to come down this way." She left him before he could ask more questions.

Josh Manning.

It had been nearly two years since Travis heard that name. Josh Manning was the best staff sergeant he'd ever had. Ironically, he was wounded one month before Travis. Manning's injuries, in fact, were the reason Travis had been in Afghanistan to check on the Rangers who were training and working with their Afghanistan counterparts.

He punched in the number.

"Manning," the former staff sergeant said in his usual no-nonsense manner.

"How did you find me?" Travis asked without a greeting.

"I didn't. A psychologist at Fort Hood did. I'd heard you'd been wounded and asked him for help. It's hell trying to get information from the army. He asked his colleagues at other hospitals. I learned you're about to be released."

Why in the hell would Josh Manning track him down? No one else had. "Still cutting corners, Sergeant?" he asked.

"I had a good instructor," Josh retorted.

Travis got down to business. "If you went to all that trouble, I assume you had a reason."

He heard Manning chuckle. It surprised him. He couldn't remember the man even smiling much before. But then Manning surprised him even more with his next words. "Are you staying in the service? If not, I need you."

I need you. Hell, it was the first time in nearly two years he'd heard those words. It was especially surprising from Manning, who'd never admitted to needing anything, except maybe better equipment.

"Not sure," Travis replied. "I have three months' medical leave coming. There could be a staff job available but…"

His voice trailed off.

"Maybe my offer will help," Manning said.

Travis couldn't imagine how, but he'd never known Manning to waste time or words. Manning had been the most competent noncom who'd served under him.

They had become friends during the ten years they had worked together, both moving up the military ladder. When they first met, Sergeant Manning was a squad leader, and Travis was a lieutenant. Travis made sure Manning stayed with him. He'd been his go-to guy in the most difficult and dangerous missions. He not only thought strategically, but his fellow soldiers would follow him to hell and back.

Travis realized he'd been silent for more than a few seconds. "How?" he asked dubiously.

"I remember you telling me you were a college athlete and studied sports management in Indiana. That included business, didn't it?"

"Some," Travis admitted.

"A friend of mine, a former navy SEAL—yeah, I know, strange friend for a Ranger—just bought a small ranch where I live. He's thinking about starting a horse therapy program for vets. He's knee deep in getting it started and needs help with the business aspects, particularly possible grants, regulations, staffing…"

"Why me?"

"Because I know how you cared about your men. The job needs someone who would be committed as well as having some knowledge of athletics and business."

It definitely sounded interesting, particularly Manning's participation, but he wasn't qualified. "I don't get it," he said. "I don't know anything about grants."

"But you know about physical therapy and organization. I also remember how you used to work the system to get what you needed. You never took no for an answer. That's what we need now."

"We?"

"It's kinda a joint effort. You have to see it

for yourself to believe it," Manning said. "It would just be temporary, and we can't afford to pay much."

"In other words, you want someone cheap."

"More like free, except for the use of a really nice cabin, as long as you stay."

"You really know how to sell a job," Travis replied. Could it be that Manning had somehow discovered that Travis had no family, no plans?

Being a desk jockey held little appeal for him. "Where?" he asked.

"A little town in Colorado. It's...unusual."

"You living there now?"

"About eighteen months. After I recovered, I found Amos. He's with me now."

"That's great." Travis remembered the military dog, how the animal mourned when his handler, Manning's best friend, died. The dog was eventually sent back stateside.

"Call it a working vacation," Josh said. "I have a cabin that will be all yours. It's on a lake, next to a mountain. The town is vet-friendly."

"How long?"

"A few months. We have volunteers, enthusiasm, horses. Just no expertise."

Travis looked around the room. Danny was still here, supporting the others.

"You said there's a ranch?"

"Yeah."

"Any jobs available there for a young amputee?"

"We could find something. You have a prospect?"

"A corporal. Lost his right leg. He's a foster kid. No family. No place to go. But he's a damn hard worker and has encouraged everyone around here."

"Sounds like someone we can use," Manning said. "We'll figure something out."

"You sound…" Travis couldn't find the right word.

"Content? I am. I have a wife, a kid, five or six dogs—it changes by the day—two horses and a crazy cat. I'm even an innkeeper," Manning said with a humor that was definitely new.

"This I have to see," Travis replied, signaling his acceptance. They discussed the logistics for a moment more, and then he hung up.

Stunned, Travis stood there for a moment. His thoughts raced ahead as he looked at too many warriors struggling to get their lives back.

For the first time in two years, he felt a sense of excitement. He had a challenge, another battle, even if the campaign might be brief. He'd seen so many fellow patients sink into hopelessness. He'd felt it himself. Maybe, just maybe, he could do something worthwhile, both for himself and others fighting for a new life.

He whistled as he limped down the hall. It was the first time he had whistled since his injury.

CHAPTER TWO

Denver

A LITTLE GIRL RUNNING. *Blood everywhere. Spreading like a river. Edging nearer and nearer...*

Panicked, Jenny woke, soaked in her own sweat. The jerk of her body as she woke renewed intense pain in her shoulder. Disoriented, she looked around, trying to control the trembling. The night-light, now necessary for sleep, was just strong enough to reveal the shadowed bedroom, rather than the rubble of a once prosperous city.

Had she screamed again? God, she hoped not.

Her brief prayer was not answered. She heard a tentative knock on the door, and her mother inched the door open and entered the room. Her hair was in rare disarray, her robe partly open, her face slathered with some kind of cream.

"Jennifer?" Her mother's voice was loud, and Jenny smelled alcohol on her breath as she leaned over. "Another nightmare?"

Jenny struggled to sit upright. Even after four months, the pain in her shoulder could stop her cold.

"It's okay, Mother. It's gone."

She'd never told her mother the truth of the nightmares, that they always revolved around the child standing bewildered in a blood-soaked street. Had the little girl survived? The question wouldn't leave her. "I'm okay now. Really. Just a bad dream. Remember, I used to have them as a child." Jenny looked at the clock. A little after 4:00 a.m. "You go back to bed. I know you have that luncheon today. I'll read for a while, then go back to sleep."

"If you're sure…"

"I am. It's gone now."

"Maybe a sleeping pill…"

"Maybe," she said, although she had no plans of taking one. She had watched others in pain become reliant on pills. That would not happen to her. She knew her recuperating time would be long and painful. It was too easy to become addicted to pain meds.

"I'll get you a glass of water, okay?" her mother persisted.

Jenny nodded. She could do that on her own, but the small chore would satisfy her mother.

After her mother brought the water, Jenny went to her bathroom and took a hot, and then cold, shower to shake off the nightmare.

She knew she couldn't go back to sleep. Not yet. The horror of those moments was still too real. She went to the corner of her room, where she kept the physical therapy equipment. She selected a rod, turned on the portable TV to an all-news station and sat down in front of it. Her injury didn't seem to hurt so much when she was occupied with news.

She started moving the rod from side to side as she watched. An upset election in Europe, Congress fighting again, riots in a Middle Eastern country. She ached to be in the middle of it. She didn't belong in a luxurious bedroom, in a gated community.

She held the rod across her body like a vaudevillian dancing with a cane. She moved it to the left and then to the right. It was one of the excruciatingly painful exercises to expand the mobility of her right shoulder. She smothered a cry as she impatiently shoved the rod too far.

The news turned back again to the Middle East, reporting on the refugees fleeing from wars in Iraq and Syria. She wanted to cry. Scream. Do something. She kept seeing that bombing and the children and adults running for cover where there was none. Did the volunteer medical workers make it to safety? If so, what about the next day? And the one after that?

The scenes haunted her.

Yet despite her injury, she wanted to go back.

She needed to record what was happening. She wanted the world to know. To care, dammit.

She didn't know now whether she *could* ever return, with her shattered rotator cuff and damaged tendons and muscles. The wrong movement sent rivers of pain through her. She also experienced flashbacks and nightmares. Though less frequent now, she couldn't take the chance of endangering others during one of her episodes.

Where was Rick now? She hadn't heard from him in a month. He had stayed with her that day and somehow managed to get her across the border to a hospital. He'd called from a cell phone, somewhere in the field, three weeks later. She'd been barely coherent after her surgery, but she told him she would be back.

She missed him. He was fearless and always had a joke on his lips. He was probably the only person who'd ever understood her need to write stories that needed to be told. That was *her* source of adrenaline, just as photography was his…

Stop thinking about the past.

She dropped the rod and went to the window. She stared out at the manicured lawn and towering trees in the backyard. The vivid reds and oranges stood in stark contrast to the colorless rocks and sand of much of the Middle East. So why couldn't she appreciate it? The house and grounds felt like a prison.

It had been nearly four months since that bloody afternoon in Syria. She was lucky not to have bled to death. The red-hot metal had cauterized the wound, and Rick had cradled her body to keep the metal from moving until they found a doctor among the refugees. She'd been patched up enough to get to Turkey, where she received further medical treatment, and was sent home to Colorado.

Following two operations on her shoulder, she'd needed weeks of intense therapy. Her mother begged her to move into the family home, which was close to the rehab center.

She'd resisted at first. With the exception of several brief visits with her mother, she'd not been home since college. She'd been overseas for the last eight years, five of them in the Middle East. Moving back at thirty-two was humiliating.

But staying there for a few weeks was the logical decision. She couldn't even dress herself without going into elaborate contortions.

Recuperating in a happy home would have been difficult enough, but this house was not happy. Her father was rarely there, and when he was, he usually went straight to his study. Her mother drank too much wine when she wasn't at charity functions, and probably when she was, too. Her smile was a little too bright. Jenny's journalistic eye saw the pain she tried to hide.

On the rare weekends her father returned from San Francisco, where his company kept an apartment for him, he couldn't stop reminding her that he had warned her not to go. The Middle East was no place for a woman. Why couldn't she be like her two sisters?

According to her father, journalism was no profession for his daughter. No opportunity to marry an up-and-coming husband, as her sisters had, and have children.

But then Jenny knew she'd always been a disappointment to him.

From the time she was old enough to walk, she'd run after fire engines or any other kind of excitement. At ten, she'd saved her allowance to buy a battered set of encyclopedias at a used book sale, and by twelve she'd read through them, along with finishing the reading list for the fifth, sixth and seventh grades. In lieu of dancing lessons, she headed for the library. The librarian was her best friend.

Her parents hadn't been concerned when she announced at age eleven that she wanted to wander the world, rather than get married, assuming her declaration was just a child's wild fancy. They became more concerned when, at sixteen, she announced she was going to be a journalist and, at seventeen, attended a lecture by a renowned journalist at the University of Colorado, instead of going to the junior prom.

More than anything else, she'd wanted to be on her own, free to fly like a bird…

And she had.

Would she ever fly again?

THREE MORNINGS LATER, Jenny woke to pounding at the door. Her brain was foggy. Daylight poured through the window. She glanced at the clock and jerked upright. It was ten in the morning, but then she hadn't gone to sleep until 4:00 a.m. She'd been caught up in an idea for a story.

More impatient knocking, and then the door burst open. Her sister Lenore walked in.

Jenny stared at her. "I thought you were in San Francisco."

"Charlie and I flew in this morning," she said.

"Charlie?"

"Charlotte, your niece. She announced last year she wants to be called Charlie."

"How did our parents take the announcement?"

"They ignored Charlie's edict, of course, and warned me that she might, of all horrors, take after you."

Jenny chuckled. This was a different side of Lenore. But then, except for a brief visit at the hospital a few months ago, she hadn't seen her sister in more than five years. "Mother didn't say you were coming," she said.

"She didn't know," Lenore said. "Charlie's downstairs with her now." She scrutinized Jenny. "You look a lot better than you did a few months ago. But you really have to do something with that hair."

"Gee, thanks. I missed you, too," Jenny replied. Her hair probably *was* a mess after sleeping on it. It was uncontrollably curly and a real pain to brush with her left hand.

"You never did like lies. Even little ones," Lenore said as she eyed Jenny critically. "You know, your hair would look really cute if you cut it shorter."

"I would look like Little Orphan Annie," Jenny retorted, not admitting that she needed a new hairstyle, one that she could manage with her injury.

Lenore laughed, but it sounded hollow. "No, you wouldn't. It would look great on you. I couldn't get away with it, but you could." She paused, and then she added awkwardly, "How are you feeling? Really?"

"Good," Jenny lied. "I'm hoping to leave soon. I want to get back to work."

"Is your shoulder healed enough?"

"I can manage most activities now. The problem

is driving. A sudden movement can nearly paralyze my arm, but I'm working on it."

"You're not planning to go back to the Middle East?"

"I'm not that delusional," Jenny said. "But I haven't completely been idle. Thanks to the internet, I've been researching some stories I can do here in the States."

"Anything in particular?"

She nodded. "Horse therapy."

"Horse therapy?" Lenore echoed. "Therapy for horses?"

"No," Jenny said patiently, unsure whether her sister was kidding. "Equine therapy for veterans. I was looking at various therapy programs and found a number that involved horses. I knew there were equine programs for kids with autism and disabilities. I didn't know how many are available for veterans. It could make a great story."

Lenore studied her for a moment. "Does this interest have anything to do with your nightmares?"

"Mom told you?" Jenny asked.

"She's worried about you."

"I'm worried about *her*, or I would have left by now," Jenny said. "She's drinking too much. I suppose you know our father rarely comes home these days. He's living full time in San Francisco."

"I might be able to help you there. Charlie and I are moving back to Denver. Doug and I are getting a divorce." It was said in a monotone voice, but Jenny saw the pain in her eyes.

"A divorce?" Jenny couldn't hold back her surprise. "I thought you and Doug were the perfect couple. What happened?"

Lenore shrugged. "The old, old story. He found someone younger. And thinner. A friend told me he was cheating. I didn't believe it at first, but I hired a private investigator. He produced a lot of photos. Doug didn't even try to deny it. I think he was actually relieved. He just didn't have the guts to ask for a divorce, and he didn't want to share any money. The photos, though, bought me a nice settlement."

"I'm sorry, Lenore. I really am." Jenny didn't add that she thought Lenore was better off without Doug. She'd never liked him. He was an executive in their father's company. Too good-looking. Too oblivious to other people, unless they could do something for him. Too much like her father.

"The settlement will give me enough to buy a condo," Lenore said, "and Charlie and I are moving here to be close to Mother. I'll have to go to work." She hesitated. "I got a real estate license in California and made some sales. I was pretty good at it. More important, it's the kind of job where you control your own hours. I can be there for Charlie and for Mother."

Jenny nodded. Her sister *would* be good at real estate. She was attractive and smart. She'd studied business in school until she met Doug and married him before finishing her degree.

"What does Father think about that?"

Lenore shrugged. "He disapproved, of course, but all he really cares about is the company."

"I wish Mother would leave him."

"She's afraid of being alone. He's convinced her that a woman is worthless without a husband." Lenore grinned suddenly and added, "That's why he was always on your case. You disproved the theory. Unfortunately, I was a slow learner."

"But now I support myself and I've got to get back to work, starting with the equine therapy programs. I'm only too familiar with the military and the burdens they carry when they leave. I really want to tell that story."

"Well, you'll have a place to hang your hat if you need one," Lenore said. "You can move in with us. Charlie would love to spend time with you. She reminds me a lot of you when you were a kid, although she's more withdrawn. She's curious and reads all the time. She's read everything she could find about you and written by you on the internet." Lenore paused, and then said sadly,

"Spending time with you would take some of the sting away from the move. Sometimes, no matter how rotten the father, the daughter forgives him."

Jenny wondered if Lenore was talking about herself, as well as her daughter. It warmed her heart that Charlotte—Charlie—was interested in what she did. Jenny hadn't seen much of her niece, but she remembered a pretty blonde girl who looked at her shyly and was very polite.

"She's hurting," Lenore continued. "But I don't want her around our father or my ex-husband. I remember how Father tried to make you into something you weren't. So did I, and I regret all those lessons I forced on you about makeup and dressing to attract the opposite sex. And some of the comments I made about you being a nerd."

"I was," Jenny said with a grin. "I still am."

"I don't think so," Lenore said. "I've kept up with you. You have a powerful voice. I'm really proud of you."

Jenny didn't know what to say. She finally found her voice. "What about Mom."

"The condo I'm buying is just a few blocks away. We can see her often and avoid the house when Father's around. In the meantime I'm going to try to convince Mother to ask Father for a divorce, or at least leave him and move in with us. She's so unhappy although she doesn't want to admit it."

"How's our sister, Stacy? I haven't seen her since I went overseas?"

Lenore just shrugged. "She says everything is fine. Stacy started a home decoration business which is why she couldn't get away to see you. Mac supports her and the kids are doing well." She hesitated, then added, "I don't want to push you, but I'd really love for you to move in with us after closing on the condo. You wouldn't have to worry about looking after Charlie. At ten, almost eleven, she's quite responsible."

Touched by the unexpected offer, Jenny nodded. "Thanks. I'm not sure what I'm going to do next but it might well be a godsend." She changed the subject. "Have you mentioned your move here to Mother and Father?"

"I told Father before coming here. My ex didn't have the guts to tell him about the divorce so I gave him the unhappy news. He disapproved. Of the divorce of course, not the behavior that prompted it. I'm telling Mother tonight."

"She'll be happy to have you here and disappointed by the divorce," Jenny predicted. Like Father, their mother would rather be miserable—which she was—than admit a failed marriage.

"I'll stay out of the way unless you need support. How does Stacy feel about it?"

"Stacy echoes Father. As always. It's my fault and I wasn't a good enough wife." She paused, then added, "It's ridiculous to still feel like a child asking permission to go to a movie."

"Well, I certainly never expected to be here when I hit thirty-two," Jenny said.

"Just think about moving in with us," Lenore pled and left the room.

Perhaps now *was* the time to explore some possibilities. If she moved in with Lenore, their mother would still have them both nearby for company. It was time to start thinking about subjects she could sell to various publications. In addition to the horse therapy idea, another came to mind: *rehab and family challenges*. For the first time since the injury, she felt excited. Stimulated. It wouldn't be what she had been doing, but it would be writing. Travel pieces, human interest stuff. A lot of papers used stringers or freelancers. She knew how to find stories, to look under a headline and find something no one else had.

Her thoughts turned back to Lenore. Maybe the move would be good for both of them. Maybe she would get to know her sister and niece better in the bargain.

CHAPTER THREE

Two weeks after his last rehab appointment, Travis limped through the Denver airport, using a cane, but no brace or crutches.

He hated the looks tossed his way. Pity. Curiosity.

The cane wasn't necessary for short walks, but on the longer ones, he sometimes needed assistance.

There was one advantage, though. The agent at the check-in desk in Dulles International Airport took one glance at his military identification and then his cane, and upgraded him to first class. He'd dreaded the long flight from Washington to Denver with his bad leg scrunched up.

He didn't have any baggage other than his carry-on with an extra pair of jeans, shirt, skivvies and a toilet kit. He didn't think he'd stay more than two or three days. He just wanted to meet the participants, listen to their plans and then make up his mind as to whether he wanted to return for a longer stay.

In the meantime, he'd looked up other vet programs around the country. They'd ranged from small mom-and-pop programs with weekend stays for the veteran and family to months-long stints aimed at teaching skills that could turn into civilian jobs.

He hadn't mentioned anything to Danny, who had not yet been released from the hospital. He didn't want to get the kid's hopes up. Except he knew Josh Manning well. Manning wouldn't have contacted him, certainly wouldn't have paid for his airfare, if he was not deadly serious.

Once aboard the plane, Travis gratefully slid into the window seat and placed his cane underneath. He leaned back and sighed in relief as he stretched his legs out in front of him. The right one ached from the long walk. It was galling to remember the ease with which he used to make a ten-mile trek.

The spacious room meant he could sleep. He had taken a cab to the airport at 5:00 a.m. for the 8:00 a.m. flight and then the flight was delayed.

Once in the air, he closed his eyes and tried to sleep. He wanted to be fully awake when he arrived. He'd looked up Covenant Falls on the internet and knew it was located on the plateau, in the shadow of the San Juan Mountains. Manning said he would pick him up at the Denver airport and drive him to Covenant Falls.

Not for the first time, he doubted the wisdom

of the trip. Was it simply a do-good ploy on his ex-sergeant's part? And what qualifications did Travis really have aside from a seventeen-year-old college degree? His confidence had melted away over the past two years. Still, the invitation got him out of his nondescript furnished apartment, and he looked forward to seeing Manning. Most important: this program might give him a real goal.

He still hung onto a thread of hope that maybe his career wasn't over. Maybe—just maybe—a desk job could lead back to the battlefield. He didn't like war, but he respected the men under his command, and he felt he should be out there with them. A loss of one was like a loss in his own family. Hell, they *were* his family.

He slept until lunch. The small steak that arrived was tough, and he cut the meat awkwardly with his left hand. The loss of two fingers on his right hand made it unsteady despite all the rehab. He was still learning, still retraining what remained of his hand. He was grateful the woman seated next to him didn't ask if he wanted help, but he was all too aware of her curious gaze.

TRAVIS SPOTTED JOSH MANNING the moment he entered the Denver airport baggage area. Josh and he were both around six-two, and though his former sergeant looked relaxed in a pair of jeans, blue denim shirt and jacket, his green eyes held the same steely edge they always had as he studied the incoming passengers.

Josh grinned when he saw him and walked over. "Major, it's damned good to see you."

Travis nodded. "Same here, but I'm not Major to you any longer. It's Travis." He held out his maimed hand and Josh took it in a strong handshake.

"I was damn sorry to hear about what happened to you," Josh said. "Are you out now?"

"I'm on medical leave now. I have a little time to decide whether to accept a desk job, if one becomes available. You know how army budget cuts are. There's no certainty that they'll have a job for me."

"Is a desk job something you even want?"

Travis shrugged his shoulders and accompanied Josh toward the door. There was an ease about him that had not been there before, a peace in his eyes that Travis envied. After a long walk, they reached a weathered Jeep with the top up, and he saw a dog sitting like a sentinel in the front seat.

"Amos?" he asked. The former military dog wagged his tail enthusiastically.

Josh grinned. "Sure enough. I found him a year and a half after Dave died. He was a mess.

So was I. It was hard to tell which one of us was the worse."

Travis leaned over and offered his good hand to the dog. Amos licked him.

"He remembers you," Josh said. "He doesn't do that with strangers." Josh made a gesture, and the dog scrambled over the seat and sat alertly in the back seat.

Travis awkwardly fit himself inside and looked back. "Sorry I took your place," he apologized to Amos, who barked and wagged his tail again.

"It's okay with him. He knows you're an old friend."

"I'm glad you found him," Travis said. "Lieutenant Warner told me how he'd mourned for Dave. It got so bad, he had to be sent back to the States."

"Well, he ended up being my savior, along with a kid and his mother."

"I can't imagine you with a wife and kid."

"I can't either. It's been a year and a half since I married Eve, and I still have to pinch myself to realize it's real. Me, married to the mayor of the town?"

"Have to admit it shocked me, too."

"I was in pretty bad shape when I arrived. Neither Dave nor I had any family, so we made each other the beneficiary in our wills. He owned a cabin in a place called Covenant Falls and all he talked about was moving there after the service and starting a wilderness adventure business with me. When he died, I inherited it."

He paused. Then he added with obvious pain, "It was a virtual wreck, just like me and Amos were. Dave was like a brother to me, and he died saving my life. I think the only thing that kept me from hitting bottom was thinking I was responsible for saving the damn cabin."

Travis was caught up in the story now. "Go on."

Josh fell silent for a moment, and then he shrugged. "Covenant Falls is…unique. There's about three thousand people in and around town. Then there's a number of small ranches within a fifty-mile radius. Probably three quarters of the population are over fifty and have lived there all their lives. Its history is interesting—it was one of the earliest trading posts in Colorado. The founder was a Scotsman who saved the life of a Ute chief and in return received protection from the tribe. Thus the name Covenant Falls."

"Sounds interesting," Travis said and meant it. He'd always liked history, especially American history.

Josh gave him a crooked smile. "Yeah, but all I wanted was to be left alone, fix the cabin, sell it and get the hell out, especially when brownies and cookies and other baked stuff started appearing on my doorstep. I really didn't want to have anything to do with anyone, particularly civilians. Then a very pretty mayor ambushed me in the backyard," he continued. "I'd decided to resign from the human race, but it turned out the town had different ideas. Before I knew it, I was volunteering to join other vets in reroofing houses. For free."

He sounded chagrined and Travis laughed. Josh had been all warrior and all business. To think of him turning from tiger to pussycat was intriguing. Maybe Covenant Falls *was* unique. The man looked years younger.

"You're staying then."

"Yeah. I'm even part owner of an inn. It's part of what Jubal and I are thinking about."

"Jubal? Not Jubal Pierce?"

"You know him?"

"I know of him. There's not many Jubals in the world. He had one hell of a reputation in the Special Forces community until he disappeared several years ago. It was big news when he returned from the dead. How did he end up here?"

"I mentioned on the phone it was complicated. When Eve and I got married, I moved in with her and her son. I wanted Dave's cabin to be used by a veteran. An army chopper pilot named Clint was recommended by a military psychologist I knew. He was followed by Lieutenant Andrea Stuart, an army surgical nurse, and then Jubal, who was invited by Clint. They went way back. We're all in on this project, but Jubal is the driving force."

Travis looked out at the mountains to their right as they drove south. "Looks like great horse country."

"The land around Covenant Falls is even better," Josh replied. "It hugs the mountains and is off the beaten path. There's some really fine ranches in the area. At least five want to be included in our project. But we don't know where to start. We've been researching different Horses for Heroes programs, including several that include multiple ranches. Now we need a battle plan and you were damn good at that."

"How did this all get started?" Travis asked.

"Riding helped Jubal immensely after he returned. He'd lost his team in Africa and was aimless until a rancher invited him to ride one of his horses. He says it changed his life, gave him a purpose. I think it's important to him to help other veterans now. He knows how difficult it is to come back. All of us do. We decided to participate, but none of us knew how to start, what we would need, what kind of program works best for veterans. And us."

"And you think I do?" Travis said with a raised eyebrow.

"I know you're damned good at planning and

implementing plans. All we know is that contact with horses seems to be very therapeutic. We know there's different types of programs but they don't come close to meeting the demand.

"Right now," Josh continued, "he's thinking of a long-term project, teaching vets the care of horses along with horsemanship. There's jobs available in the field. But he's open to other ideas. What we would like you to do is visit ongoing programs, learn about their pros and cons, staffing needs, requirements for a nonprofit and VA Administration grants."

"Is that all?" Travis asked incredulously.

It was startling to see the smile spread across Josh's face. "Probably not," he said. "But it's the beginning."

"Can you find a job for the young soldier I told you about?"

"I'm sure we can. Jubal is working with another rancher on the program, and they both need help with horses. You think your soldier will be interested? If not, I'm sure we can find someone in town."

"I'll talk to him. He's a city boy but I think he'll grab anything. He's really a good kid and smart. And scared."

"He'll have a lot of support here. The town loves its veterans."

Travis nodded.

"I'll take you to the cabin first," Josh said. "I know you must be tired from the early flight. If you're up to it, we'll have supper later at Jubal's ranch. Some other folks will be there."

"I'll be up for it," Travis said. He'd been growing more and more interested as Josh spoke.

They arrived in Covenant Falls late in the afternoon after stopping for lunch along the way. There were no traffic lights, only a few stop signs. Josh pointed out the City Hall, medical clinic, veterinarian's office, bank and real estate office. With a glance at the back seat, Travis noticed Amos was regarding the world outside with intense interest. It was good to see the dog thriving. Maybe now that he was in the United States again, he would adopt a dog.

He was struck with a sudden loneliness. He certainly didn't begrudge Josh's obvious happiness, but his own future didn't look promising. Dinah's expression when she first saw him haunted him.

"Major…?" Josh's voice was a welcome intrusion on dark thoughts.

"Travis," Travis corrected again.

"That's going to be difficult to get used to," Josh said as they followed a road that bordered a very blue lake. He turned into the last driveway on the street and stopped in front of a cabin with a wide screened porch.

They walked up to the door, and Josh opened it. "The key is in the kitchen."

"You don't keep it locked?"

"Crime is rare here, especially since Chris, one of the vets, became police chief."

Travis looked around. A large stone fireplace filled one end of the room. A wall of windows filled another side. Through them, he could see that the backyard was large and backed onto a forest. A large rock barbecue pit was surrounded by three lounge chairs. The cabin was much more than he'd expected.

"I'm going to let you settle in and get some rest," his host said. "I'll pick you up at six. Come hungry."

After Josh left, Travis explored the cabin. If he accepted the offer, it would be a great place to stay. The cabin was immensely comfortable, and the lake outside was a gem. He grabbed a beer from the fridge and took it out to the screened porch and its comfortable chairs.

Covenant Falls looked like a nice town, but he had grown up near an even smaller one and was familiar with its pitfalls. Everyone knew everyone's business, and Travis preferred the anonymity of a large town.

But this project of Josh Manning's was intriguing. Travis was fully aware of the problems vets often had when returning home. Many, if not most, soldiers joined to learn a skill, earn an education or make it a lifetime career. Deployments were long and frequent, and your buddies became your lifeline, as well as your family. Leaving due to injury was devastating.

He knew that first-hand. He would listen tonight, but he already knew he wanted to be involved.

He needed a mission, and this sounded like a good one.

JENNY'S SISTER LOST no time in finding a three bedroom condo she loved. The owner was being transferred overseas, needed a quick sale and was more than happy to add his furniture to the sale.

Jenny moved in with her two weeks later after her father returned to the family home and railed against both sisters, Lenore for ending her marriage and Jenny for taking Lenore's side.

In the next few weeks, Jenny found an unexpected friend in her sister and a special kinship with Charlie, who was, as Lenore said, very much like herself. They spent a lot of time together as Lenore studied for the Colorado real estate exam.

They shared books and discussed the news on television, and Jenny recounted stories of overseas adventures minus the bad ones.

But as much as she enjoyed the new relationships, her restlessness returned. She wanted to roam again. Visit new places, meet new people. Charlie seemed to understand, and together they combed newspapers, magazines and the internet to find that special "something."

It was Charlie who found it in one of Lenore's Colorado travel magazines that her mother was collecting for future clients.

"Look," Charlie said excitedly. "Here's a story about an inn in a town named Covenant Falls. I've never heard of it, but it's in Colorado. It mentions a horse therapy program."

The article featured an inn with the catchy name of the Camel Trail Inn. One line in the short article really struck her. "Innkeeper Susan Hall said many of the town's outdoor activities are operated by veterans, and plans are underway to develop an equine therapy program for veterans."

The latter paragraph struck her like lightning. It was exactly what she'd been searching for.

She smiled. A little-known town named Covenant Falls. An inn named the Camel Trail Inn, veterans offering outdoor activities and possibly an equine therapy program.

It was the story she was looking for.

CHAPTER FOUR

"You have to be kidding!" Travis exclaimed.

"Afraid not," Josh Manning said over the phone.

Three weeks after Travis's first trip to Covenant Falls, he'd finally moved into Josh's cabin.

He hadn't known at first whether he was the right person for the job. He liked the ideas he'd heard at supper that first night. He liked Jubal Pierce and his business partner, Luke, and their commitment to an equine therapy program. He'd seen enough vets in Walter Reed and rehab to know how debilitating the aftermath of war could be.

But he'd wanted to do some research on his own first. He'd spent three weeks back in Washington on his laptop, getting to know equine therapy programs available for veterans. Some received grants, some fees from the VA and some public support. Still, there was more need than availability.

Jubal, though, was impatient. He wanted to get moving. Riding and a horse named Jacko had helped him survive the rough months after leaving the SEALs. He was determined to do the same for others. He'd read about and talked to providers. He knew the need.

Jubal's commitment to hire Danny was the deciding factor. The kid had been uncertain, having never lived in a small town nor worked with horses. He wasn't sure what he could do with one leg, and he didn't want to let Travis down. Travis felt it was the other way around. He didn't want to let the kid down.

So Travis was there to work on the details, and Danny had moved out to Jubal's ranch and was now helping to build a bunkhouse of sorts for single participants in the program. Other vets in town had pledged to help, and Danny would learn about construction, as well as horses.

Danny had been awed by working with a SEAL, and Jubal had been pleased with his work ethic and eagerness to learn. For the time being, he used a spare room at Jubal's ranch, but would move into the bunkhouse once it was finished. The job offered a small salary, as well as room and board.

Everything seemed fine until Travis received the phone call from Josh.

"I have some news," Josh said, sounding unhappy.

Travis waited for the other shoe to drop.

"A reporter called my wife, as well as the manager of our inn," Josh said. "She'd heard about Covenant Falls and the veterans here. She wants to do a story."

"A reporter?" An image of his ex-fiancé skipped through his mind.

"Yeah. I checked on her, and she's pretty high-powered. Jennifer Talbot. She works for several news agencies. Did some reporting in Afghanistan, Iraq and Syria."

"I know the name," Travis said. "Concentrated on soldiers and civilians more than tactics. But why the interest in Covenant Falls? It's peanuts compared to what she's been doing. We don't even know *if* there will be an equine therapy program yet, much less what it might look like. It's a hell of a long way from being a reality."

"Eve told her, but she was insistent. Long story short, she wouldn't take no for an answer."

"Dammit," Travis said. He'd had contact with reporters before. Many went for the headline, not the meat of the story. And too many got the meat wrong.

"My sentiments exactly. It's much too early. But she made a reservation at the inn. Indefinite stay starting on Thursday."

"What is she doing back here in the States?"

"She didn't say. Susan was too busy answering the reporter's questions. I gather this Jennifer

Talbot is interested in doing a story about veterans coming here, and Susan mentioned the equine therapy project and Jubal's name. Talbot apparently seized on it." Josh hesitated, then added, "Talbot then called my wife for more details. Eve was cautious. She knows how we feel about our privacy and that Jubal definitely does not want this project to be about him. One reason he moved here was to get away from the publicity about his captivity and escape. He went through hell, and he doesn't want to live through it again in the newspapers."

"It might be hard to avoid it now," Travis said. After a moment of consideration, he added, "Publicity would probably help bring in donations."

"We don't want that kind of publicity," Josh said. "First of all, we don't even know if we'll go ahead. Second, if we do go ahead, the wrong kind of publicity could scare vets away. We'll want word of mouth through the military community. We don't want it to be about us."

"Got it," Travis said.

"Maybe you can talk to her. I think you might be more diplomatic than the rest of us, you being an officer and all," Josh suggested. "Tell her to come back in a year or two."

"Not going to be easy. A missing SEAL who suddenly reappears out of the jungle to open a therapy program, not to mention the army nurse, chopper pilot and you," Travis said. "Even I know it's a great human interest story."

"And a spotlight would be on any program we come up with. We're thinking about applying for grants, not spreading it all over newspapers."

"What do you suggest?" Travis asked.

"Pick her up at the Pueblo airport," Josh said. "Susan apparently offered. She would do anything to make the inn a success, and I'm usually all for that since I'm a co-owner. Except this time."

"I don't think that's in my job description," Travis said wryly.

"You're a hell of a lot more diplomatic than I am. As your staff sergeant, I saw you manipulate superior officers and make them think your idea was theirs more than once."

Travis couldn't really deny that. He'd gotten Josh out of several scrapes with superior officers.

"I'm just not sure what I can do."

"Take her by the Falls. Get her interested in the town rather than the veterans."

"I've only been here a few days," Travis protested.

"But you've had a crash course. I tried to get Andy, but she had previous commitments."

"I still don't understand why she can't drive herself here. Must be a prima donna."

"Susan offered," Josh said.

Travis knew ambitious reporters. After all, Dinah had been one. He knew her obsession with a good news story. There was little she wouldn't do to get an exclusive.

Handling another reporter was the last thing Travis wanted to do, but he understood the danger this posed to the program they might develop. Veterans were fighting enough demons without having a spotlight on them.

He wanted to say no. He was still very aware of his own injuries and scars, but he had to get over it sometime. And he was a part of this now.

"I can't guarantee results," he warned.

"Understood," Josh said. "You'll meet her at the airport then?"

"Reluctantly," Travis said. "I would call it hazardous duty."

Josh chuckled on the phone. "Why don't you come to our house for dinner tonight?"

"A bribe?"

"Now, would I do that?" Josh asked in a wounded tone.

"Not two years ago. I'm not so certain now. This town has corrupted you. Remind me not to stay long."

Upon landing at Pueblo's small airport, Jenny used her good arm to open the overhead storage and take out her carry-on. She was accustomed to traveling light and washing clothes in a bath-room sink. Despite the pain in her shoulder, she was excited. She had a story, one her gut told her was good.

A moment of unaccustomed nervousness hit her as she walked through the terminal area. Was she ready for this? Susan Hall had offered to meet her, but she didn't see a woman who appeared to be watching for someone. She did notice in-stead, a tall well-built man, who appeared to be studying every figure coming through the door, He stepped toward her.

"Miss Talbot?"

Interesting looking. His hair was sandy, short and neatly cut. His eyes were an intriguing mix-ture of green and amber and brown. Difficult to read. He had the alertness of a soldier and the authority of an officer. A faint scar ran down his cheek and turned one side of his lip upward in a perpetual half smile. Rather than marring a handsome face, she thought it made him more in-teresting. As he approached, she noticed a limp.

She turned on a smile that usually brought one in return. This one just brought a slight twist of the lips that was barely welcoming.

"I'm Jenny."

"Travis Hammond," he said in a deep voice. "I'm substituting for Susan Hall."

She thrust out her hand. His large right hand

wrapped around hers, and she noticed he was missing the two middle fingers. It was different from other handshakes, but she was used to seeing injuries and their aftermath. She shook his hand the way she would with anyone else.

"Thanks for picking me up," she said.

"No problem," he said, but his expression was challenging.

"I have a small issue with my shoulder. The doctor said I shouldn't drive yet. Otherwise I would have rented a car. So I truly appreciate you picking me up." She hated explaining, but she didn't want him to think she was a diva.

He nodded and reached for her carry-on. For a brief moment, their hands met again, and an odd recognition flashed between them. It was weird and even a bit discomforting. For her, anyway.

After a slight hesitation, she handed her carry-on to him, and he shouldered it. She preferred to carry her own stuff, even now. She'd been doing it for years. She never wanted to be considered weaker or less able than a guy. In the field, you carried your own weight if you wanted respect. Sometimes, she knew she carried it to extremes.

On the other hand, she didn't want him to believe she didn't think he could handle it with his hand. There was, she admitted to herself, some irony in that. "Thanks again," she said simply.

"Any other luggage, Miss Talbot?" he asked.

She gave him her usually effective smile. "It's Jenny," she said. "And no. I travel light."

He didn't return the smile. Just nodded. "My car's not far," he said. "I understand you're staying at the inn in Covenant Falls."

"Who could resist staying at a place called the Camel Trail Inn?" she said as he steered her out the door, across the taxi and pickup line and down a row of cars to a silver sedan.

"Too many people, according to the manager," he replied drily.

He opened the back door and put her carry-on in the back seat. She didn't wait for him to come around but opened the passenger door and slid inside. He joined her a second later in the driver's seat and drove out of the lot after paying the parking fee.

She disliked depending on a stranger, especially one who didn't appear thrilled with the chore. She had no idea what she would do about transportation in Covenant Falls. Probably no taxis or Uber. She only hoped she could walk most places and beg a ride for longer distances. Maybe, just maybe, she would try driving. Wouldn't be so hard on near-empty streets.

She looked at her driver, only too aware of his intriguing scent of soap and outdoors and after-shave lotion. He was quiet and controlled, and there was a natural confidence about him. He was polite but a little wary. She wondered why.

"Are you one of the veterans who moved here?" she asked, twisting as much as she could to study him.

"No. I'm just here temporarily. Arrived five days ago."

She tried again. "What happened to Susan Hall?" His short, cryptic answers were beginning to annoy her.

"Apparently she had an influx of customers."

"And you volunteered?"

"Not exactly," he said with a wry grimace.

"You were requisitioned?"

"Yes, ma'am."

An honest answer. She liked that. "Reluctantly, I take it."

His silence answered that question.

"Are you active or retired?"

"A little of both, I guess. I'm not quite out yet." He didn't ask how she knew.

"Well, thank you for picking me up," she said with a grin. "Can we stop for lunch on the way? I'm starved." She wanted him out of the car. Face-to-face.

"Sure. What do you like?"

"A hamburger. A nice, big juicy one with a large plate of fries."

"I think I can manage that," he said with the

smallest crack of a smile. "But why do you sound as if you've been deprived?"

"Long, sad tale that I'm sure would bore you."

"I doubt that."

She retreated. She wanted to know about *him*. He had turned the tables. She wasn't accustomed to that.

"If you can wait, the best burger in Colorado is in Covenant Falls," he said. "Maude's. I personally vouch for that."

"Okay. I can tolerate a growling stomach if you can."

"On the way, maybe you can tell me about that long, sad tale."

Dammit. Perhaps, if she answered, he would reveal more himself. She wanted that. More and more every moment. "Hospitals," she said, "and a family that believes hamburgers are…well… plebeian. And before that there was Syria and a few other places that didn't count hamburgers as part of their daily diet."

"How long were you in the hospital?"

"Weeks. There were several surgeries on my right shoulder. It's improving, but not as fast as I would like." She didn't want to talk about it. "What about you? Have you been to Syria?"

She was dangling her fishing rod, hoping to catch some clues about him. Ally or obstacle? She had been thrown off by his appearance. After reading a short news story about Covenant Falls and the opening of the inn, she'd been expecting the very nice, very helpful woman she'd spoken with on the phone. That she'd been replaced by a cautious newcomer did not bode well. This was a warning flag. She felt it in her bones.

"The government says I haven't been," he replied.

"I'm aware of what the government says. What do *you* say?"

"What the government says."

She hid a smile and changed topics. "Are you a Ranger?" she asked. She'd met a lot of them. She would bet her last dollar he was Special Forces. There was a confidence about them that was unmistakable. They were among the best and knew it.

"Yes," he said simply.

"And you're on leave?"

"Yes."

He was a master at brevity. "Why are you in Covenant Falls?" she persisted.

"Seeing a friend."

"One of the veterans?"

He glanced at her. "You're just full of questions."

"I'm a reporter," she said, as if that explained everything. "Didn't anyone warn you?"

"Not completely."

His answers were frustrating. She thought from his tone he knew that and was thoroughly enjoying it. She looked out the window at the mountains looming ahead. "I find it very interesting that I've never heard anything about Covenant Falls, even though I lived in Denver."

"Maybe because the people there don't care whether you did or not."

"I find that even more interesting."

He chuckled. It had a very nice tone to it.

She studied the barely visible scar that turned the right corner of his mouth up slightly. It would have been a classically handsome face minus the scar. She wondered whether he minded that imperfection.

"Tell me about the town," she said.

"What do you want to know?"

"How many veterans live there?"

"Susan didn't tell you?" Susan had apparently told her altogether too much.

"No. She just said there were a lot."

"That's my answer, too. I don't have numbers but it's a small town, and small towns typically send more of their young people to the military than cities. Call it patriotism or lack of opportunity where they are. And I suppose most return to their roots after their service…"

"How many are not native to the area?" she asked. "Susan said there were more than a few."

"I've only been here a few days," he said. "Susan can probably help you with that more than I can."

He paused, then added, "Answered all your questions now?"

She knew he was trying to frustrate her into asking fewer questions. Wasn't working. "I'm a reporter, so the answer is no. Not even close."

"Can we at least have a reprieve?"

"Five minutes," she offered.

"I can work with that," he said drily.

She bit her tongue and examined the car. Obviously a rental. It was too clean inside to be otherwise. She wanted to ask why. In four more minutes.

Then she studied her surroundings. Since the north–south interstate ran through Pueblo, she'd driven through the city several times. It was an attractive city with numerous parks, but several miles outside the city limits, Travis turned onto a two-lane road that ran through ranch country.

"How far is Covenant Falls?" she asked although she already knew, having done extensive research. But it was a natural enough question and she wanted to keep him talking.

He glanced at her with a raised eyebrow and she suspected he knew what she was doing. "It's only been two minutes," he pointed out.

"Sorry, I couldn't help myself."

"About an hour and a half."

"Are you staying at the Camel Trail Inn, too?"

He sighed and didn't answer.

Now questions were busting out of her brain. She'd rarely met such an unhelpful male.

She knew she wasn't pretty, with her untamable hair, a complexion that burned easily and a figure that was more stick than curvy, but she was usually interested in what guys were interested in, and easily became buddies with those she met. She was rarely in one place long enough to build a romantic relationship, though, and if one started budding, she ran as though the devil was after her. Marriage was her worst nightmare. She only knew of bad ones.

She looked at her watch. Five minutes were up.

"Where *are* you staying?" she asked. As far as she knew, the town had several bed and breakfasts, the inn and nothing else.

"A private cabin," he said. "It belongs to a friend."

"Was answering that hard?"

"I'm not particularly fond of reporters," he said.

"Why?"

"The truth?"

"Always."

"It's not you, individually. It's just that the vets here do not want publicity. One of the reasons they've stayed is because people here respect that. They're no different than the pharmacist or woodworker or mechanic. They want Covenant Falls to grow because it's a great place to live, not because they are some kind of oddity."

"I can respect that," she said.

"Can you? Aren't you here for a story?"

"Won't you need publicity if you go ahead with a therapy program?"

"No. We would work through military sources."

"Is this why you came to pick me up? To diplomatically deliver a message?"

"I don't think I was that diplomatic."

She was silent for a moment. "What if I promise not to submit anything you or the other vets don't approve?"

"I didn't think reporters did that."

"We usually don't. Practically never, in fact," she admitted. "But this subject is personally important to me. I want to do it. And I want to do it right."

He took his eyes off the road and looked at her. She expected him to ask why. He didn't. His gaze went back to the road.

She waited.

"No one can force you to leave," he said.

"But I don't want to run around chasing my tail either. I don't break confidences or promises. If I did, no one would talk to me again."

He didn't say anything for a few minutes. She was beginning to think he wouldn't. He'd obviously been sent to dissuade her. What he didn't know was how badly she wanted to do the story. She'd been clutching the prospect like a lifeline.

Everything about it intrigued her: warriors ending up in a small town, healing, joining together to help others. It had everything…

But only if she could gain their trust. And the first gatekeeper to get by was the obviously wary man next to her.

CHAPTER FIVE

THEY WEREN'T MORE than a mile out of Pueblo when Travis realized he was in trouble.

He had been from the first moment he saw her.

He'd tried to avoid glancing at his passenger as he drove the nearly empty two-lane road from Pueblo to Covenant Falls, but his gaze kept wandering from the road to Jenny Talbot.

She was not at all what he'd expected when Josh asked him to pick her up. She looked younger than the black-and-white photo he'd found online. Plus, in the photo her hair had been pulled back and it looked dark. Now it was short and fiery.

Neither had the photo done justice to the green eyes that danced with warmth and curiosity. She was medium height but looked taller, maybe because her body was lean rather than curvy. She radiated energy.

When he agreed to meet her, he'd expected someone like his ex-fiancé—cool and poised.

Jennifer Talbot was definitely not that. She wore worn jeans, a T-shirt and a denim jacket that looked great on her lanky figure. She didn't try to hide the freckles on her nose. Her mouth was too wide for beauty, and her jaw too stubborn, but when she smiled, it was as if the sun just came out.

But she did have something in common with Dinah. Persistence.

He recalled the first time he'd met Dinah. As a commander in the field, he'd had contact with reporters and perfected the art of saying little and doing it politely.

That talent had been noted, and while he was stationed in Georgia, between deployments, he was often asked to be a spokesman. He'd met Dinah at a news conference. She was beautiful, charming...and persistent.

The memory of their last meeting still stung. It had, no doubt, made him leery of other journalists. But there was something different about this one.

He'd immediately noticed the way she avoided using her right arm and liked the fact that she stated the injury from the start without elaboration or expecting anything because of it. He'd also found, and liked, several of her articles. They demonstrated that she had a real understanding of the places and people she was covering. He didn't have much time to think about it, though. He was too busy fending off questions after his five-minute moratorium was over. She didn't hesitate to bore in. She obviously wanted a story. But he sensed the interest went deeper. Although he was usually cautious of civilians, especially reporters, he was attracted to her positive vibes and low-key humor.

But he was also cautious. He didn't know what his next steps would be after this short—and virtually nonpaying—job. He was in no position to get interested in a woman. Any woman. Particularly one who was obviously consumed by her own career. Been there, done that.

His thoughts were suddenly interrupted by a loud *ahem* sound.

She started her questions again, and to his surprise, he enjoyed dueling with her. As the questions continued, the car seemed to heat despite the cool air floating from the air-conditioning. He hadn't felt it in a long time but he knew it was trouble. Chemistry? Electricity sparking between them? Whatever it was, it scared the hell out of him.

He was pretty sure she felt it, too. A quick glance revealed rosier cheeks than when she'd stepped into the luggage area.

Caution flags started flying. He could probably ignore the physical attraction if he wasn't equally fascinated by the way her mind worked. Something about her was compelling, and it prompted him to say more than he intended.

He also sensed she knew far more about Covenant Falls than he did. But then, a good reporter would do his or her research. The question was how much.

"Tell me about the veterans who are thinking about developing an equine therapy program."

"I haven't been here much longer than you have," he countered. "It's probably best if you meet them first." He didn't add that they all might go into hiding. Josh had not been enthusiastic about her interest.

"Okay, I've met *you*," she countered. "I know you're a Ranger. What's next for you?"

"I have no idea," he said honestly. "What are *you* going to do?"

"I'll keep finding stories."

"You're lucky, then. I'm trying to figure it out." He had no idea why he blurted that out. She had a way of digging into a person without them being aware of how deep she was going.

"Where's home for you?" she asked.

"The army and wherever they send me."

"Then why are you here?" she persisted. "I take it the army didn't send you."

He shook his head. "Does anything come out of your mouth that's not a question?"

"Not often," she replied. "I'm curious. Always have been. I drive some people crazy."

"Just some?"

"That's not polite," she said with a grin. "But probably true." She hesitated for a moment. Then she continued, "I'm not just here for a story. I know the price you guys pay. I know you don't like to talk about it. I don't either. It's important, though, that your stories be told."

Her voice had suddenly become determined and serious—the playfulness was completely gone. He also heard pain in it. That intrigued him far more than it should.

"I've read some articles you wrote on Syria." He didn't add that he thought they were good. Better than good. He didn't want to give her an opening until he talked to Josh and the others. He suspected Josh had wanted him to pick her up to get a read on her.

She didn't ask what he thought about them. Instead, she went back to her obvious default position: questions. That second of vulnerability was gone.

"Tell me about the town," she said. "How did it get so many incoming veterans? I understand what you said about small towns producing a lot of veterans but from what Ms. Hall told me you have a lot of new ones."

"What else did Ms. Hall tell you?" he asked in return.

"Just that it was home to some veterans who are thinking about starting a Horses for Heroes program," Jenny said. "The name, I learned, covers a number of equine therapy programs. I'd been reading about them and think it's a great idea. I wanted to know more."

"That's all it is now," Travis said. "Just an idea. Certainly not ready for publicity. There's other programs that are already active and would make a good story."

"But the fact that nearly the whole town might be involved is...intriguing."

"Is that what Susan said?"

"Now who's asking the questions?"

He smiled. "It's a request for clarification," he replied in a smug tone.

"Nifty answer," she said. "But you're deflecting. Are you connected with the 'idea' in some way? Or are you just visiting?"

It was unnerving at the way she cut through to the chase so easily. Travis didn't like lying and so far he'd avoided actually doing so. He inwardly groaned. She would find out soon anyway.

"I'm doing some research," he said.

"I'm very good at research," she said with that infectious smile of hers. "It's how I found Covenant Falls."

He believed her. His silence was his answer.

She sighed. Tried again. "You've been here a few days. What do you think about Covenant Falls?"

He shrugged. "Haven't been here long enough to think much of anything. It's like any small town, I suppose, except it seems to have survived better than mine did." The words escaped him before he could call them back.

"You're from a small town?"

"I was," he admitted.

"Bigger or smaller than Covenant Falls?"

Travis inwardly groaned. In trying to avoid one topic, he'd opened an old wound. But in this short time, he could already tell she would continue pressing him.

"Smaller."

"Where?" She was like a bee buzzing inside his head, jabbing at memories he preferred to forget.

"Midwest."

"What did you play? Baseball or football?"

"Baseball. How did you know?"

She shrugged. "There's an athleticism in the way your body moves," she said.

Not anymore.

"Yes, there is," she said, apparently reading his mind. She changed the subject. "Susan said the town was full of veterans, even before Iraq and Afghanistan and Syria."

He shrugged. "Like many small towns, there aren't many job opportunities here. The military is an option."

"But they come back. There couldn't be many more options after they return?"

"Their roots are here," he said. He'd brought up the subject three weeks ago on his first trip. "Some of them for generations. Friends and family are here. I think some people feel it even stronger after being away for years. They've learned skills in the army or saved up enough money to start a small business. They do all right."

"What about your more recent military arrivals? The ones who aren't natives of the area?"

"How recent do you mean?"

"Say, the last two years. Ms. Hall said there are several newcomers. They didn't have generations of history here."

"There's no secret about it. Josh Manning was the first. He was also a Ranger. He was wounded in Afghanistan, was medically discharged and inherited a cabin here."

"And then?"

"Josh married the mayor and became a businessman. He's part owner of the inn where you're staying and the cabin was passed on to another vet."

"Who came next?"

"Susan Hall didn't tell you all this?" In his mind, he was thinking that the innkeeper had said altogether too much.

"Nope."

"And you didn't ask?"

"She had a paying guest who interrupted us," Jenny said with a grin. "Tell me about the others."

He sighed and ran down the list of temporary guests at the cabin.

"And you're using it now."

"For a few weeks only."

"But they were all coming temporarily. Right? What changed?"

The innkeeper again. "Why am I telling you everything you already know?" he asked.

"But I don't. Just bits and pieces of a fascinating puzzle. Why did they all stay?"

He hesitated. Covenant Falls was a welcoming place, but he sure as hell wasn't going to say that. In addition to protecting the privacy of the vets, he knew Josh didn't want the town to turn into some weird fairy tale that attracted people for all the wrong reasons.

He'd been incredulous himself when he'd learned of the marriages and engagements of the recent vets in Covenant Falls. Clint, whom he'd met on the previous trip, had joked that there was something in the water.

They were nearing the outskirts of the town. Maybe a short detour would answer some questions, or deter them. He would take Josh's suggestion and show her the waterfall. Maybe he could interest her in writing about the town and forget about the veterans. And maybe that was too many *maybes*.

"Want to see the falls of Covenant Falls?"

"The falls? That's an affirmative. I've missed them where I've been."

He circled the town and took the road to the falls. They passed the Rusty Nail, with its half-filled parking lot. "I haven't been here yet," he said, "but I'm told their burgers are good."

She had stopped asking questions and looked around with interest. The road was steadily going upward now and the trees ahead were starting to change color. Patches of gold and red were highlighted by the sun. Travis followed a twisting, newly paved road up a sharp incline, and then he turned into a parking area.

He might have offered to open the door for her, but she was out the second the car came to a stop. They could hear the falls from where they were, but they could not see them. He led the way to a wooden fence and stood back as she looked down at the meandering river below.

"Nice," she said.

He gave her a moment, and then he led the way

around a stand of trees, and suddenly they faced the falls. Water tumbled over a high cliff to the rocks below. A rainbow arched above it. A cool breeze carried spray to where they stood, sprinkling them. A look of pure enchantment crossed her face, turning it from attractive into beautiful. He had the damnedest urge to take her in his arms and hold her against him.

If it had been just a physical reaction, he could step away. Her delight, though, made him smile inside—and he hadn't done that in a long time. He started to reach for her, to touch her. *Snap out of it. Keep it strictly business.*

Travis stepped back. Away from temptation. *It was the rainbow.* Nothing else. When Josh brought him here on his first visit, Travis had been impressed, particularly with the rainbow that Josh said was almost always visible during the day. Hell, even to a has-been warrior like himself, it seemed to wave a banner of new chances, new opportunities.

"It's beautiful," Jenny said, licking at the moisture around her lips with her tongue. It was a natural enough reaction, but it was sensuous without intent, and that made the action even more sensuous. He was suddenly warmer. He wanted to put an arm around her and share that sense of awe.

Bad idea. He backed away. He sure as hell

wasn't ready for another relationship, even a short one, and suspected she wasn't either. Just as important, he saw in her a free spirit. She'd been injured and was using this time to heal. He'd met many military correspondents during his years overseas, and most were as addicted to the adrenaline as the soldiers were.

She would be here briefly, and apparently it was his job to guide her away from the proposed horse therapy program. He sensed that it could be difficult to guide Jennifer Talbot away from anything that interested her.

Jenny turned to him and put her hand on his arm. "I've seen larger falls, far more powerful ones, but this is so...untouched. And the rainbow—is it always there?"

"Josh says it is, as long as the sun is shining."

"I can't believe I haven't heard of it before," she exclaimed. "It's almost...mystic."

Mystic? He didn't believe in that stuff, and yet it'd helped change the lives of three hardened warriors and one war-experienced nurse...not to mention a Scotsman nearly a hundred and fifty years ago. At least that was what Josh contended.

"What can you tell me about it?" she asked. "Why isn't it on a map? Isn't it in the national forest?"

"Nope, that's the odd part of it. You haven't heard about it because the town wanted to keep it to themselves. The founder of Covenant Falls, who had substantial political pull at the time Colorado became a state, had the area incorporated into the city limits. The family had enough pull to keep it from being included in the national forest. At least, that's the story. The city has never tried to keep outsiders out. It just never advertised the fact. That's changing, according to Josh. The town needs revitalization. There's not many jobs for young people, and the population is aging."

"I can understand why they might want to keep it private," she said. "It's so peaceful here. I feel I could reach out and touch the end of the rainbow."

"I thought you were an action junkie."

"Is that your impression?" she said. "I do like to be where things are happening. I also like full moons, soft misty days, ocean sunsets and especially rainbows. Quiet things. They center me. Especially after being in a war-torn area."

"How long have you been back in the States?"

"Four months, nearly five."

"Planning to go back to Syria?" he asked.

"If I can. My shoulder was damaged by a piece of shrapnel during a 'truce' there. The shoulder joint was injured, and the rotator cuff torn. My shoulder is getting stronger, but then I make a move and wow, it feels like someone is tearing it off. I'm working up to driving again."

He liked the way she replied frankly. No drama. Just how it was.

"But I do want to go back," she repeated. "Someone needs to tell the story there. The civilian population is being slaughtered. I was accompanying a medical group during a promised cease-fire. They—we—were bombed. I keep reliving it."

There it was again. No self-pity. Damned if he didn't like her.

"I didn't advertise it," she continued. "I was afraid it might scare off some of the news services I worked with. I just told them I needed time off."

He didn't ask any questions. It was none of his business, and he sure as hell didn't want to talk about his own injuries. But he empathized with her. More than he wanted.

"Tell me more about the town," she said, changing the subject. "It sounds even more interesting than I thought."

"I don't know that much. The two people who can help you are Andy Stuart, the army nurse, and Eve Manning, Josh's wife. She's also the mayor."

"Special Operations?" she asked suddenly.

She did it again. Threw out a question, seemingly out of the blue. She was smart. Too smart. He hesitated.

"Forget I asked that," she said. But he knew she had her answer by his silence.

He looked as his watch. "It's nearly four," he said. "What about those burgers?"

"You heard my stomach," she accused him.

"I heard my own."

"A duet," she said with that quick, open smile.

As they walked back, he saw her stop and turn. She hesitated. It was obvious she didn't want to leave.

He didn't want to either. For a moment, he'd felt alive again, more alive than he had in years. He wanted to catch her hand, as a high school kid would.

Instead, he walked in silence beside her, reminding himself of another newswoman. Jennifer Talbot was here for a few days, no more. Then she'd hopefully get back to her life, although he was very aware of how difficult shoulder wounds could be. He liked that she wasn't giving up.

Hell, he liked her too much. But then, he'd liked his ex-fiancé immediately, too.

Hopefully, she would talk to Eve and Josh and Andy and write a story on Covenant Falls, minus Jubal's pet project.

He'd done his part. There shouldn't be a need

to meet again, although Covenant Falls' size made that unlikely.

Unless he sped up his plans to go on the road. Like maybe tomorrow.

CHAPTER SIX

WHAT IS HAPPENING?

Jenny tried to keep her cool. From the moment Travis Hammond met her at the airport, bells began to ring, bells that had grown louder and more persistent as they walked to the waterfall. When she felt the spray and saw the sky filled with color, she'd almost leaned against him. She wanted to.

She didn't believe in romantic bells. She could admire a good-looking guy from a distance and enjoy social time, but any internal reaction? Not really. No blood rushing inside. No confusion. No craving to touch.

She tried to shrug it off now, especially since he didn't seem afflicted with the same reactions. He was cool, and even amused at times, but nothing seemed to penetrate his shell.

That was a good thing.

He stopped the car on what looked like the main street. Maude's was proclaimed on a sign above the glass front. It looked like many of the small-town diners she'd seen throughout the

United States, and she'd always sought them out over the franchise restaurants.

It was getting late in the afternoon and she hadn't had anything but toast since breakfast. When he parked, she slid out of her seat and had started for the diner before he caught up with her. "You really are hungry," he said.

"I warned you earlier," she said as they reached the door.

A middle-aged woman with a maternal air immediately came from behind a counter and greeted them. "Welcome back, Major Hammond," she said with a wide smile. "And who is this?"

"Jennifer Talbot," Travis said. "She's a reporter. She flew in from Denver today and claims to be in dire need of a hamburger."

"Or two," Jenny added. "With fries and pickles. And everyone calls me Jenny."

"I'm Maude," the woman said, "and I'm delighted to meet you, Jenny Talbot. Why don't you take the back booth? Hopefully, no one will bother you there."

Jenny felt her face flame at the intimation that they might want to be alone. "No need," she said.

"I'm giving her a ride," Travis explained. "Josh asked me to pick her up at the Pueblo airport. She's staying at the Camel Trail Inn."

Maude nodded, but Jenny noted a gleam in her eyes.

"Well, welcome to Covenant Falls," Maude said as she plucked two menus from the counter and led the way to the back. Jenny noticed five tables were occupied and another four people were at the counter. They all turned, and she felt their eyes on her as she and Travis followed Maude to a booth set against the window and the back wall.

Jenny slipped in ahead of Travis to grab the seat against the wall. He looked startled but grinned ruefully and took the seat across from her. She had learned from her time in dangerous countries to always take a corner seat where you had full view of the interior. She couldn't help but feel a ripple of satisfaction at beating him to it.

If Maude noticed anything, she kept it to herself as she handed them worn menus. "We have great hamburgers," Maude said. "The beef is fresh, and we use a mix of ground sirloin for taste and chuck for texture. But the steaks are great, too, as the major can testify to."

"The burger," Jenny said. "Two of them with cheddar cheese, if you have it, and onions and ketchup on the side. And french fries."

"You have a keeper here, Major," Maude said. "Steak or hamburger for you?"

"She ordered with such relish, I guess I'll have the same," he told Maude. "And unsweetened iced tea for me." He glanced at Jenny with a raised eyebrow.

"With lots of lemon," Jenny said.

Maude laughed. "I'll have to hire her to sit at the door and eat cheeseburgers. I bet my business would double." She turned back to Travis. "I heard you brought a young man with you."

Travis turned to Jenny. "There's no secrets here. Not for long." He turned back to Maude. "His name is Danny Ware," he said. "First time he comes in here is on me, okay?"

"Nope. Heard he's a wounded vet. First visit is on me. You can have the second. Deal?"

"Deal."

"Who is Danny?" Jenny asked as Maude walked away.

Travis felt uncomfortable. "A kid I met in rehab. Lost his leg in Afghanistan. One of the ranchers hired him to do some work."

"Jubal or Josh?" she asked.

"Didn't Susan tell you that, too?"

"No, but it makes sense. He came with you. Josh is your friend and he's working with Jubal."

The drinks came immediately in tall, frosted glasses with lemon. She took an appreciative sip. "Hmm. I can tell I'll like this place."

"You'll also like the inn," he said. "Susan's great, and so is the food. I ate there when I was here a couple of months ago."

"How long were you in Covenant Falls then?"

"Three days. Then I came back a few days ago."

"With Danny?"

"Yeah."

"I'd like to meet him."

"He's a little shy."

"I'm good with shy."

Travis sighed. Hell, she was probably good with everyone. It was downright scary. He changed the subject. "How long are you going to be here?" he asked.

"As long as it takes."

He considered that. He felt like smiling—and groaning. He liked her. He liked her very much. He couldn't remember the last time a woman had affected him like this. Yes, he could. Never.

He'd been infatuated with Dinah, but had he ever really liked her? He'd been proud to have her on his arm. He was impressed with her accomplishments. She was damned good in bed, too. He even thought he was in love, but now he wondered whether he'd ever really known her. Some of the attraction, he'd realized while recuperating, had been wanting to know someone was waiting for him back home.

That seemed kind of sad now. But he should have been far more devastated at her reaction than he was. Still, it had burned into his consciousness that other women could feel the same.

This woman didn't appear to notice his limp, nor the missing fingers on his hand. Nor was she obsessed with her own looks. She'd applied only a touch of lipstick and was dressed in comfortable, well-worn jeans—unlike his former fiancé, who wouldn't be caught dead in them.

"Why are you really interested in Covenant Falls?" he asked abruptly. "It's just another small town. It seems way below your league."

She squinted at him as if he had three heads. "There's always a story," she replied.

He took it as an invitation for find out more about her. She had been interrogating him. Time to turn the tables.

"Then why go all the way to the Middle East?"

"Good question," she said. "I asked myself that many times, especially when I was in the hospital."

"Any answers?"

"Hard to explain," she said. "Why did you join the army?"

"You first," he insisted.

She took a long sip of tea before answering.

She shrugged. "I always had wanderlust. When I was a kid, I could travel through books and movies and television. But that wasn't enough. I wanted to see places and events through my own eyes, not someone else's. I majored in journalism in college, helped put myself through by writing for the university television station and stringing for state newspapers.

"When I graduated, reality hit," she said with a wry grimace. "Jobs were hard to come by in the business. Newspapers were consolidating all over the country. Really fine, experienced reporters couldn't find jobs. The entire field was in withdrawal.

"I auditioned for several television stations," she continued with that spark of defiance in her eyes, "but I turned down being a weather girl."

He couldn't help but smile at that. Just from the few hours he'd spent with her, he realized she wouldn't be satisfied in a nine to five job even on television. He had a damn hard job thinking of one for himself. "No," he said. "I can't picture you standing in front of a board, day after day."

Her brow furrowed. "You're right. Instead, I worked at making contacts with editors through press clubs and friends. I made a nuisance out of myself. Through pure persistence, I got a job with a small city newspaper. Interesting, but not what I wanted. I wanted to cover more big news, and I wanted to travel." She paused. "I'm talking too much."

"No, you're not," he replied. "Go on."

"Maybe *you* should have been a reporter,"

she said with that quick, heart-stopping grin. "I discovered that my newspaper was paying freelancers for travel articles. I investigated and discovered a lot of travel magazines as well as newspapers used freelancers. I also discovered that, unlike newspapers, travel magazines are doing very well and looking for contributors. I'd saved enough money to take a sailboat cruise to some off-the-beaten-trail Caribbean Islands and wrote three different stories and sent them to three different travel publications. All three bought them and wanted more."

She paused, but now he was caught up in her story. She sipped her tea.

"How did you go from travel writer to war correspondent?" Travis asked. He wanted to keep the conversation away from Covenant Falls and himself, and turnaround from all her questions was only fair. He also liked watching her as she spoke. Her green eyes lit with life and humor. Determination and restlessness radiated from her. It was even in the way her fingers wandered from her glass to the silverware. They were always in motion.

He realized one thing. It was going to be nearly impossible to deflect her from whatever she was seeking.

She played with the napkin, another indication of suppressed energy. "I spent two years as a travel writer, both for magazines and newspapers. I could always find quirky people and odd bits of history and out-of-the-way places. Most of my expenses were paid by hotels or ships or travel agencies. I saved money. I was satisfying my travel drive, but not the part of me that wanted to be where important things were happening.

"When I'd saved enough money and made contacts with major news organizations, I decided to go out on my own. I had a college friend who worked with refugees in Jordan and I was able to get a visa. That was before everything blew up there. Once in the Middle East, I started writing stories about ordinary people caught up in war and a growing number were picked up by several news services. Few of them wanted to pay for a full-time reporter with all the risks involved."

It sounded easy, but Travis knew how difficult it was to get permission to enter Middle Eastern countries. He wondered whether it was that smile or the obvious never-say-quit determination. Whatever it was, it did not bode well for trying to discourage her from whatever she wanted here.

"You did more than a few articles," he said.

"You did some research, too," she tossed back.

"A little," he admitted. "But I suspect there's more to the story."

"I was in the right place at the wrong time,"

she said. "I was staying in a hotel in Iraq when terrorists hit a popular restaurant on the same street. I emailed it to a news service that had picked up some of my travel articles. The news manager bought it, pushed it and it got wide distribution. He said he would take whatever else I could give him. Through him, I was able to get press credentials and go pretty much wherever I wanted to go. And that's pretty much the whole story."

"And what about your family?" he asked.

She shrugged. "No husband. No children. As for my parents, they disapproved of almost everything I did. My father's expectation was a proper marriage to a very eligible and preferably wealthy man. He was sadly disappointed with my wandering ways. We don't speak much."

"Mother?" he asked.

"She thinks like Father thinks."

The food came. Jenny grabbed one of the two cheeseburgers the second the plate was down, but she paused before eating long enough to look up at Maude with a blinding smile. "Heavens, but that smells good."

He was just as hungry, and they both concentrated on hamburgers and fries. He was impressed. When she finished with the first burger and french fries, she fastened her gaze on him. "Your turn to tell your life story."

"You still have a burger left."

"That's dessert. A dignified pause is warranted," she explained patiently.

He chuckled. He was both relieved and yet oddly saddened to be leaving Covenant Falls the day after tomorrow.

"Fair's fair," Jenny persisted. "I get to ask a question now."

"Okay," he said. "Ask."

"How long have you been in the army?"

"Seventeen years in September."

"Do you want to stay in?"

"Depends on the job. My injuries, both leg and hand, will keep me out of the field."

She studied him for a long moment. "Why did you join the army?"

He shrugged. "Nine-Eleven, like a lot of people my age. A close friend died in the South Tower."

"What *were* you planning to do?"

"Sports management. High school or college athletics. I'd just received my undergrad degree and was planning to get my master's, but sports didn't seem that important after Kevin died. Instead, I went into officer candidate school."

"What about *your* family?"

"There isn't any," he said in a flat tone that ordinarily would have warned most people off. He'd already said more to her than he remembered telling anyone else. More explanation would carry too much pain.

They were trading some pretty personal stuff, and ordinarily he would have retreated, but it seemed a natural exchange with her. *Watch it*, he told himself. *Don't forget she's a reporter.*

"You were manufactured?" Her quick rebuke took him by surprise.

He should have known she wouldn't let him get away so lightly.

He shrugged. "My mother died when I was fourteen. My dad died seven years ago." He anticipated the next question, the one he didn't want to answer, the one that tore him apart.

"No brothers or sisters?" she persisted.

He had invited the questions by asking some of her. "One brother," he said shortly. "He died in Iraq."

"Your family's military?"

"My father was a farmer." It was a short, curt answer, which was meant to discourage more questions.

She grinned. "I can't imagine you as a farmer."

"Neither could I," he said. "So I concentrated on baseball to get me through college."

"Pitcher," she guessed.

He looked at her in surprise.

"I like sports," she said. "I watched a lot of them when I was growing up and whenever I was within range of television. Pitchers have a certain look about them."

He didn't think he wanted to ask more about that. Damn but she was uncanny. It was as if she reached inside him and jerked out information. But he wasn't going to give her the satisfaction of knowing it. He simply nodded.

Maude was back at their table, holding two pieces of pie. "Apple," she said. "Just from the oven. On the house. It's a welcome to Jenny. Miss or Mrs.?" Maude asked.

"Ms.," Jenny replied without offense. In fact, Travis saw a smile starting on her lips.

"Sorry to ask," Maude said, "but everyone is going to want to know, especially the guys." She raised an eyebrow in Travis's direction and hurried off.

"It's a small town," Travis said with a grin. "A visitor is big news. I ran smack into it on my first trip here. Before the afternoon is over, everyone will know that a new lady's in town and she's a Ms."

"I'm just a temporary *lady in town*," she protested. Despite the fact she'd just consumed a huge cheeseburger and a mound of french fries, she eyed the apple pie topped with real whipped cream and took a mouthful.

"Doesn't matter," Travis said while watching in amazement. "You ought to hear Josh Manning's account of his first few days here. It's enough to scare off the bravest of newcomers."

"I look forward to hearing it."

"Are you a native of Denver?" he asked.

"Born and raised," she said. "I always wondered what it would be like to live in a small town."

"And people from a small town always wish they lived in a big one."

"Grass is always greener," Jenny observed with a smile that slowly faded away. "Unless you live in a war zone, then there's no grass on either side. Just rubble. And bombs and death..."

A glazed look came over her, and she went still. A tear fell. He realized she was having a flashback. He'd had enough of them to know.

"Jenny?" he said gently. He reached over and touched her hand. Her fork had fallen onto the plate. She blinked and then shook her head as if to erase the image.

She glanced up at him, obviously trying to focus on where she was. It was the first vulnerability he'd noticed in her. Still another side to what he realized was a very complex person. "Are you all right?" he asked. "Do you want to leave?"

"No," she replied softly. "I'll be all right in a minute. It's just...sometimes it hits me...images." She searched his face. "You must have seen the children wherever you were. How can you forget them?" It wasn't an accusation. She was asking for help.

"You don't," he said. "You live with them, just like I live with the faces of men I sent into action and who didn't come back."

She took a deep breath. "I'm sorry."

"Don't be sorry about caring."

He didn't know where those words came from. He was supposed to be the objective shepherd charged with guiding her away from the project. He was beginning to think it might be impossible.

Not knowing what else to say, he took a bite of pie. *Back to today.* He was on the receiving end of a searching glance before she picked her fork back up. "So when do I get to meet all your fellow vets?"

"You still have a burger to eat," he reminded her.

"So I do. I'll save the rest of the pie for later." True to her word, she demolished the second burger in record time.

"Where do you put that?"

"My stomach is used to feast and famine," she replied. "Not my fault you starved me before we got here."

"I'll remember that in the future," he said.

"Good," she replied. Then she excused herself to find the restroom.

Travis reminded himself that he probably wouldn't see her again. He had to prepare for his trip, and then he would be traveling for nearly a week. Hopefully, she would be gone when he returned. She was far too appealing. Far too challenging. He looked at his watch. After five. He had planned to visit Jubal's ranch by now and check on Danny. He'd completely lost track of time. The truth was, he needed help. He made a quick call to Andy, the former army surgical nurse who was head of the chamber of commerce, as well as curator of the town's small museum.

"Hi," he said. "I have the reporter at Maude's, but I need to leave. I know it's late, but can I run her over to the center so you can tell her more about Covenant Falls, then take her to the inn?"

"Sure," Andy said.

"We'll be there in about fifteen minutes or less."

"Is she that bad?"

"Before she gets to the inn, she'll know your life story."

"The hell she will."

"Just wait," he said and hung up as Jenny returned.

Maude reappeared with the check and handed it to Travis.

Jenny frowned. "I want to pay my share."

"Nope," he said firmly.

Maude beamed down on them. Approving. "Yours is on the house. Are you staying long?"

Jenny shrugged. "Not sure."

Travis stood. It took a moment for him to get his balance. Jenny stood with him.

"You wanted to meet one of the Covenant Falls veterans," he said. "I called Andy Stuart. She's at the community center, which doubles as the town museum and chamber of commerce. She'll take you to the inn." He could hear how curt his tone was. Self-protection. She had rocked him to the core in the time they had spent together. He saw the surprise in her eyes.

He softened his voice. "She knows a lot more about this town than I do," he said. "Ask her about the diary."

He hoped the tidbit would grab her interest in the few minutes it would take to get her to the community center. Then he would drive to Jubal's ranch, tell him what happened and complete the plans for his own fact-finding road trip. He might even leave early. Like tomorrow.

"Okay," she said simply. "Thanks for lunch."

"It ended up as dinner," he corrected as they walked to his car. The community center was less than a mile from the restaurant, and they drove in uncomfortable silence. His sudden stiffness had destroyed the easy companionship between them. Unfortunately, it had no effect on the underlying sexual tension that made him ache in sensitive places.

The center's parking lot was nearly empty when they arrived. He watched as Jenny's gaze sweep the park in front of the lake, before examining the brick building that he understood had once been a restaurant.

As before, Jenny didn't wait for him to open the door. Instead, she matched his halting walk to the door. Just outside, Jenny turned to him. "Thank you for the ride, the visit to the falls, Maude's."

God help him, but her eyes were gorgeous. And penetrating. "You're welcome."

"I'll see you again?"

"Possibly," he said. *Not if he could help it.*

She nodded.

He opened the door. Andy was at the information desk at the foot of the staircase. He knew by now that the library was on the left and a community room on the right. The museum was upstairs.

He introduced them, and then he escaped before he said something dumb, like he would see her again.

Yeah, he would move his trip up.

CHAPTER SEVEN

JENNY LIKED ANDY and she was immediately taken with Andy's dog, Joseph, a medium-sized black, brown and gray Australian shepherd that offered his paw when they were introduced.

Jenny accepted it and looked up at Andy. "He's very well-mannered."

"Thank you," Andy said. "He's a therapy dog. He keeps the nightmares at bay."

"Travis said you were in the army," Jenny said. He hadn't mentioned her PTSD.

Andy nodded. "Surgical nurse until injuries to my hand made it impossible." She hesitated as if deciding whether to continue. Then she said, "Others were killed in the same attack. It was hard to get back on track."

She ran a hand over Joseph's thick fur. "I had PTSD and severe depression. No interest in anything. My doctor practically shanghaied me to visit a woman who trained rescues to become therapy dogs. Had to stay nearly a week with her before she decided I was worthy of Joseph."

She leaned over and rubbed Joseph's fur. "He

senses when I'm about to have a flashback and comforts me. He wakes me up when I have a nightmare. He's been a lifesaver. I can't believe I fought the idea. I didn't want to think I needed help."

Sounded all too familiar. She hadn't wanted to admit that her nightmares were a problem either. "I've had nightmares, too," she confided. "I was in Syria during a bombing of a hospital." She didn't go into the details. It seemed...minor compared to what actual combatants like Andy experienced.

"Stephanie Phillips, the local veterinarian, always knows about dogs available for adoption," Andy said. "She has two search-and-rescue dogs of her own. You might want to talk to her."

"I always wanted a dog," Jenny admitted, "but my parents didn't want the bother when I was young, and then I was traveling all the time. I still have that wanderlust, and it's not fair to a dog."

"If you change your mind, Stephanie is involved with a number of dog rescue groups in Colorado," Andy said. Then she confessed, "I was reluctant at first. I didn't want to care about anyone or anything again, but Joseph is well worth the effort. I learned I *could* care again, that the rewards more than make up for the pain of loss."

Jenny was beginning to wonder if Travis had brought her here to learn more than Covenant

Falls' history. He hadn't made the suggestion until after she'd had that flashback.

She tried to shoo the thought away. It was none of his business. "I like Joseph's name. Was it your idea?"

"Nope, he was already named for Joseph's coat of many colors. It suits him."

Jenny rubbed the dog's ears and received a quick lick of a tongue in return. It delighted her. She did it again.

"He likes you," Andy said. "He's cautious. He was apparently dumped in the middle of no-where."

"I can't imagine anyone doing something like that to an animal, especially one so intelligent." Jenny changed subjects. "How long have you lived here? And why here?"

Andy grinned. "Travis said you're a reporter and would probably know more about me than I did after a conversation." She shrugged. "I moved here a little less than a year ago. The same doc-tor who tempted me with Joseph treated Josh Manning. You might have heard something about him. From what I understand, Josh was a real loner when he came here to heal from some bad wounds. He'd inherited a lake cabin from his best friend. When he married Eve, he wanted other vets to use the cabin to transition…or whatever. I was the third occupant."

Andy hesitated, and then she asked, "Are you thinking about going back to the Middle East?"

Word certainly got around fast. Jenny shrugged. "I don't know. I want to. I don't know if I'll be physically able." It was the first time Jenny admitted it to anyone. Even to herself.

"Covenant Falls must be rather tame next to where you've been. How did you find us?"

"I'm from Denver. I was recuperating—kinda still am—from a shrapnel wound to my shoulder. I read a review of the inn in a state travel magazine and realized I didn't know anything about Covenant Falls. I called the inn, and Susan told me about all the vets here, and that they're considering starting an equine therapy program. I thought it would make a great story."

"Way premature," Andy said. "It's still in the talking stage."

"But the fact there's so many veterans here… that's a story in itself."

"I don't think they'll think so," Andy said in a friendly tone that took any sting from the words. "We just seemed to fit in. The people here not only accepted us but drew us into their lives, made us a part of the community. We don't want to be different or special or whatever."

It was a warning.

"But," Andy added, "Covenant Falls has a

fascinating history, and that *would* make a good story."

The travel-writer part of Jenny responded to that suggestion, even though she recognized the attempt at diversion. She'd always been able to find good stories in what seemed the most prosaic places. "Tell me about it," she said.

"I can do better than that. I can show you," Andy said. She led the way up the stairs and unlocked a door to a large room. Glass cases lined three sides of the room, broken only by a desk in the middle of one side. A chair was in front. A leather-bound book sat on the top of the desk. It was a little larger and thicker than a typical hardback.

"It's an accurate replica of the journal written by the founder of Covenant Falls," Andy said. "He started writing in it in Scotland and carried it all the way from the east coast to what is now Covenant Falls. All the words are his. I wanted visitors to get the feeling of the original. You can take it with you tonight."

"Really?"

"Sure. Then you'll understand why we feel Covenant Falls is special."

"Sounds terrific. Thank you," Jenny said. She could hardly wait to get her hands on it. She loved journals and diaries. It didn't, however, quash her interest in the veterans as, apparently, Andy and Travis hoped.

"Joseph and I will run you over to the Camel Trail Inn. I think you'll really like it."

"Thanks. It sounds interesting."

"If you have any questions or want more information, call me. My number is on a slip of paper in the book. If you lose it, ask anyone for it."

"I'm sure I'll have a lot of questions. I warn you, I can be pesky—if Travis hasn't already told you."

Andy's smile told her that Travis had. "You need anything, ask Susan. If you want a few minutes to look around up here, go ahead."

"I think I would rather read the journal first," Jenny replied. It was after six. She had kept Andy long enough. "I appreciate you staying late and giving me a ride."

"Hey, I've been trying to get publicity for the town. It deserves it. The history is mind-boggling, at least to me."

As long as it wasn't about the veterans. Jenny was getting the message loud and clear. She was beginning to wonder whether there was a conspiracy. Andy handed her the journal. They left the museum, Joseph padding beside them and happily jumping into the back seat of the car.

Five minutes later, Andy drove up to the Camel Trail Inn. A sketch and photo of the inn's exterior had been on its website, but it hadn't done the place justice. The rustic exterior, with its sign of a grinning camel, was welcoming. Only a few cars were parked in its lot. Jenny wondered out loud how the inn survived.

"We have a growing tourist trade," Andy said. "It started with a pageant we initiated last summer. It drew crowds from the surrounding areas and attracted attention in the state travel industry. Since then, we've been adding attractions— horseback riding trips, visits to old mines, fishing contests. The summer and weekends are pretty good. During the rest of the year, there's entertainment in the dining room on weekends, and that draws a good crowd from ranches around here."

Jenny grabbed the journal in both hands as they walked inside. It was heavy but manageable. She paused at the entrance. The lobby was just as inviting as the exterior. Rustic yet attractive, with a giant stone fireplace taking up one side of the room. She could envision a roaring fire on a wintry day.

She went to the registration counter and was met by an attractive woman in a white blouse and black slacks.

"Ms. Talbot?"

"It's Jenny."

"And I'm Susan," the woman said. "Welcome to the Camel Trail Inn."

It wasn't just words. There was real warmth behind them, as Jenny had noticed during their earlier call.

While she signed in and handed over her credit card, Susan explained the inn's offerings.

"There's fresh coffee at 6:00 a.m. here in the lobby, along with some pastries, and from four to six in the afternoon, we have wine and cheese. It's self-serve.

"If you're here Friday and Saturday, the dining room is open for breakfast and dinner. In between, you can order for delivery from either Maude's or the Rusty Nail. Menus are in the rooms."

"That sounds good," Jenny said. She had been wondering what to do about food since she had no transportation.

She turned to Andy. "Thanks for the information, the journal and the ride."

"You're very welcome," Andy said. "Don't hesitate to call if you want more information."

Jenny wanted a lot more, but she reined herself in. She didn't want to scare her most friendly contact off.

After Andy left, Susan picked up Jenny's carry-on and showed her to a small library. "This is where we serve wine and cheese in the afternoon," she said. "We move to the lobby when we're full. You're welcome to read and take a book with you when you leave. In fact, we're delighted when you do. Our guests leave them for that purpose."

Jenny followed Susan to the room. It was large and comfortable. A horseshoe was nailed above the door—a whimsy that appealed to her.

"It's delightful," she exclaimed. It had character and comfort.

"There's still time for a glass of wine when you get settled," Susan said.

"Are you here all the time?" Jenny asked.

"I try to be out front when guests are expected to check in, but there's always someone in the office. Just ring the bell." She left, closing the door behind her.

Jenny unpacked her carry-on and checked out the bathroom. It was large, with an oversize tub and shower. The room and service were more than she'd expected, although she knew the value of spending a few dollars on a glass of wine and cheese to bring back customers and garner recommendations on travel sites. No matter what else she found on this trip, she would write and submit a travel piece on the Camel Trail Inn as an example of how to do things right.

She changed to a pair of shorts and T-shirt and walked to the small library. Two couples had arrived while she was checking out her room. A counter held three bottles of wine, including a white wine in an ice bucket. A plate with several kinds of cheeses and gourmet crackers had been placed next to it.

She had meant to pour a glass of wine and head back to her room, but she wanted to know why others had landed in this out-of-the-way town. In minutes she felt as if she knew the couples. Both were celebrating the husbands' return from deployments and heard, through word of mouth, that it was a vet-friendly town with outdoor activities available for a reasonable price. They had booked a Jeep trip up into some old gold camps and a horseback riding trek into the mountains.

"We loved every minute," Teresa, one of the wives, said. "The guide for the Jeep trip was an old-timer with a lot of stories, and one of the local ranchers took us for a day-long horseback trip up to the falls. They were breathtaking. The finishing touch was to come back to wine and cheese."

Andy felt a rare tug of her heart as the couples left hand in hand for dinner at the Rusty Nail. *What had she missed?* She wondered how it felt, to love like that. But then wouldn't she miss the freedom of going where she wanted and when she wanted? She'd fought hard for that independence. She'd never regretted it.

When she returned to her room, there was a

message on her room phone from Eve Manning. Could she come over for dinner tomorrow night?

She called the number on the message. "Mrs. Manning? This is Jenny Talbot. Thank you for the invitation. I would be delighted to come."

"Good. It'll be a small group. One of us will pick you up at six thirty if that's okay. My husband will be barbecuing, and it's very casual."

"Thank you," Jenny said. "I'm looking forward to it." She hung up, unable to believe her luck. Eve Manning had been on her list of people to call tomorrow. She wondered if Travis had anything to do with it—and what the mayor of Covenant Falls wanted.

She took a shower and pulled on a long T-shirt. She then settled down in bed with the journal. But her thoughts kept turning to the man with whom she'd spent so much of the day.

She had truly enjoyed his company, until he abruptly applied the brakes on their easy communication. She'd been charmed by his openness, his ease with himself and the unexpected humor that made her smile. She'd liked the way he interacted with Maude and the unobtrusive way he'd discovered more about her than she about him. She couldn't remember when she'd blurted out personal information in so short a time. It was disconcerting.

It doesn't matter. She wouldn't be here more

than a few days. But Travis Hammond remained in her head. Maybe she'd just imagined the heat that rose between them in the car and that electric connection at the waterfall. Dammit, she still felt it when she mentally revisited those hours with him.

The journal. *Read the journal.*

She opened it. The writing was cursive. Neat. Precise. In minutes, she was carried away by the words of a man who lived more than a hundred and fifty years earlier. It started with an entry from November 5, 1848, which read, "Today I leave my beloved Scotland…"

As she turned the pages, she felt as if she were traveling with Angus Monroe, first on the voyage from Scotland to New York to find his wayward brother, and then across half a continent to establish a trading post. She reached the part where he buried his brother just east of Covenant Falls, the brother he'd traveled so far to find…

"It is a sad day," Monroe's entry stated. "My brother, Liam, died just days from the mountains he longed to see… With a heavy heart, we gave him a Christian burial as the sun set. God give him rest…"

Caught up in the drama, she ignored the clock next to her bed and continued to read as Angus started his trading business and risked his life to save an Ute chief.

Many pages later, he married the chief's sister, and the Ute tribe made a covenant of peace with him.

She was more than halfway through the journal when the day caught up with her and the words seemed to blur.

Jenny looked at the clock. It was after 2:00 a.m.

She understood why Andy wanted her to read the journal. It revealed the mystique of Covenant Falls. There were legends about many towns and cities, but few with this kind of authenticity.

But it didn't explain why so many veterans came here. And stayed. So far, she knew of Josh Manning, Jubal Pierce, Clint Morgan, the chopper pilot, and now Andy. She had a story. She had the intriguing history of Covenant Falls for a travel piece, but she sensed a much larger story, the kind of human interest that had always been her strength. All she had to do was earn some trust.

She sensed it wasn't going to be easy.

AFTER TRAVIS LEFT Jenny Talbot at the community center, he drove to see Josh. His former sergeant had added an office to the small ranch he now called home.

One of the Mannings' two horses neighed to announce his arrival. Josh Manning emerged from the house, followed by a gang of dogs. Josh calmed the dogs that raced to see who would greet Travis first, invited him inside and grabbed two beers from the fridge. They went outside to several lounge chairs.

Travis downed half of his beer in one pull.

"She's that bad?" Josh said with amusement.

"Worse," Travis said ruefully. He paused, and then he ventured, "Maybe some publicity could be beneficial."

Josh raised an eyebrow. "So she's persuasive?"

"Let's say she's damn persistent."

"Obnoxious?"

A pause. "I wish," Travis replied. "I could handle that."

"I look forward to meeting her," Josh said. "I think the Covenant Falls cupid is ready to strike again."

"No," Travis insisted. "It's just difficult—no, make that impossible—to shut the door." He finished the beer. "Oh well, I'm leaving soon, and she'll be gone when I get back. I'm going to head out early, on Sunday." The more he thought about Sunday, the more he liked the idea. Unfortunately, it was only Thursday, and the appointments were already set in stone.

"Retreating from the battlefield?" Josh asked with a humor he'd apparently acquired with his marriage.

Travis grinned. It must have come along with

Josh's wife, new son, two horses, a motley bunch of rescue dogs and one crazy cat. He certainly had not noticed it in the years they'd served together.

"You could probably say that," he answered. "You haven't met her yet."

Josh shrugged. "I will. Susan told Eve about her, and my wife invited her to dinner tomorrow night. You're invited, too, along with Stephanie and Clint. I think Eve hopes she can steer our reporter into doing a story on Steph's search-and-rescue group."

"Can I decline?" Travis said.

"Nope," Josh replied.

Travis inwardly groaned. *That's all he needed. More Jennifer Talbot.* He could refuse, of course, but that would be cowardly. No excuse would do. As he'd told Jenny, everyone knew everyone's business here.

"Maybe Eve could show her around tomorrow," Travis suggested hopefully. "They have a lot in common, mainly drive and persistence. Hell, I don't know much more about the town than Jenny does."

"Jenny?" Josh asked, an eyebrow raised. "It sounds kinda…easy on your tongue."

"Well, I couldn't keep calling her Ms. Talbot," he said defensively.

"Why not Jennifer?"

Josh got him there. He shrugged.

"Pretty?"

"I bet you looked her up, just as I did," Travis said.

"Couldn't tell much from a black-and-white photo," Josh shot back.

"She's...well, attractive."

"I don't believe this," Josh said. "You're stuttering."

"No, I'm not," Travis replied indignantly, then tried to answer. "She's...certainly full of questions. In fact, they never stop. But she's likable. She had Maude eating out of her hand the minute we walked into the restaurant. She could probably tame a tiger."

"I thought you were just going to pick her up and take her to the inn, maybe by the waterfall. What's this about Maude's?"

Travis felt his face burning. "She was hungry. I also took her to the falls. Thought that might get her mind off the vets."

Josh didn't say anything more, but his expression did. "Another beer?"

"I better not. I'm driving out to Jubal's ranch, see how Danny's doing and tell Jubal what to expect. I think Jenny Talbot's going to be knocking on his door soon."

Josh nodded. "I'll see you tomorrow night.

In the meantime, I'll ask Eve to divert Ms. Talbot tomorrow."

Travis had had dinner with Josh and his wife several times since Josh had contacted him about the study. Mayor Eve *would* be a good match for Jenny. The thought of the two of them together was truly frightening.

Travis had looked forward to the trip, to a fresh look at the country. He liked driving in the Western United States, with the ever-changing landscapes, and he liked driving alone. It gave him time to think and a chance to meet new people.

Travis got up and limped to his car. "She kept me moving today," he explained. "Tell Eve I said hello. How you ever got her to marry you, I don't know."

"She said it was my winning personality."

Travis raised an eyebrow. He still couldn't believe his no-nonsense staff sergeant was relaxing in a lawn chair, surrounded by dogs and sporting a big grin on his face.

He left, stopping long enough to call Jubal to alert him to his arrival. When he arrived, he punched a number on the security gate leading to the stable and drove inside. Five horses were grazing in the front pasture. He didn't recognize two of them, and they looked thinner than the others. Must be new arrivals. He knew that Jubal and his partner, Luke, were acquiring rescued horses for the program. The theory was the vets and horses would help each other to heal.

When he pulled up, a dog barked and ran several feet toward him, and then it retreated to the side of a tall, lanky man who appeared from the side of the ranch house. Sweat covered his forehead.

Former SEAL Jubal Pierce approached Travis, his hand outstretched. "How did the pickup go?"

"Interesting," he said. "How's Danny doing?"

"He's a great worker. Learns fast and never stops. He and the horses get along just fine, and he's already learned to saddle them. Right now, he's working with Nate and Craig Stokes, who are adding new stalls and a room for an employee in the stable. We plan to start on the bunkhouse when we agree on how many participants we want."

"That's why I'm here. I thought he might like to use Josh's cabin while I'm gone."

"We can ask him what he wants to do, but he's now using an extra room in the house," Jubal said. "He's made fast friends with this dog. Roger is one of Stephanie's rescues she foisted off on me. The kid has a way with animals, although he says he's never been around any."

"Two orphaned souls," Travis mused aloud. "He has no family, other than the army. Thanks for taking him in."

"I'm the grateful one. He's shy but good with the horses. He's already been in the saddle. He needs help with that leg, but I rigged a kind of harness. He's still a bit tentative, which is good. It's hard to tell this early, but I'm thinking he's a keeper. Hardworking kids like that are hard to find."

Relief and gratitude flooded Travis.

"That's great. Thanks."

"I think I'm the one thanking you. Since he arrived, I've been looking up info on horseback riding for amputees and learning a lot. I want to include them in whatever we do. Now, come on back and you can see how much we got done."

Travis followed him to the rear of the stable. The bones of the addition were in place. He'd met Nate, another vet who had partnered with Josh on some projects in and around Covenant Falls, but he hadn't met the other man.

Danny was standing on his new prosthetic and pounding nails into a cross-section. He finished and turned. "Major," he said, his face lighting up.

"It's Travis now. How's it going?"

"Just fine," Danny said as he knelt and rubbed the fur of the dog that trotted up to him. "I'm learning a lot, and the horses, they're fine. Real fine."

"Your leg?"

"It's okay."

But Travis could tell from the way the boy limped that it was still painful. He had grit, but then, he'd been a soldier.

Danny looked him straight in the eyes. "Thank you, Major." He didn't have to elaborate.

Travis just nodded, feeling like a fraud. He'd done damned little. Jubal led him back through the stable and offered him a sandwich, but Travis was still full of cheeseburger.

"I ate at Maude's," he explained.

"I heard," Jubal said.

"Of course you did." Travis sighed. "Why am I not surprised?"

He followed Jubal back out the stable. "Looks like you have some newcomers," he said.

"Four," Jubal said. "Two are in the pasture. These two need some extra attention."

"How many horses do you have now?"

"I have Jacko—I bought him from Luke, and he's my personal horse. He's probably most responsible for this effort. I was drifting until I met him. Two more came with the ranch. Well-behaved riding horses. And I bought three mares I can breed to Luke's stallion. In the meantime, they're good riding horses. I just adopted the four new horses from a horse rescue group. The two in the pasture need to be fattened but are gentle. The ones in the stalls are skittish and need a lot of attention."

"So ten on hand?" Travis said.

Jubal nodded. "I hope to add several mustangs before we open. And Luke and other ranchers are eager to participate so we're not limited in numbers."

Travis had hoped for more guidance. It was damn little to go on and a hell of a lot on his shoulders. "What exactly do you want me to do," Travis said.

"Simply put," Travis said, "assess existing programs and give us options with pros and cons. Josh has great faith in your ability to do both."

Travis inwardly groaned. It was a huge task and lives could depend on it. He was only too aware of the suicide rate among veterans, not to mention divorces and homelessness, but he didn't feel qualified for it.

Jubal must have sensed his hesitancy. "The goal in visiting the ranches is determining which seems the most effective for the greatest number of veterans along with the costs."

They were questions that challenged and intrigued Travis. He knew about training soldiers. But helping them heal? He was only too aware of the problems they faced. After multiple years of deployments, soldiers returned to families and communities that couldn't possibly understand what they'd experienced and continued to experience. The most difficult part was losing buddies who had become as close, or even closer than, family members. They'd lived together, depended on each other, protected each other. The band of brothers was a reality, not just a book title.

That loss along with the fierceness of nightmares and flashbacks, the reflexive response to loud noises, the inability to sleep and the pain of survivor's guilt made it all but impossible to return to a "normal" life for many. Could horses really be that livesaving?

Travis knew something of Jubal's history. After years of dangerous missions, the SEAL had lost his team and been held captive for two years. He saw the raw edges in Jubal and wondered whether the former SEAL wasn't trying to rid himself of ghosts by banishing them from others.

"I'd better go," he said. "I have a lot of work to do. I'm heading out Sunday, instead of Monday."

"How did your meeting with the journalist go?" Jubal asked.

"Interesting," he said. "It might be difficult to dissuade her from writing about the program and you, and God help you if she connects all the recent marriages and engagements. Covenant Falls will become the Western Love Boat."

"Is that why you're starting early? Getting out of Dodge?"

"I wasn't employed to run interference with

a reporter," Travis said. "The salary is way too low. Besides, I'm an outsider. I don't know anything about anything."

To his surprise, Jubal grinned. "Now, that's the best reason *for* you to handle her."

Handle her? Good luck to anyone who tried.

"I'm through," he said flatly. "I picked her up as asked. I suggested to Josh that Eve take over now."

"I hear she's pretty busy with the city budget now."

Travis shook his head. He couldn't wrap his mind around this town and the number of warriors reduced to, well, putty in the hands of the opposite sex.

Just as well he planned to leave as soon as he fulfilled his obligation to the group.

"I'm heading back to the cabin," he said. He left before Jubal could protest. He was not, absolutely not, going to be the go-to person for a reporter.

Didn't matter how damned appealing she might be.

CHAPTER EIGHT

THE NIGHTMARE RETURNED with a vengeance. It was the first time in a month.

Jenny heard the approaching rumble of the planes. The whistle of bombs and explosions mixed with screams. The air was full of dust and fire and death. She jerked awake.

Light seeped in from the bathroom. She'd left the light on inside and closed the door halfway. She hadn't wanted to wake in darkness. She only hoped she hadn't made any noise.

She held her breath for a few minutes. There was no pounding on the door, no ringing of the room phone.

She looked at the clock. A little after four. She knew from experience that she wouldn't go back to sleep again. Every sense was awake now. She picked up the journal and placed it on the night table. She'd read more than three-quarters of it last night.

She took a shower. Hot water first to wash away the sweat, and then cold water to wipe away the cobwebs in her head. After she dried herself off, she worked on her shoulder exercises with the folding rod she'd brought with her. She kept at it until the muscles and ligaments in her shoulder hurt so much that she almost screamed.

She wanted to go outside. Feel fresh air on her face. Wash away the lingering memory of dust and desperation and death. As comfortable as the room was, she felt trapped.

She pulled on some clothes. Then she left without locking the door. She doubted there were burglars in Covenant Falls. It looked like a model of a small town in a film from the 1960s. Was it real?

Was Travis Hammond real? She didn't need complications. She just wanted to heal and get back to where she belonged.

No one was in the lobby, although it was well lit. She opened the door and took a deep breath of the fresh air. A nearly full moon sat atop the mountains.

It was clean. Bright. So beautiful it hurt. She knew the mountains. She'd skied and climbed and walked the nearby Rockies while in college, but never had she known the peace she felt here. Maybe Covenant Falls did have a magic of its own.

She started walking. The streets were quiet, the houses dark. After walking about a mile, she turned back. She went to her room. It was still not time for the fresh coffee and pastries, but she had a coffee machine in her room. She didn't particularly care for the tiny packages and drip machines, but she needed the jolt.

She planned the day ahead. After breakfast she would walk back through town, meet whoever she could. Spend more time at the community center. She wanted to discover the heart of Covenant Falls.

She picked up the journal and tried to read, but her thoughts kept turning to Travis and hazel eyes that never seemed to be the same color. They'd changed with his moods. He'd been cautious around her, but he had a quick sense of humor that emerged when she least expected it.

She tried the journal again, reading the words of the Scottish trader who'd journeyed half a continent for a brother who didn't live to see their dream come true. Charlie, the romantic, would love the tale.

Her niece would love everything about the town. It held a strange pull for her, too. Maybe she was ready for a little peace.

Did she really want to go back to the Middle East? There were so many stories to be told there, but the loss and suffering of the people had drained her.

Maybe there were important stories here, as well. Stories not about wars, but people like

Angus, who saved the life of an enemy, or a small town working to make life better for veterans.

She took a chair, curled her legs under her and found the entry where she'd left off.

AFTER A RESTLESS SLEEP, Travis woke at dawn. He was relieved Danny was doing well. More than well. Danny seemed happier than at any time since he'd met him, except maybe the day he got his new prosthetic. From his few meetings with Jubal, Travis knew the former SEAL would look after Danny.

He got out of bed, pulled on a pair of jeans and walked to the dock. He sat on the bench and watched the first glimmers of dawn crawl over the horizon. The peace soothed the violence that had colored so much of his life.

An eagle, probably looking for breakfast, soared above him. He doubted it worried about the future or felt piercing loneliness. He'd had few visitors during the past two years beyond his ex-fiancé and several military friends.

He turned his thoughts back to Jenny. Despite her injury in Syria, she obviously loved her independence. He knew from the articles he'd found that she'd been in many of the Middle East hotspots. A lot of the stories were about civilians trying to exist in a war zone or surviving a terrorist bomb. There was empathy in the stories, a connection to the people she wrote about.

Her experiences, though, hadn't dimmed a contagious smile that had probably lured many people to say more than they'd ever intended.

Dammit, he wanted to see her again, spend time with her and discover more about her. But this was no time to get involved with a woman, particularly when he knew it would be temporary. He needed to start building some permanence now, whether it was the army or academics or something else. She had made it clear that she liked her freedom.

So why couldn't he get her out of his mind?

Time to get back to work. Today was Friday. He had a lot to do before Sunday. He'd ordered and read books on equine therapy and rehab programs and accumulated a growing file of different programs in the country. He kept finding new ones. The demand was strong. In his usual methodical way, he'd jotted down questions as he researched.

He left the dock and walked toward a path winding up the mountain, located behind the cabin. He hesitated once he reached the foot of the path. He'd tried it on his first visit to Covenant Falls, but it was steep, and he'd stumbled several times before heading back down. He was better at walking now, more aware of his ankle's limitations. Maybe he would try it later.

Once back at the cabin, his thoughts turned to his trip ahead. He'd already checked the mileage from Covenant Falls to Fort Hood. It was a long car trip but he really looked forward to it. He'd been cooped up in hospitals and rehab for two years. The freedom of the road was enticing.

He made coffee, fried three eggs and toasted some bread, then settled into one of Josh's extraordinarily comfortable chairs and started reviewing the materials he'd gathered.

There seemed to be no competition between the programs. By their very nature, participants were limited, and there was an ongoing demand.

Travis felt a responsibility to them. He'd been the person who sent men and women to train unreliable allies in hostile territory. He'd watched them cry over a fallen comrade but rarely for themselves when they went home without legs or arms or prospects of a job or future.

It was midafternoon when the phone rang. It was Josh. "You *are* coming for steaks tonight, right?" Josh asked.

"Sure," Travis said.

"I think I told you Eve invited Jennifer Talbot."

"I think your steaks overcome any reservations I have. What time?"

"Six thirty good for you?"

"Fine."

There was a pause. Then Josh said, "Can you pick her up and drive her here? Stephanie and Clint were going to do it, but she's been called out on a lost person, and Clint is going along with her. No telling how long the search will last."

After accepting the dinner invite, he couldn't very well say no—as much as he wanted to.

Or did he?

He didn't answer immediately.

"Don't worry," Josh said, interpreting the silence. "Eve's not matchmaking. Both of you are here temporarily. Eve knows that. It's just that Ms. Talbot doesn't drive, and we'll be busy cooking."

What could he say? That he was smitten with her, like a teenager?

He surrendered, feeling a jolt of anticipation. "I think I can manage that," he conceded.

After the call ended, Travis looked up the number of the inn on a list next to the phone and called Jenny. She wasn't in, and he left a message that he would pick her up at a quarter after six. He hoped that Eve had reached her about dinner.

He drank another cup of coffee and decided to try the path up the mountain again. It was just as steep as he remembered, but he was careful. By the time he reached a lookout about halfway up, he sat down and rested. Frustration filled him.

He used to run twenty miles. Now his leg ached in less than half a mile. His ankle had stiffened and didn't want to work. He looked at his watch. It was nearly five. Time to start heading back. He needed to have a good stiff drink. Then he'd check with Jenny to make sure she received the message.

HE HEADED FOR the inn. He was surprised to see Jenny step out of the doorway as he pulled up. She was wearing black slacks and an emerald green blouse that matched her eyes. Her short, copper-colored hair was damp and framed her face. As before, her only makeup appeared to be lipstick.

She opened the passenger-side door before he could get out.

"You got shanghaied again," she said with that quick smile. "Thanks for picking me up."

"You're welcome." He concentrated on driving the short distance. "How was your day?"

"Good. I spent most of the day at the community center going through newspapers, and I had another burger at Maude's. And now steaks. I'm a happy person. I wanted to meet more people but ran out of time."

"I have to warn you that, in addition to some very good steaks tonight, there's a mob of dogs."

"I like animals," she said. Then she added, "Eve said you and her husband served together."

"We did."

"Did you see about your young friend?"

He nodded. "Yeah. He's good. Learning some skills other than war."

The words popped out of his mouth without warning. *There had been so many kids, all so young. Eighteen. Nineteen. Twenty. Like his brother.*

He took a deep breath. The army had been his life and the Rangers his family. He didn't regret it. He was proud of his service, of the men who had served with him. But in the hospital, he'd seen so much loss. He'd also seen so much gallantry.

She asked softly, "Did he serve with you?"

"No. I met him in rehab."

"He has no family?"

"No. Foster kid. They throw them out of the system when they're eighteen. No education beyond high school. No stipend. Not even a ten-dollar bill. Just get the hell out. He felt his only choice was the army. Now he has to survive with one leg." He tried to suppress the anger he felt. "The problems facing foster kids would make a good story," he said. "A lot better than one about a small town."

"I'll remember that," she said, ignoring the implied criticism. "I would like to meet him."

They reached Josh's ranch. Travis smelled the smoke from the grill and steered Jenny toward the back of the ranch house once they'd both left the car. Josh was busy nursing charcoal and hickory in his grill.

She hadn't met Josh Manning before but went right to him, holding her hand out. "I'm Jenny."

Josh took it. "I'm Josh, and this fellow next to me is Amos." The Malinois standing guard next to him regarded her with cautious eyes.

"May I say hello?" she asked.

"He would be offended if you didn't," Josh said.

She stooped and Amos sniffed her. Then he licked her hand. She scratched behind the dog's ears, and he made little whining noises of approval.

"You passed the friend test," Josh said.

"He's a military dog, isn't he?"

"Was. He's retired, along with me. And if you like animals, you'll love my stepson's herd. They're undisciplined and drive me crazy, but they're lovable, and they came with the package."

"Don't believe him," came another voice from behind Travis.

He turned to see Eve behind him. "He adores them," she added. "And they return the feeling."

Eve went over to Jenny. "I'm Eve. It's so good to meet you in person."

"And I'm Jenny. Thanks for the invitation."

"I'm a little behind in the kitchen," Eve said. "Why don't you come inside and have a glass of wine while I finish the salad?"

Jenny nodded. "Sounds good."

The two women disappeared indoors.

Josh smiled at Travis. "She's pretty. She also has good taste in dogs."

Travis ignored the comment. "Where's my buddy and his menagerie?"

Josh raised an eyebrow. "I might just sue you for alienation of affection. I used to be my stepson's hero. Now it seems you are. Nick's been waiting for you all day. I finally convinced him to feed and water the horses. I'm sure he'll be here any minute to get another pitching lesson."

"He's got a good arm," Travis replied.

"Well, you created a monster. I have to catch balls every night now." Josh changed the subject. "How are you on the trip? Got it all worked out?"

"Pretty much. It's eight hundred miles to Fort Hood, and my appointment with Dr. Payne is at eleven Tuesday. Leaving Sunday will save me the pain of an eight-hundred-mile drive in one day."

"I was worried about that. You sure you don't want to fly down there and rent a car?"

"No," Travis replied. "Tell you the truth, I'm looking forward to a road trip."

"Okay. It's your choice," Josh said. "I like the programs you've selected."

"It's a good mix," Travis replied.

Josh took another sip of beer. "Wish I could go along, but I have a prospective client coming this week. A husband and wife are thinking about moving their business here. They live in California, where the business taxes are sky-high. Someone told them about our town."

"What kind of business?"

"You'll like this. Kind of ironic. It's a maker of dog and cat beds for a chain of pet stores. It's a small business but would employ ten or twelve people to start. The owners like this area and hated the traffic in Los Angeles. They also like to employ veterans, which is one of the reasons Covenant Falls caught their attention. The low taxes more than compensate for additional shipping costs. It's exactly the type of business we've been trying to draw."

"Considering the number of dogs I've met around here, they've found the right place," Travis observed. "They can make a profit just by selling to your family."

"I mentioned that," Josh replied with a grin. "They'll need a building, small but expandable. My partner, Nate, is an excellent builder and knows how to do it on a budget. I can work with the bank on financing. And, if they do move here, they'll need a house. Means a few more jobs and maybe some home sales."

"I never thought I would see the day you wore a suit," Travis said. "Or talked about financing."

"No suit yet, but I've been taking online courses in finance. The president of the bank has been working with me. Sometime I'll have to tell you that story."

"Another one?"

Josh shrugged.

Travis shook his head. "I still don't get why so many of you stayed here."

"For me, Eve is the answer. If I wanted her, I had to take the rest of the package, and that included Covenant Falls and her instinct to fix every person and every animal she encounters. There's never been a day I regretted it."

Nick appeared then from the direction of the stable and ran toward them. "Hi, Major Hammond. Will you give me some pitching tips again?"

"Sure," Travis said.

"Awesome," Nick said. He already had a baseball in hand.

Travis grinned. "You just happened to have one with you?"

"Yessir. The gloves are out here, too."

"If it's okay with Josh, let's show him what a great pitcher he's raising."

"Go to it," Josh said.

JENNY HELPED EVE finish a salad, chopping onions and tomatoes. She then accepted the offer of a glass of wine.

Andy had told her a little about Eve, that she'd been widowed when her son was still a toddler and that she'd been elected mayor four years ago. She'd married Josh Manning in an outside wedding attended by nearly the entire town.

Jenny liked everything she'd heard. A woman who was a survivor, who had lost a father to violence and a husband to a heart attack, and who'd made not only a new life but apparently a very purposeful one and who'd tamed a warrior. Or maybe became one with him.

She glanced out the kitchen window. Travis Hammond was leaning over a young boy who was holding a baseball.

"That's my son, Nick," Eve said. "He's been excited since he heard Travis was returning to Covenant Falls. Travis played baseball in college, and Nick is a Little League pitcher. Travis gave him some pointers on his last trip, and now Nick has decided he wants to be a professional baseball player. Before, he wanted to be a veterinarian."

"I can guess which you would prefer," Jenny said.

"Oh, I think he'll change his mind a dozen more times before he has to make decisions. Six months ago, he planned to be a forest ranger."

Jenny's attention returned to the tall man who held the ball with the three fingers on his right hand before giving it to Eve's son. Travis then stooped down and guided Nick's arm as the boy threw the ball to Josh. It hit the mark, and the boy looked up with such bliss her heart ached.

She reminded herself that Travis was a soldier. Yet she'd witnessed other scenes during conflicts when a soldier went out of his way to comfort or help a child caught in chaos. Why should she be surprised? He probably helped old ladies cross the street. He would stop the traffic in both directions.

"He's one of the really good guys," Eve said after they both watched for several minutes. "He and Josh are good friends, which is unusual considering the difference in ranks. Josh says Travis would have made colonel if he hadn't been so outspoken on behalf of his men." She turned away from the window. "Everything's ready except the steaks, and Josh is taking care of that. Let's join the guys."

Jenny hurried to open the back door as Eve carried their glasses of wine outside.

At seeing them, Josh left his pitching position to put the steaks on the grill, while Nick threw the ball to Travis and he threw it back. The sun hit the peaks of the mountains, and the horizon erupted with fire. The air was spiced with the scent of smoking hickory.

She could see the lure of this town, although she would probably go crazy after a few weeks. Wanderlust would catch up with her again.

She put her wineglass on an outside table and walked closer to where Travis was standing. One of Nick's pitches went wide, toward her, and she automatically reached out to catch it.

Pain shot through her, and she dropped the ball. She stood there for a moment, trying to absorb the sudden agony that ran through her.

Travis was by her side in seconds. "Your shoulder?"

"I'm fine," she insisted. "It will go away in a minute. I shouldn't have tried..."

"What can I do?" Travis said.

"What can *we* do?" Eve broke in.

Jenny was embarrassed. Everyone looked terribly concerned, but she knew the pain would gradually fade. It was Nick who worried her. He looked stricken.

She leaned down next to him. "I haven't caught a ball in a long time," she said softly. "You have one fine arm, my friend. You don't worry about mine. It will be as good as ever in a few minutes."

"Are you sure?" Nick asked.

"Absolutely. How can I not be when Josh is

grilling those steaks? You think I'd miss one of those?"

"He grills the best steaks ever," Nick bragged and started for the door. "Can I get you something, Miss Talbot?"

"After dinner, I'd like to meet the dogs I've heard about."

"They'd like that," Nick said, his worried expression fading.

"Why don't you go inside and put the salad on the table," Eve said.

"Okay," Nick said. He turned to Jenny again. "I sure am sorry if I hurt you."

"Not to worry another second, or you *will* hurt me."

"I like you a lot," Nick confided. Then he darted inside the house.

Eve looked at her. "Thank you."

"He's a nice kid."

"Yes, he is," Eve said. "*Now*, what can I do for you?"

"Serve me one of those steaks. You might have to cut mine tonight, but tomorrow my shoulder will be fine."

Eve gave her a slow smile. "Done," she said as she handed Jenny her glass of wine.

Travis hovered as Jenny held the glass in her left hand while trying not to let the others know how much her shoulder ached. She would take an anti-inflammatory tonight and it should be down to a dull ache in the morning.

Meanwhile, Jenny tried to concentrate on watching Josh's culinary skills as he added some kind of sauce to the meat. "Smells great," she said.

"Steak suppers have become a tradition for newcomers," Eve said. "It's our way of welcoming new friends. We usually don't try to injure our guests, though. Are you sure I can't get you something, or call the doctor?"

"Not necessary," Jenny said. "Truly, it's already fading away, and I wouldn't miss that steak for anything."

"If you're sure…"

"I am," Jenny said in a tone that, while pleasant, made it clear the subject was closed.

Eve nodded and turned to Travis. "Have you decided when you're leaving?"

"Sunday morning," Travis answered.

Jenny's ears perked up. "You're leaving?"

"Temporarily," Josh said.

Jenny raised an eyebrow.

"He's going to visit ranches that helps veterans," Nick, who'd just returned, said proudly. "I wanted to go, too, but I have to go to school."

Jenny's antenna went straight up and she turned to Travis. "That's interesting," she said. "You didn't mention that."

"No reason to," he said.

She was used to rebuffs but this one stung. She'd liked him and he knew about her interest in veterans and had said nothing. She wasn't going to show her disappointment, but that didn't mean she wasn't going to drop it.

"Equine therapy programs?" she asked.

He nodded warily.

"How long will you be gone?" she persisted.

"Not sure. Five, maybe six days," Travis replied.

She started to ask another question when Josh interrupted. "The steaks are ready. Travis, you want to help take them inside?"

Travis stood, and he and Josh went to the grill while Nick and Eve headed toward the house. She followed them inside.

But if Travis thought the subject was dropped he was in for a shock. Now her interest was thoroughly stirred and when that happened she would go to almost any lengths to satisfy it.

CHAPTER NINE

JENNY TRIED TO keep her thoughts to herself as she sat down at the table. The steaks did smell wonderful. An ambush would come later.

Eve apparently sensed something because she turned to Jenny. "Do you ride horses?" she asked.

"Not since a pony at a birthday party when I was ten, but it's on my bucket list."

"If your shoulder is better, come over tomorrow and ride Beauty. She's very gentle, and her gait is great for a new rider."

"I would love that. Thank you," Jenny said, her green eyes brightening. "The shoulder is already better."

"Good. What about 10:00 a.m.? The town doctor will be here, too. Her daughter is learning to ride. Lisa Redding might make a good story for you. She went from being a pediatric surgeon in a Chicago hospital to a small-town doc, and we're very lucky to have her. Small-town and rural areas have a rough time attracting doctors."

It probably *would* be a good story. Jenny was aware of the shortage of GPs, particularly in rural areas. At this rate, she could probably stay here for years. Everone wanted to give her a story except the one she really wanted. Still…

"Do you have a newspaper here?" she asked. "I didn't see one on the town website, but I saw an empty rack in Maude's restaurant."

"You might say we do," Eve said. "*The Covenant Falls Herald.* It exists, but that's about it. The editor/owner died and left it to a nephew who had no interest in running it. He's hoping to find someone willing to pay a far too high price for it. Right now, it carries canned material, like how to decorate a pumpkin or old recipes, a gossip column by the town's biggest nuisance and legal notices, which are cheaper than placing them in a larger county paper."

Jenny laughed. She liked Eve.

"I can tell Eve is a fan," Travis added wryly.

"I would give a lot to bring a new owner here," her hostess said. "The paper is more than a hundred years old. It's incredibly sad to see it deteriorate."

Jenny didn't like the direction the conversation had suddenly taken. From what she'd observed in the past two days, this town had a way of sucking people into its web. She wondered how it had acquired a coveted doctor. She hoped they didn't have a similar idea about her.

Supper was extraordinary. Because Jenny still

had pain in her shoulder, Eve had cut up one of the steaks, which melted in Jenny's mouth. The baked potatoes were perfect, and the salad just right. Jenny chose iced tea over more wine, since she might need a pain pill that night.

"Does everyone in Covenant Falls eat this well?" Jenny asked. "I think I've gained five pounds since I arrived."

"Just when there's company," Nick piped up.

"Yeah, and we starve you the rest of the time," Josh said.

"Well, there's more vegetables."

"You don't like vegetables?" Jenny asked.

"Not nearly as well as meat and pie."

Jenny was fascinated with the gentle banter between the adults and the boy. She hadn't had that. Dinner at her house had always been formal. Input from the younger members was not encouraged.

"What do you think about Covenant Falls?" Eve said.

"It's not a place to come to lose weight," Jenny replied. "But I think it's one of the state's best-kept secrets. I met two couples last night at the inn, and they told me they had a great time going to the old mining camps and then horseback riding up to the falls. They said they heard about it from other veterans."

"I like that," Josh said. "Particularly the fact they had a great time."

"Maybe you should target your marketing at veteran magazines," Jenny suggested. "Get quotes from some of the guests who are veterans, even offer free weekends as some kind of prize. If the inn isn't full, it's not going to cost you much. The main thing is getting people talking about it."

"That's a good idea," Eve said. "I'll mention it to Susan. In the meantime, let's go out and see Beauty and the Beast."

Jenny looked at her in surprise.

"My horses," Eve explained. "Josh and Nick can clean up the dishes."

Travis had been quiet during most of the dinner. "I'll help the guys."

"Sounds good to me," Eve said.

Jenny started to protest.

"They don't mind doing it," Eve said. "They make a contest as to who can finish the fastest. Men like competition."

Nick thrust out his chest at being called a man.

"Then I won't complain," Jenny said. She liked Eve and Josh more every minute. She noticed the ease and obvious respect between them, how they touched each other in passing, their exchange of smiles. Love visibly flowed between them and Nick.

"It took me a while to convince Josh that helping in the kitchen was a manly thing to do," Eve said.

"On occasion," Josh corrected as he put an arm around Eve and hugged her.

For a second, Jenny felt envy for something she'd always rejected. She didn't believe in love or marriage. Her father was a bully, her mother an alcoholic; her older sister had, from what she had seen, married a man just like her father. And Lenore's recent disaster only solidified everything she'd believed.

She viewed marriage as a millstone and had avoided any relationships other than short ones with guys who felt the same. She usually hadn't been in one place long to even start a relationship. But watching Josh Manning, a tough Ranger sergeant, collecting dishes challenged that very strong belief. Maybe it wouldn't last, but there was no doubting the love between the Mannings.

She accompanied Eve out to the stable. As they walked inside, two white horses poked their heads over the stall gate. Eve plucked two carrots from a box and handed one to Jenny. "This is the first step in making friends for life. This is Beauty." Eve stopped in front of the first one. "She's my love. The Beast can be a little surly sometimes, but never Beauty. She has a gait like a rocking horse."

Jenny offered Beauty the carrot. The horse accepted it gently and quickly chomped it down. They moved to the Beast, who leaned over the stall door to get his carrot. He took it more greedily.

"They're beautiful," Jenny said.

"They're good horses," Eve said, "but then most horses are, if properly treated. Jubal firmly believes that and is acquiring rescue horses for his ranch. He hopes to add some mustangs."

"Mustangs?"

"The federal government is rounding up the last of them. They're for sale cheap because they're wild. Don't even know what a human is."

"I read something recently about mustangs," Jenny said. "There was a story in the newspaper about a prison program… Wild Horse Inmate Program or something like that. They've discovered that in gentling the horses, the inmates themselves change."

Eve nodded. "I'm familiar with the program. The prison even makes money by then selling the trained mustangs. It's a win-win-win program. The mustangs are saved. The prisoners learn a skill and undergo rehabilitation, and people can buy reasonably priced, well-trained horses."

Beauty nuzzled Jenny for another carrot.

"I've been researching equine therapy. Some of the programs for vets are using wild mustangs. Do you know if Travis is planning to visit any of those ranches?"

"I really don't know," Eve said. "This is all pretty preliminary now."

Jenny paused, and then she plunged in. "I think the idea of creating an equine therapy program is great. Do you think Travis would agree to take me along on his trip? I would pay my expenses and share of the gas. I wouldn't publish anything prematurely and would fact check any story with your group. I don't usually do that, but I understand how sensitive this can be and the last thing I would want is to harm or delay this project."

"It's not up to me," Eve said. "It's Travis's decision."

"I think he would say no," Jenny said.

"Why?" Eve asked.

"He's been very…polite but…eager to get rid of me."

Eve smiled. "You should have seen Josh when I met him. He was mad as hell at the world. Didn't want anything to do with me or the town. He was just going to rehab his cabin and leave."

"And what happened to change his mind?"

"My son did. He was bit by a rattlesnake at Josh's cottage. It kinda smashed the ice."

"I don't have a son," Jenny said.

"Then you'll just have to ask Travis," Eve countered.

"I thought you might say that."

Eve hesitated. "He's a good guy but a private one. He was Josh's commanding officer for years, and yet Josh knows very little about his background or family, except he seems to have none. I do know there's no one Josh respects as much as Travis."

It was a warning. Subtle but clear.

Jenny nodded. "I'm going to give it a try."

Eve grinned. "Good luck."

IT WAS NEARLY ten that night when Travis and Jenny left the ranch and headed toward the Camel Trail Inn.

Travis had enjoyed the evening more than any he could remember. The food was great, the wine fine and the company even better. And coaching Nick brought Travis a satisfaction he hadn't felt in a long time.

Jenny, without any previous ties to the other four, had been the odd person out in the group, and yet she seemed to fit so easily, she might have been there many times earlier. She was warm, bright and curious with the adults, and he liked the way she treated Nick as someone important.

He felt warmer as he drove toward the inn. Damn but he wanted to touch her, kiss her, have her look at him with the same warmth he felt. He reminded himself they were going down different paths, and he had the feeling that if he kissed her, he couldn't end it there.

Down boy. Maybe it was just too damn long since he'd been with a woman. After he got engaged, he had been deployed for a year before being wounded and ending up in the hospital on and off for two years. He'd been self-conscious about his leg, his missing fingers and the scars on his body.

Jenny Talbot would probably be as repulsed as his former fiancé had been when she saw the full extent of the damage. But the attraction was there, dancing between them like a flame building all too rapidly. He was sure she felt it, too. He shouldn't start something he was unable to finish.

They arrived at the inn to find the parking lot almost full.

Neither of them made a move to get out of the car. "I'm sorry about your arm," he said. "I didn't think…"

"Neither did I," she said. "It doesn't always react that way. Every once in a while it just lets me know there's a demon still poking around in my shoulder. It will be fine in the morning."

"Maybe you shouldn't try to ride tomorrow."

"Maybe I should never try to ride or throw a ball or lift something, but then I would miss a lot."

He couldn't really argue with that. He'd tried to do activities he shouldn't either. He understood. And he sensed she didn't want to talk about it. Instead, he tried to change the subject to something neutral.

"Josh said they get a lot of townspeople and ranchers here on Friday and Saturday night. There's usually some entertainment and dancing."

He saw a momentary wistfulness in her face. If she had been out of the country in war zones for the past few years, it would have been a long time since she'd been on a dance floor. It had been a long time for Travis for other reasons.

She was silent for a moment, and then she asked, "Will you take me along on your trip to visit the equine therapy ranches?"

He was too startled to say anything.

"I'll pay my share of expenses, of course," she hurried on. "I won't be a bother. I won't butt in. I won't complain. About anything. And I won't publish anything without your and Josh's approval. Or whoever else's you want."

"You can do all that?" he asked, not without a touch of humor. "Not be a bother or butt in or complain?"

"When I really try," she said with that blinding smile of hers.

"I don't know if the word *try* convinces me."

She was silent for a few seconds. "Okay, I'll delete *try*. I'll do it."

"Including no story at all?"

"Yes," she said simply.

"Then you would be the first reporter ever. At least in my experience."

"Maybe," she said, "but that's how badly I want to do the story. Not just a short piece, but in-depth. What kind of programs are available? Do they have lasting effects?" She hesitated. Then she added, "I knew a lot of guys overseas. I know what many of them experienced, and I'm aware of the problems many face when they come home."

He didn't question her sincerity. She'd also experienced the violence of war. But the simple fact was Jubal and Josh were in the early stages. If there wasn't a need, or if they didn't think they could develop an effective program, they would not begin one.

"When I read a story about the Camel Trail Inn," Jenny continued, "and Susan mentioned the veterans here and the possibility of starting an equine therapy program, I knew I had to come."

"Why?" he asked.

"I'd already done a lot of research on PTSD

and therapy dogs for a possible article," she said. "I wasn't aware there are equine therapy programs designed specifically for veterans." She paused, and he knew there was something she wasn't saying. It was in the intensity with which she spoke. Had she loved someone with PTSD? That might account for her interest. He didn't like the sudden burst of jealousy that exploded inside.

"It goes deeper than that, doesn't it?" he guessed.

She stared at him for a moment and then sighed. "My interest is personal, as well as professional. When we were at Maude's, I'm sure you noticed those seconds at Maude's when I... went missing. I've been diagnosed with PTSD although I'm sure it's not anything like it is for those who have been fighting for years."

He realized the admission came reluctantly, but then a lot of veterans didn't like to admit it. He hadn't. It was admitting a vulnerability, and soldiers weren't supposed to do that. His was pretty much under control, but he knew a flashback could occur at any time. "What happened?" he asked gently.

She hesitated, obviously reluctant, and then said slowly, "I saw a lot of violence and the results of violence. I could live with that. I was reporting on stories that needed to be told. It was important because there wasn't much media around to record it."

"And?" he pressed when she took a deep breath.

"In April, I was in Syria, traveling with a medical team headed for an overcrowded hospital during a cease-fire. Someone apparently forgot it *was* a cease-fire and bombed the hospital and the streets around it. There was a little girl—four… five—running down the street…screaming.

"I can't forget her," she continued. "Or the doctors. There's something obscene about murdering doctors and nurses risking their lives to help others. But it's the girl in the nightmares. I'll never know what happened to her—or the doctors—because I was hit by shrapnel from one of the bombs. A friend got me to a medic, but that little girl still haunts me."

She looked at him, her eyes now filled with tears that didn't fall. "I don't like it," she said in a sudden outburst. "I don't like not being in control. Or fearing sleep. Or jumping at a loud noise. I can relate to soldiers who have the same anger and reluctance to get help or share those feelings with others, particularly family. No one can really understand until they've been there and watched children being starved or killed, or being so afraid you start shaking. You especially don't talk about fear. So you don't talk about any of it, and the bad memories grow and shadow any good moments and sometimes take over completely. I want to know what *can* help."

He could have said no to any other answer, but not this one. Jennifer Talbot was talented, confident and driven, but she had her demons, too. And the fact she had admitted so much to him, a virtual stranger, told him how much she wanted, and needed, some closure of her own.

"This is Jubal and Josh's project, not mine. They would have to approve." By not saying no immediately, he was asking for trouble.

"Thank you," she said simply.

It was probably one of the worse mistakes he'd ever made, and he wanted reassurance. "You do agree not to write anything Jubal and Josh don't approve?"

"Yes."

He got out of the car then. She didn't. He walked around and opened her door, and she stepped out and looked up at him. "Thanks for driving me home tonight and for…"

He was drowning in those eyes. There was still a dampness in them. She hadn't been lying about the child. It hadn't been a bid for sympathy. He touched her face with his good hand and guided his fingers over her features. He wanted to kiss her then. Badly. He wanted to blot out those bad memories. But she was vulnerable now and damn if he would take advantage of it.

He stepped back. *Keep your cool.* Hard to do when everything in him wanted to put his arms around her and kiss away those unshed tears.

Instead, he took her hand and led her to the door of the inn. Then he brushed an errant curl that fell over her forehead. "Good night, Jenny Talbot," he said softly.

She hadn't moved her gaze from him, her eyes searching his.

Damn, he didn't want to hover, but he didn't want to leave either. What he needed was another frigid shower. Maybe he would need a bunch of them.

She broke the spell. "Thank you," she said softly. "Thank you for taking me tonight. Thank you for…well…everything."

He nodded and turned away before he did or said something he would regret.

When he reached the car and looked back, she was gone.

CHAPTER TEN

JENNY FELT CONFLICTED as she walked into the inn. She was a step closer to a good story. Visiting several equine programs, as well as a psychologist involved in the programs, would be a gold mine for her.

But she was feeling so many other emotions. The story alone didn't account for the quickening of her heart. She still felt the warmth of Travis's hand on her. It was as if her body had suddenly sprung back to life.

Some inner voice told her a trip with Travis was a bad idea. But then again, a long car trip would expose warts. Maybe they would end up hating each other, and she would still have a story. He would probably be dominating. His way or the highway.

Or not.

He didn't appear to be dominating, but he was an army officer. A Ranger. Accustomed to being in charge and obeyed...

Susan still sat behind the check-in desk.

"You're working late," Jenny observed, relieved that her musings had been interrupted.

"Just some paperwork," Susan said. "We have a group here this weekend for a fiftieth wedding anniversary party. I'm making sure everything, including the banquet tomorrow night, goes well. The couple lives here, and, along with local friends, their children and great-grandchildren are coming back to celebrate. Some have already checked in and are in the dining room. Others will be here tomorrow."

"That sounds like fun." *Fifty years? And still married?*

"It will be. The Cutlers are good people. Lived here all their lives. Their children all left town after college, but they'll be here for the party with their families. I want it to go well." Susan looked at her more closely. "You have a glow about you. Covenant Falls must suit you."

A glow? She didn't glow, except maybe sometimes when she got a good story. It couldn't be for any other reason. "I think I'll be leaving Sunday for a few days. Then I'll be back at the end of the week."

"Just let me know," Susan said. "I'll have plenty of rooms next week. I should warn you, though, it'll probably be noisy tomorrow night. The dining room is totally booked, but you can order from the menu for room service. Best trout around."

"I'll remember that. Is there any place to buy clothes in town?"

"The General Store has some. Not a bad selection for a small town. Need a ride over there tomorrow?"

"I'll walk," Jenny said. "After a huge dinner tonight, I need the exercise."

She went to her room and took a long shower to wash Travis out of her mind. Especially that slow half smile that hid what he was really thinking. But then her mind wandered to the patient way he coached Nick.

Even if her father had a son, she couldn't imagine him ever taking time to play ball with him.

Darn, but she'd liked Travis when he drove her to Covenant Falls. Now she really liked him. More than liked him. *Admit it.* His touch had left a painful craving deep inside, one she'd never felt before. Sure, she'd felt passion and need before, but never any that ran this deep and strong.

It's just been two days.

Feeling suddenly uncertain, she called her sister. Lenore was usually up late. In the past few months, they had become friends. Her only friend stateside. She had been on the move too much to establish any long-lasting relationships.

"Hi," she said when Lenore answered. "I just came back from dinner."

"With anyone interesting?" Lenore asked.

"A married couple and their son. How's my niece doing?"

"She misses you. She's been looking up everything she can find about Covenant Falls."

"Tell her I'll bring her down when she has a school break. Lots of history here. She'll love it. I'm not so sure you would. The only place to buy clothes is a general store."

"Are you saying I'm shallow?" Lenore asked, a sharp edge to her tone.

A year ago, Jenny would have gotten defensive at that tone. Now she said mildly, "Nope, you just like to dress well as opposed to my jeans and fatigues."

"With your figure, you would look good in a burlap bag if there are such things now."

"I have *no* shape, Lenore," Jenny corrected her.

"Better than too much of one," Lenore said, and Jenny heard sadness in her voice. Had weight been one of the problems with Lenore's marriage? Not that Lenore was overweight, but she had gained a few pounds since the time she was a high school cheerleader. Jenny thought she looked just right. But Lenore's ex-husband liked perfect, or at least his idea of perfect. *Jerk*.

"If I keep eating as much as I have in the past

two days, I'm going to swell up like a blimp," Jenny said. "The food is good. Great, in fact."

"Maybe I'll come with Charlie after all," Lenore said.

"I'd like that. We'll plan on it."

After they said goodbye, Jenny wondered if Lenore would like Covenant Falls for more than a day or two. She would love the waterfall. Who wouldn't with its perpetual rainbow? Maybe a place like Covenant Falls was exactly what Lenore needed.

Jenny stayed up late to continue researching equine therapy programs. She guessed at which ones Travis planned to visit and picked out several that particularly interested her.

She thought about Jubal. She wanted to meet the ex-SEAL in any event. She knew his history. It was all over the newspapers when he returned from the dead. She wondered how he was adjusting to the peaceful life of a rancher.

She made a mental list of things to do tomorrow. She had to get Angus Monroe's journal back to Andy, go shopping for clothes, have the riding lesson at Eve's and take a trip to Jubal Pierce's ranch.

If Travis convinced Jubal to let her go with him. If he really tried.

She glanced at the clock. It was eleven now, and she was tired. She hadn't had much sleep last night, and tomorrow would be a busy day. The sharp pain in her shoulder had reduced to a throb, but the anti-inflammatory should help further. It was important that she appeared well tomorrow.

She had to get some sleep if she wanted to be sharp tomorrow, and she needed to be that. She might have a lot of persuading left to do.

She closed her eyes, willing sleep to come and trying to banish warm hazel eyes from her mind.

JOSH AND JUBAL had both sworn to the benefits of swimming in the lake. Travis hadn't been so sure.

Jubal was a former SEAL. Frigid water swimming was something he did, even liked, according to Josh. It was included in Ranger training, but not to the extent of what the SEALs did. To Travis, it had been the worst part of training. Why swim in icy water if you didn't have to? Pain for pain's sake did not appeal to him.

Still, a little pain right now might knock some sense into him.

He didn't have a suit with him, but he cut the legs off a pair of jeans. He certainly didn't want to be arrested for indecent exposure, even if he doubted anyone would see him at this time of night. Still… he was the guest of the mayor's husband.

He selected the newest pair of jeans rather than the oldest. The oldest were more comfortable.

He found a pair of scissors and hacked off the legs, wondering as he did so whether he'd lost his mind in even thinking about taking Jenny with him next week.

Seven days of temptation, and it *would* be temptation.

But the look in her eyes when she told him about the bombing made it impossible for him to say no. He hadn't experienced the worst effects of PTSD, although there was the occasional nightmare. But he'd seen enough in rehab to know how it ravaged lives. He had no doubt that she had it.

It was eleven. The temperature was around seventy degrees, with a cooling breeze.

He walked to the lake and plunged in.

He froze at first, but then his body grew accustomed to it, and his strokes warmed his body. His bad foot didn't matter. His missing fingers were inconsequential. He concentrated on each stroke, reached halfway and turned back.

When Travis got to shore, he toweled off, understanding now why Josh and Jubal recommended the swim. He had some measure of control back. Travis moved as quickly as he could back to the cabin as the breeze strengthened. He would call Josh and Jubal in the morning about Jenny's request. He would express no opinion on it except, maybe, a lack of enthusiasm.

JENNY WOKE WITH a jerk. She panicked for a moment, uncertain as to where she was. Then, slowly, everything came into focus, and she remembered. Covenant Falls was a safe place, probably the most peaceful she'd ever visited. She looked at the clock. It was a few minutes past six.

She tested her arm. It was still a little sore, but far better than the night before. She pulled on her jeans and a clean T-shirt, ran a brush through her hair, brushed her teeth and grabbed her laptop before leaving the room.

As promised, hot coffee and pastries were available in the lobby. Jenny picked up a mug and filled it. Black coffee was her lifeblood, and she took an appreciative sip. Then she looked around. The room was empty, except for an older woman behind the desk.

She walked over to her. "Am I the first up?" she asked.

"Yes. That means you get first choice of the pastries. They were baked last night. I recommend the cinnamon rolls," the woman said. "I'm Mary Reid, assistant manager."

"I'm happy to see that Susan isn't here twenty-four hours."

"She has been at times."

Jenny grabbed one of the rolls. *How could an inn feel so much like a home?* Or was it just warmer than her own home had been? The employees seemed to adopt their visitors rather than just serve them. Several tables and chairs had been placed in the lobby, and she took a seat.

She opened up her laptop. News was her drug. She usually kept a television on an all-news station as well as trolling the internet several times a day. She was often doing something else at the same time, such as shoulder exercises, reading or writing. But she always kept one eye on the news.

Not since she arrived in Covenant Falls, though. It was weird. Out of character. And yet, she didn't care. It was like being in some kind of Neverland for the hard-driving realist she'd been these past few years.

She finished her coffee and refilled the mug. Then she tasted the cinnamon roll and thought she'd died and gone to heaven. She thanked Mary and took the coffee and another pastry to her room to watch the news. Time to get back to normal.

She was anxious. Would Jubal, whom she'd never met, veto her inclusion on the trip? Would she have a chance to plead her case? Or would Travis veto it himself when he rethought it?

She finished the cinnamon roll and then did her shoulder exercises while watching the news. Her shoulder ached more than usual, but at least she could use it.

She was pretty sure she could still ride a horse. Her phone rang.

"Hope I didn't wake you," Eve said.

"No. I'm an early riser."

"I suspected as much. Plans have changed. Instead of a ride at my house, how about taking it at Jubal's ranch today? If that's okay with you, I'll pick you up at eleven and drive you there."

Jenny was stunned and then elated. In addition to needing his approval for the trip, Jubal Pierce would make a great story subject. "Sounds good," she said, trying to contain her excitement, although a small voice inside said it was a test.

"Wear jeans," Eve said. "And some kind of boots or laced shoes if you have them."

"Can do," Jenny replied.

"Great. See you at eleven." Eve hung up.

Then Jenny called her mother to say she might be on the road for a while. Before her injury, she'd gone months without contacting her family. But during her stay at her parents' house, she'd noticed how hard her mother had tried to connect with her.

"Why don't you come back?" her mother said. "I miss you. It was so nice having you here for a while."

Maybe for her mother, not so much her father. In the weeks she'd spent there, he'd been gone ninety percent of the time and had little time for her when he was present—except to tell her she'd brought her wounds on herself. "I have to get back to work," Jenny said.

"We can give you money if that's the problem," her mother said.

"I'm fine," Jenny said. "My shoulder is better, and I'm working on several stories."

"Well…if you're sure…" Her voice trailed off.

"I am, but thanks for offering."

"You're my youngest. If you need anything…"

She heard the ache of loneliness in her mother's voice, and it ripped into her heart. "I know," she said softly. "And I'll be back to see you in a few weeks." Maybe, she thought, she'd been selfish not to notice her mother's unhappiness. Was it new? Or had it been there twelve years ago when she finished college and took off on her own? She'd felt so alienated then, after years of criticism from her father and little or no support from her mother. She hung up the phone and glanced at the clock. It was nearly nine thirty. She went out to the lobby.

Susan was back at the desk. "Good morning."

"I'm off to the General Store. Can I get riding boots there?"

"You certainly can."

"Is it just a general store or is it named General Store?"

"The latter," Susan said with a smile.

Jenny had noticed the store earlier and knew how to get there. It was a cool morning, with wispy clouds floating through a deep blue sky. It was going to be a good day. She sauntered rather than walking briskly. She wasn't in a hurry, and it was a sheer pleasure to smell the scent of pine and look up at the mountains. She noted everything around her. The houses in this neighborhood were modest but well-tended. Grass was mowed, house exteriors painted.

She passed a drug store, a clinic and Maude's, which looked full. She thought about going into the restaurant, but she was still full of cinnamon rolls. She passed up the temptation and found the General Store.

Inside, she wandered to the clothing racks in the back and selected a wash-and-wear red skirt and a white short-sleeved blouse, along with a red sweater for chilly nights.

A woman approached her. "I'm Heather. Can I help you?"

"I'm looking for some footwear. I have a horseback riding lesson today, and all I have is a pair of sandals and some canvas sneakers."

"Where are you going?" Heather asked.

"Jubal Pierce's ranch."

"Ah…you must be the reporter."

She tried to figure out how the clerk knew.

"I'm *a* reporter," she said good-naturedly. "I don't know if I'm *the* reporter."

Heather grinned. "You must be. Word is a reporter is in town. No mention of two. News travels fast around here. But let's solve your problem. You really need boots, especially if you keep on riding."

Now that was an interesting assumption. "I don't know if I will," she said, "but I'd like to look at them." If she was going to be walking around ranches, she would need something tougher than the footwear she'd brought with her. She was certainly familiar with boots. She'd often worn army surplus boots in the Mideast.

Heather led her over to a sizable shoe and boot area. Jenny was impressed at the variety.

Heather asked her size, and then she selected three different styles of boots. "I would suggest paddock boots rather than tall riding boots. They're less expensive, more versatile and a lot easier to put on because they zip up."

Jenny eyed an elegant pair of riding boots, tall with supple leather and an engraved Western pattern, but realized immediately that buying them would be foolish. In addition to being awkward to carry, she might be wearing them only once. They were also three-times more expensive than the paddock boots.

She had to watch her money. She had savings,

but she knew how fast they could run out. It was essential to sell some stories, both for income and to keep her name out there.

"I'll take the paddock boots," she said after trying them on.

"A good decision since you're just beginning," Heather said. "Both Luke and Jubal are good instructors. My daughter is going to them. They have adjoining ranches, you know. Jubal teaches beginning riders and Luke teaches advanced ones."

"Is Luke a veteran, too?" she asked.

"Yup, Vietnam. We have loads of veterans, one going back as far as World War II. He's in his '90s."

Before long, Jenny was going to have to expand her mental file cabinet. Possible stories were crowding inside.

"Luke's wife also teaches and is a well-known barrel racing coach," Heather continued. "She's won several barrel racing championships."

Jenny couldn't wait to get back to the inn and jot down notes on her iPad. She finished shopping and left the store with the boots plus some additional clothes she might need on a road trip, including a nice skirt and blouse along with an additional pair of jeans and a checkered shirt for riding. She still had some time before Eve was to pick her up. She only hoped she wouldn't make a complete fool of herself and fall off the horse. Or was Jubal Pierce waiting for an excuse to say no?

She saw the veterinarian office and remembered from last night that the vet had gone on a search-and-rescue mission. She wondered how it turned out.

When she tried the door, it opened. A bell rang, and a pretty young girl came from the back.

"Is the veterinarian in?"

"Stephanie?"

Jenny nodded, noting how the girl didn't include the title *Doctor* or Stephanie's last name. Everyone in Covenant Falls seemed amazingly casual with titles.

"Yes."

"She didn't get back until early this morning. She's sleeping. I'm Beth Malloy, her vet tech. Can I help you?"

"No, thanks. I was passing and thought I'd like to meet her. I've heard a lot about Dr. Phillips. Did the search go well?"

"Yes. They found the woman alive. She took a wrong turn in the mountains, ran out of gas and started walking. She'd wandered way off the road. She should have stayed with the car. It's usually easier to locate. I'll tell Stephanie you came by."

Jenny thanked her and headed back to the inn. She changed into a clean pair of jeans, the new shirt and the new boots. She reached the inn's entrance just as Eve drove up.

"Hi," Jenny said as she got into the car.

Eve nodded with approval as she surveyed her clothes.

"Heather helped me," Jenny explained. "She recommended the boots."

"She has an unerring instinct with customers," Eve said. "She and her husband own the store. He does the business part. She selects the inventory."

"And they're still married?" Jenny exclaimed.

"Oh, yes, they adore each other."

Damn, what was it about Covenant Falls that kept turning all her beliefs on their head?

She changed the subject. "Tell me about Jubal Pierce."

"Doesn't talk much, but he's a good instructor. He's great with kids. Not so sure about reporters," Eve added with a grin. "But he just got engaged to the town doctor, so he might be more mellow."

A challenge? Well, she liked challenges. They were what drove her—always had and probably always would. She would be darned if she allowed her injury or PTSD to stop her.

CHAPTER ELEVEN

As Eve drove up to a fenced property, Jenny's gaze was drawn to a young pinto frolicking in the pasture with an older horse. They left the car and approached a neat two-story brick house. Jenny noticed several cars and trucks—including Travis's rental car—parked in what appeared to be a recently expanded parking lot.

Had he been invited as well? Was he riding?

Eve led the way to a stable that was obviously being enlarged. A riding ring had been recently constructed next to it. The lumber was fresh.

A tall man with dark hair was talking to Travis and a thin young man with a prothesis for his right leg.

It must be the Danny whom Travis had mentioned: the young soldier who'd been in foster homes. The boy—no, man—had a thatch of dirty blond hair and a wiry body. His jeans were coated with dust, and he had a big smile on his face.

Danny said something to the older man, and they both turned. Jeans and boots were the uniform of the day, and she fit right in. She was grateful for Eve's advice.

Even if she hadn't already met Travis and heard about Danny, she would have known which of them was Jubal Pierce. He was a little taller than Travis and looked all muscle. His face was hard, his features strong, and he had the most piercing blue eyes she'd ever seen. He didn't smile as she approached, but studied her as if she was an odd specimen.

Jenny was not easily impressed, but she was now. Jubal Pierce was one of the very few American servicemen to escape after being captured by terrorists. She had visited the SEAL training camp and had a healthy appreciation of what it took to be a SEAL. She knew better than to mention it, but she had a million questions for him.

"Eve said you're interested in riding," he said in a gruff voice. It was a statement more than a question.

"Yes."

"Ever been on a horse?"

"Not since I was a kid, and that was a very tame pony."

"Never had an interest?" It was more an accusation than a statement.

"It's not that. More like no opportunity."

He turned to the young soldier. "This is Danny.

He's learning to ride in between working for his keep."

"Hi, Danny," she said. "It's good to meet you."

"Yes, ma'am. Me, too. I mean…meet you," he stuttered.

"He'll be learning with you," the former SEAL said. "He's already made friends with the horse he'll be riding, and I picked one out for you. Why don't you go meet Lucy, become familiar with her. Danny will show you how to saddle her."

She saw Danny's surprised face as Jubal Pierce turned away. He apparently hadn't expected to be given the responsibility. Jubal Pierce was obviously a swim or sink kind of teacher.

Without comment, Danny led the way into the stable. Jenny realized that this was, in some way, a test for both of them. Just inside the stable, the young soldier plucked a carrot from a box and handed it to Jenny. "This is for Lucy. She's a rescue horse. Jubal says she apparently was abandoned by her owners and nearly starved to death, but she's gaining weight and happy now. I rode her yesterday. She's small but a good riding horse."

"Great," she said. "I want a nice horse for my first ride."

He grinned. "Talk to her for a few minutes. Let her get used to your scent, your voice, your touch. You might want to stroke her face." He went to the next stall and gave its inhabitant a carrot as he hummed.

She heard the comforting tone of his voice and tried to imitate it as she whispered nonsense to Lucy, who nuzzled her, looking for another treat. She wished she had one as she looked into Lucy's large brown eyes. *Note to self: always carry carrots when approaching a horse.*

Jenny watched Danny attach a lead to his horse's halter and lead him out. She did the same and followed. He led her to what she recognized from films as a tack room.

Was she really going to saddle her horse?

"First," Danny said as he handed her a brush, "you groom the area where the saddle will sit." He demonstrated with his horse, and she followed his lead.

"Then check the saddle pad to make sure there aren't any burrs, straw or anything else that might cause saddle sores."

He went through the saddling process step by step, but when she came to lifting the heavy Western saddle, agonizing pain shot through her shoulder, and she dropped it, startling the horse.

"Here, ma'am, I'll do it," Danny said.

Her face flamed. She wasn't used to failing, and she particularly didn't want to fail in front of Jubal and Travis. She shook her head and waited for the pain to pass. She would be prepared for it next time.

"I'll help," Travis, who'd apparently been watching from the door, said. "I don't want you to do more damage to that shoulder."

"I can do it," she insisted. She was used to doing for herself. She took pride in it, even if it was painful. Stupid, she knew, but there it was.

"I don't doubt that, but then what would you do if it caused more damage? I should have realized... Jubal didn't know."

He took the saddle and, with one smooth motion, placed it on the horse. "There," he said. "You can buckle the cinch. Reach down with your left hand and tighten the cinch until it's snug. You should be just able to slip your hand in between your horse's belly and the cinch."

She followed the instructions, despite the pain in her shoulder. She hated that Travis had seen her fail. She hoped it wouldn't affect his decision to take her along with him.

"Danny can lead you through the last steps. He's apparently learning fast. He didn't know one end of a horse from the other when he came here a week ago. When you finish, lead him out."

Danny watched him leave, a look of hero worship on his face.

"You really like him, don't you?" she asked.

"I would follow him to hell and back," Danny

said. "I was just a corporal at the army rehab center, a nobody who didn't know what he was going to do with one leg and not much education. It was the major who started challenging me, convincing me I could be anything I wanted to be. And he didn't forget me. When he was released, he continued to come and see me. He got me this job, even paid my airfare here—although I'm going to pay it back."

All she could do was nod. She listened to Danny and followed the rest of his instructions. Despite his claim he didn't have much education, he seemed a wickedly smart young man. And determined. She knew he'd only been here a few days and guessed from what Travis had said he hadn't known anything about horses before he arrived.

When they finished, the two of them led their horses out of the stable. Jubal was leaning against the fence. He inspected her saddle and bridle, and then nodded approval at Danny. "That's a good job, Danny."

"Thank you, sir." Danny seemed to grow taller. It was obvious he was in awe of Jubal.

Jubal turned his attention to Jenny. "Do you think you can ride with that shoulder?"

So Travis had said something to him about her shoulder.

"I'm going to try."

"What's the injury?"

She told him.

"Is it still hurting from lifting the saddle?"

"Not much."

He smiled for the first time and nodded. "Good. Take hold of the saddle horn with both hands. Don't try to put weight on the right one." He held out his locked fingers for her left leg and, with one easy gesture, vaulted her into the saddle. It was all she could do to keep from going over the other side. She looked at Travis and found him grinning.

She would have liked to sock both of them, but she straightened up in the saddle and tried to look dignified.

The lesson started.

TRAVIS CLIMBED UP to sit on the corral fence and watched as Jubal instructed both Danny and Jenny. He was equally tough on both, although Danny, who'd had several days of lessons, rode with more confidence. He certainly had tacked his horse with a level of comfort that surprised Travis.

Jubal was obviously feeling Jenny Talbot out. He had not been happy when Travis had told him about Jenny's proposal. The former SEAL didn't care much for reporters. He'd been hounded when he first returned and refused to give any interviews. His team had died. He had survived. That didn't make him a hero, and he deeply resented any attempt to publicize the situation. Travis completely understood those feelings.

But Jubal obviously sensed Travis's ambivalence about Jenny's request to go with him. They had discussed her request before she arrived and, Jubal apparently decided to learn more about Jenny Talbot through the riding lesson.

Jenny was more than up to the test. Travis watched as she did everything Jubal asked without complaint, although she asked a few questions to make sure she was doing everything correctly. Her body moved easily with the horse, and she praised the mare frequently. When they finished, Jubal nodded his approval. With Jubal, that was the best anyone could get.

As Jenny and Danny led their horses inside the stable to cool them off, Jubal walked over to the fence. "She's a natural," he said.

"I would have guessed that," Travis agreed. "This is your project. You're the boss. But I think you can trust her to do as she promises. If she says she won't write anything you don't approve, I don't think she will." He paused before saying, "Quite honestly, she'll probably be helpful and come up with questions I wouldn't."

Jubal raised an eyebrow.

Travis shrugged his shoulders. "She has a way of getting people to talk…"

"I noticed," Jubal said with a slight smile.

"You're paying for the trip," Travis said, "although she said she would pay her share of expenses."

Jubal shrugged. "Josh trusts your instincts and judgment. I have to admit that what little I've seen of Jenny Talbot, I liked. But whether you take her or not is up to you."

"Thanks," Travis said sarcastically.

"Did you want me to be the bad guy?"

Maybe. He sure as hell didn't want to admit it. He was growing fond of the idea of having a companion on the trip. At least, this companion. This woman who made him laugh. He hadn't done much of that in a long time.

"She *is* attractive," Jubal observed, his gaze fixed on Travis. When Travis didn't answer, he said, "She's obviously smart and capable and apparently determined to take care of herself."

"I kinda noticed that about her."

"That could be a problem. She never should have tried to lift that saddle."

Travis nodded.

"Well, she certainly connects with people. Josh and Eve like her, and that means a lot. But like I said, it's your decision. I'm not going to make it for you. Come on inside. I've set up an account for the project and have a credit card for you. If you decide to take Miss Talbot, share the costs. That wouldn't compromise either the program or her. Travis followed Jubal into the ranch house.

"Hopefully, by the end of next week, we'll finish enlarging the stable," Jubal said. "When we decide exactly what size bunkhouse we'll need, we'll have an old-fashioned barn raising. Every veteran in town will be here." Jubal walked through the living room to the kitchen, opened the fridge, took out two beers and tossed one to Travis. "I have to thank you for Danny. He's a real asset. Luke is working with him. He thinks Danny can be a good instructor, and younger participants can relate to him better than to Luke or me."

Carrying the beers, they went back to Jubal's office and he gave Travis the credit card. "Call me if you have any problems. Thanks for doing this."

The two of them finished the beers and returned to the corral just as Jenny and Eve emerged from the barn and joined them.

"You might be sore for the next few days," Eve warned her. "You've just used muscles you probably didn't know you had. Soak in a hot bath tonight."

"It's worth it," Jenny said. "Horseback riding is—or was—on my bucket list. I understand why it can be therapeutic." She turned to Jubal. "Thank you," she said, and Jubal nodded.

She hesitated for a moment, and then she asked, "Did your name come from the southern general?"

"You know some history," Jubal said with approval. "Jubal Early. He was a Texan and a hero to my family, who lived in the same community during the early days of Texas. My father and grandfather were Jubals, too."

"Is your father still alive?"

Jubal hesitated, and then he shrugged. "He was a rodeo cowboy. Rode broncs. He was killed by one when I was seven."

"I'm so sorry," Jenny said. "I always ask too many questions."

"So I've been warned," Jubal replied.

Travis watched as Jenny thanked Jubal. "I learned a lot today," she added. "I expect that this will be the first of many rides. By the way," she said, "I noticed a pinto foal having a fine time in the pasture. How old is he or she?"

"Five months. I was present when he was born. It's an experience that humbles you."

"I would love to see a birth," Jenny said.

"One of us can alert you when the next is due," Jubal said, surprising Travis even more. "I think Luke has a mare that's due soon. Luke says it makes ranching worth all the work and risk, and I agree. It's one of the reasons I bought the ranch."

Travis couldn't remember ever hearing Jubal

talk as much, or with as much emotion, as he was doing now. More Jenny magic.

He was obviously in trouble.

Jubal led them to the fence and whistled. The mare and foal immediately came to the fence. Jubal gave Jenny a carrot from one of his many pockets. "This is Melody, the proud mom," he said as Jenny gave the mare the carrot. "The colt is Promise," he added as he ran his hand along the foal's head.

Travis watched Jenny's face soften as she touched the colt. "He's handsome."

"My partner, Luke, gave me the colt as a ranch-warming gift," Jubal said. "Melody is his prize mare, though, and I couldn't pry her away from him. She's on loan at the moment."

Another car turned into the drive. "That's Lisa," Jubal said to Jenny. "Our town doctor."

Travis had met Dr. Lisa Redding on his previous visit. Josh had told him Dr. Redding and Jubal were the next thing to being engaged, but it was obvious that he wasn't mentioning it to Jenny. He was still sorting out the close-knit circle of friends made up of veterans and their wives, fiancés and soon-to-be one or the other. It had to be especially confusing to Jenny.

He watched as Jenny engaged the newcomer and soon they were chatting like old friends. He sighed. They might be here a while longer.

CHAPTER TWELVE

JENNY WAS STARVING when she left the ranch with Travis. She hadn't had anything to eat since those two cinnamon rolls at 6:00 a.m.

It was her fault. She stayed much too long talking to Dr. Lisa Redding. The conversation had revolved around moving from a big city and major hospital to a one-stop-sign town and a small clinic. She made mental notes she would transfer to her tablet. She hadn't wanted to interrupt the conversation by taking out her phone and asking to record it. That could come later.

Travis wandered away and was talking to Jubal when she finished. "Thanks for waiting for me," she said.

"You're welcome," he said solemnly, but there was a tease in his eyes.

"They're all great. Josh, Jubal, Danny."

"Yeah, they are, but it wasn't easy to get to where they are now."

"What about you?"

He shrugged. "I suppose I have a few demons.

I try not to pay any attention to them. I got off easy compared to so many others."

"Is that why you adopted Danny?"

"He's a soldier. He deserved help," he said as they walked to his car. "Hungry?"

"Starved. Maybe some takeout at Maude's?"

"I was thinking more like a steak at the Rusty Nail. They're not as good as Josh's, but they're good. The owner is a veteran."

She sighed happily. "That sounds perfect." She hesitated before she ventured, "I'm going with you, then?"

"If you follow up on your promise," he said, wondering if he was making a very big mistake. "Can you go on short notice?"

"I've been doing that all my adult life. Keeping promises *and* moving with short notice."

"It's a very long drive," he warned.

"I like road trips," she said. "I usually fly, but I've always thought that when I had time…an open road was appealing. And after today, I really want to visit the other ranches."

"Do you ever slow down?" he asked.

"I try not to."

The Rusty Nail was the typical small-town tavern with an unpaved parking lot and worn cedar exterior. They walked inside to a large room with sawdust on the floor and peanuts on the table.

They were immediately greeted by a young woman. "Hi, Major Hammond. Good to see you again."

"You have two hungry people," Travis said. "This is Jenny Talbot. She's a reporter."

"I heard. I was hoping you'd come by."

"Of course you heard," Jenny said with a smile. "I'm quickly learning that Covenant Falls works like a game of telephone."

Travis smiled and changed the subject. "I'll have your strip steak rare, with a baked potato and a side of mushrooms."

"I'll have the same, but make mine medium rare," Jenny said. "And a beer. Anything cold. You pick."

"Make it two," Travis said.

The waitress grinned. "I like trust."

"I like *her*," Jenny said after she left.

"Everyone does. She's one reason this place thrives. That and the food."

Jenny cracked a peanut shell and popped the nuts into her mouth. "That's good. I could almost have eaten one of those horses, but Jubal and Josh wouldn't approve. They're a lot alike, aren't they?"

"Josh is more pragmatic. He's really good with business, but then he was always great with details. It was what made him a fine staff sergeant. He's a lot more relaxed now. Eve and her son have really mellowed him." There he went confiding in her again. "How's your arm?"

"Fine. I hope you don't feel guilty. I have a habit of forgetting about it. Maybe because I hate any limitations. But I noticed how good you were with Nick."

"He's got a good arm. I started pitching at that age."

"Eve said you played baseball in college. Ever think about going pro?"

"Baseball provided my education, but I knew I wasn't major-league good."

"So where do you live these days?" she asked.

"Right now, I have a small apartment near Walter Reed. What about you?" It was just so damn natural talking to her. Conversation flowed between them. No wonder she was a good reporter. He warned himself to be careful.

"I don't really have one," she said. "I've been living overseas out of a duffel bag for nearly ten years. Didn't make any sense to buy or rent."

"What do the doctors say about your shoulder?"

She shrugged. "I might get full function, then again I might not. I'm doing exercises, but it's slow. I can't complain because there's a lot of people who are dead or with worse wounds for a better reason."

The beers came in frosted mugs. She touched hers to his, and they took a long draft.

She was not dainty in drinking. She chugged it down like any soldier. But then she'd been in the sun most of the day. Her cheeks were flushed, and her green eyes gleamed. She was so full of life, it seemed to radiate from her. He had already noticed how people were drawn to her. She was genuinely interested in everyone she met, ready for any adventure and obviously fearless…

He doubted if anything—or anyone—could hold her for very long.

Particularly a war-worn soldier with a bum leg and a questionable future. *Why even worry about it?* She wouldn't be here long, and neither would he. They would go back to their separate worlds in several weeks.

"You look lost in thought," she said.

"Just enjoying the beer. How did you like your first horseback ride?"

"I loved it. I just want to saddle a horse on my own."

"It'll come."

"Do you ride?" she asked.

"When I was a kid. We had an old plow horse I rode bareback. I did ride at Jubal's ranch when I was here several weeks ago."

"So…can I go with you, then?" she asked directly.

"You don't have any other obligations, no one to check in with?" he asked. It was a question he'd wanted to ask since he first dropped her off at the Camel Trail Inn.

"No," she said. "I've been on my own for a long time."

"No questions?"

"No. I'm just tailing along. And I want you to know how much I appreciate it."

"It was Jubal's decision."

"You could have said no."

He was saved from answering by the arrival of the steaks. Outside of the military, his relationships had been few and far between. He'd had little time for romance. When he wasn't deployed, he was busy stateside, overseeing training and preparing for the next deployment.

It wasn't for lack of opportunities, but he knew the pressures of a military marriage, and he knew from personal experience that other marriages had difficulties, too. Until Dinah, he'd never found anyone who'd even made him think about anything permanent...

He watched as Jenny tasted the strip steak. She ate as if she hadn't seen food in a week. He wondered where she put it. At midmeal, a band gathered in a corner of the room.

He tried to focus on the band playing good pop country. After one song, he turned, and their gazes met. It was as if lightning darted between them. He knew from the stunned expression in her eyes that she felt it, too.

Couples were dancing, and Travis felt a rare envy. He could barely walk straight, much less dance. Ordinarily that wouldn't have bothered him, but he had the damnedest need to ask her to dance. He wanted to hold her, move with her.

Could he back out of the trip now before those feelings grew? Did he want to?

"We'd better go," he said. "I have some things to get together, and I imagine you do, too."

"I want to pay my share of dinner for tonight," she said when the bill came.

He saw the stubborn look on her face. It went against all his instincts to let her pay her bill. They weren't on the trip yet, but he understood. Independence was obviously very important to her.

They paid their bills and left the noisy room.

The inn was just a few miles away, but Travis wasn't quite ready to let her go yet. He drove past the packed lot and around to the side of the inn.

"There's a 50th wedding anniversary party here," Jenny explained. "Lots of friends and family. Susan warned me it might be noisy, but hopefully it will end early," Jenny continued, and he wondered if she was feeling the growing warmth in the car. "The dining room was closed for the party, so you saved me from starvation." She paused. "Thanks for all the help and especially for agreeing to take me with you tomorrow."

He nodded, and she reached for the door. But then she turned back, and the air in the car went from warm to electric. Their hands touched. He wanted to reach over and touch her face, draw her to him.

Her eyes were so intense, so damned green. The energy in her seemed too strong to contain in the car. His heartbeat quickened. Other parts of his anatomy did, as well.

"I should go inside," Jenny said reluctantly.

He nodded. "I'll be here at oh-eight hundred."

"I'll be ready," she said, without making a move to exit the car.

"Don't forget about that bath. You'll be sore tomorrow," he said in an effort to shatter the sexual tension radiating between them. "I rode on my last visit and paid for it the next day."

"I will. Thanks again."

He got out and limped over to the passenger side as she stepped out.

"You didn't have to do that," she said.

"You forget I have papers saying I'm an officer and a gentleman. That means accompanying you to the door."

She gave him that spontaneous grin that had enchanted him from day one. He put his hands on her shoulders, leaned down and touched his lips to hers. Gently. Tentatively.

She lifted up on her toes and returned the kiss. He felt the earth rumble under him, and the bright, vivid attraction between them exploded.

He hadn't intended it. He'd meant only to walk her to the door, but he couldn't resist the smile that lit him up inside, and once their lips met, the kiss became scorching. His arms went around her and tightened.

The electricity that darted between them almost from the first moment they met was turning into a tempest, one Travis knew he had to stop for both their sakes. Neither of them was ready for anything more than a temporary partnership. He knew that much from the conversations they'd had.

She wanted her career back. She was a wanderer, and he didn't know what in hell he wanted. He stepped back, his hands falling from her shoulders. "I'm sorry," he said. "That shouldn't have happened…"

For once in her life, Jenny was speechless. Her heart pounded. She was trembling, wanting— no, needing—to explore the flames that licked between them.

But he was right. The trip was too important to them both. She didn't want to do anything that might cause him to have second thoughts. She searched his face. "I'd better go in," she said. "I'll be at the door at eight."

She waited anxiously for his answer. Was the trip still viable? There had been vibes between them from the moment they met, but tonight it had changed into something more...intimate.

"Good night," he said in an unsteady voice.

She didn't wait. She nodded, not wanting to give him a chance to change his mind about the trip. She hoped no one was in the inn's lobby because she knew her face might give away what just happened. She'd long ago discounted tales of romantic fireworks. Never happened to her. Until now.

She tried to compose herself as she crossed the lobby. Susan stepped out of the dining room, which appeared packed. "Hi," she said. "Have a good day?"

Still shaken, she nodded. "I rode my first grown-up horse, and I'll be leaving in the morning. I should be back next Saturday or Sunday. I'll let you know when."

"I should have plenty of rooms then. In any event, I'll have one for you."

"Thanks."

"I see you found some boots."

Jenny needed to get back to her room. She was still trembling inside, but she fought to keep her tone normal. "You were right about the General Store. It did have a good selection."

Susan nodded. "If that's your first ride, you might want to soak in a hot bath."

"So people keep telling me. I'm beginning to understand why. I'm already stiff. Do you ride?"

"Since I was a kid. Most of us around here do."

"You're from Covenant Falls?"

"Born and raised. That's why I want to make the inn a success. Make it a destination. That was a good idea about concentrating advertising on veterans."

"Good," Jenny said, trying desperately to keep her voice even. Calm. "Glad I can help. I would like to do a story on the inn when I get back. I have some contacts with travel magazines."

"That would be great."

She turned toward the dining room. "It sounds like the party is going well."

"Come on in," Susan said. She didn't wait for a reply, but went to the double doors and opened one. Curious, Jenny followed.

A band was playing "Tennessee Waltz," and an elderly couple was dancing, dipping and whirling. Both had white hair, but their age didn't dim the broad smiles on their faces. A boy and girl of three or four years were doing their version of the waltz, too, while others applauded.

More couples started dancing, and Jenny

backed away. Her heart lightened at watching such a celebration and recognizing the love in the room. There was also an ache for never having known this kind of family...or joy.

She was an observer. Had been one all her life. Now she wondered whether if, by being an observer, she had missed being a participant in living. "Thank you," she said to Susan.

"Have a good night," Susan said as she closed the door.

Back in her room, she took an anti-inflammatory and sank into the tub. Only then did she allow herself to think of the kiss, of its impact. She'd been kissed many times before, but she couldn't remember one that affected her in so many ways. It had the potent combination of passion and gentleness. Travis Hammond had many qualities she admired: intelligence, humor, a rapport with people ranging from little boys to navy SEALs. That a group of warriors entrusted him with a project obviously important to them said even more.

But he was also private. He answered questions, but she always had the feeling that he was leaving the most important facts out. He'd said very little about his family, where he was from, his feelings about the military. Had he ever been married, or had there been other relationships? She wanted to know everything about him.

Could she really claim it was just journalistic curiosity?

One thing she did know: she didn't need complications now. She wanted to get back to Syria. Not wanted. Had to.

The child from her nightmares haunted her. She'd previously built an emotional shield between her and the horrors she'd seen during her years as a war correspondent, but the child had broken through it and wouldn't go away. Maybe that was why she had the nightmares. She needed to tell the child's story. Not just what she saw, but what happened after.

She'd tried to find out. She'd contacted Rick who was now in Iraq, but he didn't know more than her. He'd promised, though, to try to find out.

The water had cooled, and she ran the hot water again, until she was nearly boiled. Some of the aches and soreness from riding began to fade.

She had a tablet full of books she wanted to read, but tonight she just wanted to think about the day. About the people she'd met. Jubal. Danny. Josh. Andy. Eve. They'd all faced physical and emotional challenges, and now their main focus was helping others with theirs.

She wrote the first page of a story in her head, and then she leaned back in the tub and considered her future.

Afterwards, she packed and began writing her impressions of the people she'd met in Covenant Falls. It was past midnight when she crawled into bed. Her body was tired, but her mind was too busy to sleep. She turned on the television news, but the screen blurred. Travis's face kept appearing, instead. The thin scar that gave him a crooked smile added interest to a face that might otherwise be too handsome. His wry humor attracted her, but she kept going back to his relationships with Nick and Danny. Eve had told her that a job for Danny was the one condition Travis had made to make his first visit.

Rangers were a clannish group. They looked after each other, but Danny hadn't been a Ranger. He hadn't been anything to anybody, apparently, except to a major with no previous connection to him.

That placed Travis very high in her estimation.

She could care less about his wounds. He'd learned how to manipulate his right hand to do what needed to be done with three fingers. Although he'd obviously had surgery on his leg and it must give him pain, he didn't let it stop him.

The simple fact was she liked him. She liked him more every time she was with him. He was gentle, despite being a warrior. She thought of the way he'd lifted the saddle for her. Challenged her on the day he'd picked her up. Played baseball with Eve's son. Allowed her to make her case with Jubal. He was a rare man.

That frightened her as few other things had. She didn't want ties. She wanted the freedom to go where stories took her. And right now the story was still in Syria.

CHAPTER THIRTEEN

THE WATER WAS even colder than Travis remembered. He was grateful. It took his mind off Jenny as he swam well into the lake before turning around, climbing up on the dock and wrapping a large, thick towel around his waist. He walked to the cabin as fast as his weak leg allowed.

After a hot shower, he reviewed the materials he and Jubal had accumulated. Some of it was on his laptop but there were also books, brochures, notes and other written material Jubal had gathered after talking to the equine therapy providers on the schedule.

They had all been helpful. They were reluctantly turning away vets because their programs were full. The fact he represented a SEAL, a Ranger staff sergeant, an army nurse and a Vietnam vet made it an easy sale.

He'd prepared a list of questions for the providers and Dr. Payne. He'd asked each member of the Covenant Falls group for a couple of questions and added more of his own. Several had to do with the length of the program and the number of participants at any one time. Other questions involved financial aspects and staffing. What kind of qualifications should they look for? Would a physical therapist be necessary? A mental health professional?

It was two in the morning before he finished. Lack of sleep was finally getting to him. He knew he would wake at dawn, regardless of when he went to bed, no alarm clock needed.

He tried not to think of the next day, of spending so many hours in a small space with a woman who attracted him so strongly. That kiss had been a terrible mistake. He didn't know what in the hell he'd been thinking.

If it had just been her appearance, he could handle it. She was certainly attractive, but it was her interest in everyone and everything that drew him to her. She was challenging, and he was at a point in his life where he needed that.

In the past two years, he'd had physical challenges, but no men to lead, no battle plans to draw, no logistics problems to solve, no angry exchanges with counterparts in Afghanistan and Syria and Iraq.

She'd brought that part of him alive again. It was a gift, and he should accept it during the next few days before she left for new adventures.

And she would leave. He saw the restlessness in her. She didn't seem to have any real ties anywhere and was happy that way. He, on the other hand, was tired. Years of being deployed over what seemed half the world had dulled his adventurist side.

Dammit! He didn't know what the hell he wanted in the future. He wasn't excited about any of the post-military options he was exploring right now.

He closed his eyes. The swim had exhausted his body, and reviewing the stack of materials sated his mind. He closed his eyes and willed himself to sleep.

JENNY WAS AT the door of the inn at ten minutes to eight. She'd paid her bill and gulped down two cups of coffee and two cinnamon rolls. There seemed to be more than enough for the patrons, so she took two more for Travis.

Travis drove up about three minutes to eight. Before he got out, she threw her belongings into the back seat and stepped into the front passenger seat.

"Good morning," she said as she fastened her seat belt.

"You travel lighter than any woman I've ever known."

"How many have you known?"

"Enough to know you're an oddity." He started the car.

"Did you have breakfast?" Jenny asked.

"Are you hungry already?"

"Nope, but I brought you two of the best cinnamon rolls I've ever tasted."

He held out a hand to take one.

"You're welcome," she said as she put a napkin-wrapped roll in his hand.

"Thank you," he replied a little too politely.

He took a bite and then sighed happily. "How did I not hear about these?"

"I don't know," she said. "But I'm pretty great at ferreting out good food. You're lucky to have me along."

He took his gaze from the road and gave her that slow smile that was beginning to melt something inside her. "We'll see about that," he said.

"Grumpy this morning, are we?"

"The cinnamon rolls are easing the condition."

"Will I have to provide them every morning?"

"Might work," he replied as he drove out of Covenant Falls. "There's a map in the glove compartment if you want to navigate."

"You don't have a GPS?" She felt a growing happiness. She thoroughly enjoyed fencing with him. He stimulated her in a way nothing had since her return to the United States.

"The rental company didn't have an available car with one. Besides, I don't like an electronic device telling me where to go and scolding me when I decide to deviate."

She stared at him. She hadn't expected that. He appeared to be so organized. But now he sounded...like her. She'd thought every mile would have been mapped out.

"Can we take some back roads?" she asked.

"Why not? We have the time since I'm leaving a day sooner than I expected."

"You were trying to avoid me," she accused.

"Thought about it," he admitted with disarming honesty. "It obviously didn't work."

"What changed your mind?"

"Jubal thought you might be of some help."

"Only Jubal?"

He just smiled and changed the subject. "We'll take Interstate 25 until we reach New Mexico, but after that, you can guide."

"I can pick the route?"

"Unless it takes us to Alaska."

"I think I can avoid that," she said, charmed by his banter. She had seen some of it on the drive from the airport to Covenant Falls, but since then he'd been mostly polite and businesslike.

"As long as we're in Fort Hood by 11:00 a.m. on Tuesday," he responded.

She opened the glove compartment and pulled out a map. "Before or after we hit the state line," she said, spreading it out, "maybe we can find a welcome center with more maps and information. I like out-of-the-way places and hole-in-the-wall local eateries."

She wondered if she wasn't being a bit presumptuous, but he simply nodded. She had thought he might be stiff at first, but he wasn't. He was treating her like a partner. Maybe not welcomed with open arms, but neither was there the earlier reluctance.

"When you're finished with the map, there's a binder and several books in the back seat. The binder includes information on each of the programs we'll visit, along with stuff about other equine therapy programs in the country. There's also a few books on equine therapy and a list of questions I have for Dr. Payne. You might want to add some questions of your own after reading everything."

She placed the map on the divider and twisted her body around as much as possible while held captive by the seat belt. She noticed it was a very fat binder. Three books were positioned next to it.

"No laptop?" she observed.

"I have one but I don't like to use it when talking to people. It puts a wall between us. You can't look them in the eyes. I prefer notes."

That was interesting. She worked in the same way. She wondered why he hadn't already planned every mile and stop on the trip. If the thickness of the binder was any indication of his preciseness, would he not have spent time on routing the trip?

Maybe he had. Maybe he'd planned the route down to the last mile. Then the question was why he'd tasked her with it. *Because he wanted to keep her too busy for conversation? Or was it some kind of test? If it were the latter, he might be in for a few surprises.*

She looked at the map and selected several sites that interested her. The first was Raton Pass, which was located just over the New Mexico border. She couldn't remember hearing anything about it, just as she hadn't about Covenant Falls, but the name fascinated her. She now had a renewed interest in small towns.

She guessed they would get there by about eleven. She took out her cell phone and looked it up. As she read the information, she could barely keep a smile to herself.

"Have you ever heard of Raton Pass?" she asked.

He looked at her and raised an eyebrow. "No."

"Neither have I. It's just over the border. Might be a good place to stop for lunch."

"It will be a little early for lunch," he observed.

"I'll be hungry."

"Are you always hungry?"

"It would seem so," she said. "But you do

pretty well yourself. And anyway, you appointed me cruise director. It's a duty I take seriously."

"Is there something in Raton Pass I should know about?" he asked.

"It's a mountain pass that was part of the Santa Fe Trail," she said, grateful her cell had service. "Pioneers journeying west, raids by Native Americans, Civil War skullduggery. It was laid out in 1821 and apparently played an important role in Western history. The town has historic buildings, including a theater and hotel. Also distinguishing the town, apparently, is a hat cemetery."

Travis glanced at her and raised an eyebrow. "A hat cemetery?"

"I thought that might get your attention. It's right there on the website." She couldn't stop a giggle. She never giggled, but his expression just plain earned one. "In my travels," she continued, "I thought I had heard or seen most everything. I wrote a story on a hat museum in Europe, but a cemetery? The town sounds as interesting as Covenant Falls."

She paused for a minute. Then she mused aloud, "Maybe I can do a series on the country's most fascinating small towns. There's Covenant Falls and now Raton Pass. It has everything. History, location, oddities."

"Including the hat cemetery," Travis said drily. "Absolutely a *must* stop."

"You are not sharing my enthusiasm," she retorted, "and thirst for knowledge."

He chuckled. It was a nice sound, one she wished she heard more often. "I hope," he replied, "you are not expecting me to stop at every small town along the way to discover their eccentricities."

"Maybe not every one," she agreed.

"That's comforting."

He was in a good mood. Jenny decided to take advantage of it. "You told me your father was a farmer. Did you live in a small town?"

"Pretty small."

"In the Midwest?"

"Yes."

"Did it have any eccentricities?"

"Nope, not a single one."

"And no family at all back there?"

"No."

She noticed his lips tightening. She told herself to stop, but that reporter part of her didn't want to quit. It was, she knew, a very obnoxious part of her.

But still she couldn't stop herself from asking one last question. "And no one else?"

"Just the army," he replied. The tone did not invite further intrusion.

Jenny let some time pass while she watched the scenery. They were driving through grass-lands now, and she saw an occasional ranch. She checked out the towns ahead of them on her phone: Trinidad and Walsenburg. The latter was the size of Covenant Falls and apparently had some infamy. Robert Ford, the assassin of Jesse James, operated a saloon and gambling house there.

She didn't want to press her luck with Travis, though. She didn't know whether he shared her fascination with history. Rather than mentioning it, she added its name to her phone app as deserv-ing of a visit sometime in the future. Maybe even in a possible series about small towns.

After a few moments, she announced a town was coming up if he wanted to stop for any rea-son.

"Not unless you do," he replied.

"If we stop, I could reach in back and get your binder."

He seemed to slowly relax. "I prefer the cruise director at the moment. What else is there in Raton Pass except a hat cemetery?"

Obviously he wanted to keep the conversation inpersonal. She complied. "Ghosts."

He glanced at her and smiled. "Oh, great," he said. "That's even better than a hat cemetery. Maybe there's even hat ghosts."

"I take it you're reconciled to stopping there for lunch," she said, enchanted by the unexpected humor that could be as wacky as her own.

"I have to admit I have some curiosity. Find any other irresistible small towns?"

"I've just started…" She paused and then continued, thinking out loud. "I haven't even looked, and I found one, probably two. There has to be many others."

She realized she was getting on her soapbox. That was something she did when a new project started dancing around in her head. Ideas just started popping out. She could bore people for hours.

"That mind of yours never stops, does it?" Travis said.

He got her. He understood her. But she didn't know if he accepted her. She was a tumbleweed. Was born that way. She didn't need anyone, didn't want to need anyone, because, in her experience, it meant being trapped. Her mother was trapped in alcohol, her sisters in bad marriages—Lenore had only recently gained her independence.

"I hope not," she answered.

"I don't think you have anything to worry about," he observed.

"What about you?" Jenny asked. "What are you going to do when this study is finished?"

He shrugged. "I'm still working on that."

"You're really good with Nick. Not to mention Danny. I can tell he thinks you walk on water."

"It's very shallow water," he said.

She didn't reply to that. The conversation had veered into a heavy direction and to questions she sensed neither of them wanted nor knew how to answer. That now familiar electricity filled the car. It had nothing to do with weather and everything to do with the attraction sparking between them.

Jenny needed a diversion. She checked the map again. They had just passed Walsenburg. The interstate started climbing, and they were entering the Sangre de Cristo Mountains.

She stopped talking as they continued up to the pass and spied a New Mexico welcome center. Travis parked and they got out, stretched and looked at the incredible views around them. Mountains. Green forests. A royal blue lake.

"It's beautiful, isn't it?" Jenny said in an awed voice. The rich colors captured her imagination. She could almost see wagon trains winding their way through the steep pass.

He nodded and followed her into the center, where she grabbed all the information she could find. She noticed that his limp was more pronounced than usual and knew it was a good thing to stop.

The town of Raton was off the interstate and

seven miles or so out of the way. Without comment, Travis turned.

Jenny was even more delighted than she'd imagined as they drove to the town center, past stores with names like Little Bear Gallery and Santa Fe Traders. There was a historical theater built in 1939 by the WPA that drew visits from the San Francisco Opera and The Three Tenors.

They found the hat cemetery in a Western wear store. When anyone bought a new hat, they could donate their old one to the cemetery. Each hat received a name tag and some had attached histories of their prior owners.

Jenny was enchanted, and Travis was patient. It was 1:00 p.m. before they found a barbecue restaurant and ate lunch.

They walked back to the car. Jenny left a few purchases in the back seat and grabbed the binder. When Travis was inside, she hugged the book and said, "Thank you for indulging me."

"I needed to stretch my leg," he replied. Then he added with a slight smile, "and I've never seen a hat cemetery before."

CHAPTER FOURTEEN

TRAVIS TRIED TO concentrate on the road ahead and not his passenger. It was becoming more and more difficult.

Dammit, the truth was he was falling hard for Jenny Talbot.

He couldn't remember when he'd had a more pleasurable day or when he'd smiled quite so much. Jenny's enthusiasm was contagious. She'd charmed everyone she met in Raton because, to her, everyone was the most interesting person she'd ever met.

He understood now how she wrote such powerful stories, particularly when she wrote about innocents caught up in war.

She connected with people in a way he'd never witnessed before. He understood why people talked to her when they wouldn't talk to authorities or other reporters. She wasn't just after a story. She genuinely liked and was interested in everyone.

It was a rare quality.

Once back in the car, she'd taken up his thick

binder and appeared to be thoroughly engrossed in it. She'd abandoned her role as cruise director, especially when she realized there was but one route to take to get to where they were going. But she'd also forgotten about enjoying the scenery. Forgotten about her quest for another unique small town. She was completely engrossed in the binder.

He kept his eyes on the road. He wanted to get past Amarillo today, but he missed her questions and observations.

"I was surprised when I first started looking into equine therapy to find the number and variety of programs underway," she said, breaking the silence.

"I was, too, until I talked to Josh," Travis admitted. "He credits his dog, Amos, with saving his sanity, and Jubal says a horse on Luke's ranch made him realize there was a world beyond war."

"No one said anything about that."

"They wouldn't," Travis replied. "It's difficult to talk about. Soldiers don't like admitting having a hard time coping after leaving the military, even to themselves."

"I understand that," she said. "I hate showing vulnerability."

And there it was. Not weakness but vulnerability. There was a world of difference between the two concepts, and she understood it.

He'd watched her struggle with her shoulder, but she'd never complained or asked for help. She would have continued to try that saddle if he hadn't stepped in. She had a lot of warrior in her, too.

"What about you?" she asked suddenly. "Are you having a difficult time?"

It was an intrusive question, but he was getting used to that from her. What he might resent as prying from someone else, her curiosity was as much a part of her as an arm or leg. It was an ongoing effort to understand her world and the people who lived in it.

There was a long silence while he tried to think of an answer. "I'm not out yet." But then he added, "But yeah, for the first time in my life, I'm not sure of my next step."

"You were in Iraq during the worst of it?"

"And Afghanistan. Syria. Other places you don't hear about. My guys were mostly advisors who worked with the host country's military. Problem was they had damn little protection, and the forces they trained weren't always reliable."

He was saying things he probably shouldn't be saying, but his frustration from the past years had burst out.

She seemed to understand and changed the subject. "So are you really thinking of taking a desk job, or might you stay in Covenant Falls and help with this program?"

"No plans to stay on. This is just a temporary gig for a friend."

"Options?"

"A desk job at Fort Benning. Or a medical discharge. Neither appeals to me much. But then neither does anything else. Still, I'm a hell of a lot better off than most, so I can't complain."

Jenny was quiet for a moment, and then sighed. "I really want to write stories that help. The last thing I want to do is make life more difficult for veterans who need help. I know a little about what they face."

More than most. He'd had doubts in the beginning, but no longer. He suspected that people talked to her because they knew instinctively that she would understand and protect them.

"You should do something with kids," she blurted out in an instant subject change.

"What?"

"You should do something with kids if you leave the army. You're good with them. I saw that when you were with Nick." She grinned. "You're also patient. I'm proof of that. Anyone else would probably have bought me a one-way bus ticket back to Covenant Falls after staying so long in Raton."

"To my utter amazement, I enjoyed it," he admitted.

"Good. Does that mean we can stay in Amarillo tonight? It's a great name, and there's a Cadillac museum there…"

He raised his gaze upwards. He didn't know if she was kidding or not, and this was not the first time he was amazed at how quickly her mood changed. It was disconcerting to say the least.

"I've created a monster," he observed.

"No," she retorted. "You just sorta allowed it to expand."

He sighed. Deeply. "Whatever did I do to deserve this?" he uttered to no one in particular. "What, I fear to ask, is there to see in a Cadillac museum?"

"Lots of Cadillacs," Jenny replied with that smile that was so darn hard to ignore.

"And why would we possibly want to see them?"

"Because some are halfway buried in the ground, front first. You're obviously out of touch with the whimsical."

"I admit it," Travis said. "I sense that's definitely not a problem with you."

"I hope not. It makes every day interesting. I never know what's around the corner or the bend of the river, or, if I'm in Covenant Falls, the next rainbow."

"You never want to call some place home?"

She shrugged. "Not really. I grew up in what some might call a dysfunctional house. I couldn't wait to leave, and there was always a shining object out there in front of me. I learned to live out of a duffel bag and sometimes not even that. It's liberating not having *things* to worry about."

"Ever get lonely?"

"I would be lying if I said no. But then another story comes along, and I meet a new group of people." She hesitated. Then she asked, "Were you ever married?"

"No," he said. "Almost, but then I was wounded."

"What did that have to do with anything?"

His hands tightened on the steering wheel. "I was pretty bad when I got back. They didn't know if they could save my leg. I'd lost two fingers, and my face…"

"I happen to like it. It's a very strong face," she said. He could tell she was growing angry. Not at him, but at the unnamed woman. If Dinah had been in the car, Jenny might have unbuckled the seat belt, turned around and smacked her.

"She's an idiot," Jenny continued, obviously seething.

Damn, he would have liked to have her in his

Army company. "She was a journalist," he retorted snidely. He regretted it immediately, but it had been an automatic defense mechanism.

"Ouch," Jenny said. "But she's still an idiot. Probably a terrible journalist, too."

He chuckled. He couldn't remember when he'd done that so often. "What about you? Have you ever been engaged, or close to it?"

"Nope. Never stayed in one place long enough, although I had some good buddies in the Middle East. We often teamed together. It was too dangerous to go in alone."

He was unaccountably jealous, which was ridiculous.

"And," she added, "I just always retreated when I thought I—or someone—was getting serious."

Her turn to provide a warning to one Travis Hammond.

It was just as well. He needed a jolt back to reality. He was appalled that he'd actually considered staying in Amarillo and going to a Cadillac museum.

He had a mission, such as it was, and he'd been sidetracked. It was thoroughly undisciplined on his part, but he couldn't remember when he'd felt lighthearted or smiled so easily.

He glanced at her. They were slowing down as they approached Amarillo. The traffic was heavy.

"Where now?" she asked with the road map in her hands.

"A ranch about an hour away. It wasn't originally on the schedule, but I checked with the owner last night, and he invited us over."

"Why wasn't he on the schedule?" she asked, "particularly since it's on the route."

"Time. I thought I would be driving eight hundred miles tomorrow, and this program is simpler than the others. From what I understand, it's not a rehab program per se, but a skills experience. It teaches riding and ranch work and has a very elastic schedule for participants. Since we left today, we have time to see it. We should be there around three if you don't mind missing lunch."

"Miss a meal? How awful!" Jenny said, "After the way I've eaten in the past few days, I could go weeks without another bite. Besides," she added slyly, "I kinda absconded with fruit and pastries from the breakfast room." Then she buried her head in the road map.

Travis couldn't help but chuckle. He knew the compulsion. His soldiers did it all the time and called it foraging. Once you've been very, very hungry, you become a hoarder. You take whatever you find. He imagined that she often went without food in war-torn areas.

He handed her directions. "I think we leave the interstate soon. You're navigator now."

"Okay," she said agreeably, then added, "what can you tell me about Dr. Payne?"

Travis was dizzy. Another lightning change of subject. It was difficult to keep up with her. Or was it a technique to disarm him? He recited what little he knew. "I've not met him. I only know that he treated Josh and sent both Clint and Andy to him. All three think very highly of him."

"Andy says he saved her sanity," Jenny said, obviously seeking more information.

"It's no secret in Covenant Falls. Andy was in a forward surgical unit when an Afghan soldier whom she trusted attacked her unit during an operation. She was badly wounded, the only survivor of the team—which included her fiancé. They were to be married within a month."

"I didn't know," she said. "How terrible for her."

"Dr. Payne convinced her to visit a woman who trains rescue dogs to be therapy dogs. That's where she found Joseph. Dr. Payne then put her in touch with Josh. He thought she would be a good candidate for the cabin."

"He was right, wasn't he?" Jenny asked. "She's an enthusiastic promoter of the museum and town. Covenant Falls seems to have an unusual effect on newcomers."

Travis caught himself. He had no idea why he was saying so much, but he was discovering why she was a good reporter. She didn't always ask direct questions. She often just made comments that led her victims to elaborate.

"She seems to be doing really well now," Jenny added after failing to get an answer.

"She is," he agreed, ignoring the unspoken invitation to elaborate.

"While we're near Fort Hood, can we visit the woman who trained Andy's dog?" she asked in another topic change.

"Interested in one?" Travis asked.

"No. I'm in no position to have a dog now, but it's another aspect of healing, part of the large picture."

He hesitated, then replied, "If I can arrange it."

Jenny sensed he'd had his fill of questions. She glanced at the directions he'd given her and turned her attention to them, noting as they drove the changes in the landscape. It was a little before three when she saw the road mentioned in the directions Travis had given her. Twenty minutes later, he turned into a paved road lined by fences that seemed to go as far as they could see. Cattle grazed on one side, horses on the other. At the end of the long drive, they reached an attractive two-story house and three outbuildings.

The largest outbuilding was obviously a stable. Jenny watched as a deeply-tanned middle-aged man and two younger men left the barn and headed toward them. All three wore Western hats.

"Major Hammond?" the older man said as he held out his hand to Travis. "I'm Chet Bowen." He looked curiously at Jenny.

"Call me Travis. This is Jenny Talbot. She's a reporter and is helping us with research. Thanks for seeing us on such short notice."

"Happy to do it. We can't come close to filling the need. These two young men—Jeff Reynolds and Austin O'Brian—are part of our program. I thought you might get more from them than from me."

Jenny gave all three her best smile, and Travis saw the immediate impact. They all took off their hats and looked gobsmacked.

"I'll show you around first," Chet offered. "Then you can ask these fellows and me any questions you have. Let's start with the bunkhouse…"

He talked as they walked behind the house to an elongated one-story building with a wide front porch filled with rocking chairs.

Their host opened the door to what appeared to be a gathering place. There was a kitchen area with a fridge, grill, microwave and coffee machine.

There were several lounge chairs, a sofa and tables and chairs.

"This is the common room. The room to the right is a sleeping room for our male participants. We have six bunkbeds for a total of twelve beds. We can add more. On the other side, we have a smaller room with four bunkbeds for women."

"No televisions?" Jenny noted.

"Nope," Chet said. "We don't allow computers either. One of the important parts of the program is interaction between the veterans. They need the support of each other in addition to the acceptance they find with the horses."

"How long do they stay?" Travis said.

"It varies. Our veterans have an option of participating in a resident program where they learn horsemanship and work with our cattle, or a nonresident, self-paced program that works for those with job or education commitments."

"What's the difference?" Travis asked.

"We teach basic skills by doing," he added. "The day begins with feeding the horses and cattle onsite. Then there's a full day of horsemanship. When they gain the skills, they work alongside our cowhands. After completing the initial training, some stay and become quite skilled in working cattle and horsemanship. There's still a demand for cowhands these days. Others who don't have the time for the resident program can sign up for additional sessions or just a few hours' riding."

"Any requirements for applying?" Travis asked.

"An honorable discharge. I think I should make one thing clear. We're not a therapeutic program. We do not treat PTSD, and participants have to be ambulatory. What we do is teach skills. We believe that working with horses is therapeutic in and of itself.

"Now," Chet said, "I've talked enough, and I'm going back to the barn while you talk to these two young men. You can use the front porch. There's coffee inside and soft drinks. I know you're on a schedule, but if you have any more questions, I'm certainly available now or later. We need more programs like ours. We have a waiting list which, in this case, is not good."

He left. Travis and Jenny sat on the rocking chairs, while Jeff and Austin pulled up two more, making a circle.

Travis first explained why they were there. Then Jenny started the questions. He knew she would be more effective in drawing them out than if an officer did the questioning.

She started by asking them about where they'd served. Jeff, a twenty-nine-year-old corporal, served in some of Iraq's bloodiest battles. Austin had served as a truck driver there and had watched several vehicles ahead of him and behind destroyed by roadside bombs. Although not clinically diagnosed with PTSD, they both had nightmares and difficulty adjusting to civilian life.

Jeff was in the second week of the program, while Austin was a returnee and obviously an advocate.

"It's saved my marriage," Austin said. "When I first came home, I couldn't relate to anyone in the civilian world, not even my wife. My nightmares scared her. I couldn't talk about the time I was in combat because there was no way I could explain the constant fear, the smell of death. Especially watching your best friend die. I'd completely changed. I couldn't even enjoy a good joke when I used to be a jokester."

He looked at Jeff, who nodded. "We were headed for a divorce when someone mentioned this ranch," he continued. "I'd never been on a horse before but my wife encouraged it and I owed her one last attempt to save the marriage."

He paused, and Jenny gently urged him on. "What changed?" she asked in a voice so sympathetic, it would be impossible not to reply.

"Other than marrying my wife, it was the best decision I've made. Horses don't judge. They don't have expectations. They're accepting. After the first few nervous moments, I slowly relaxed, really relaxed for the first time since coming home. Dusty, the horse I usually ride, nuzzles me when I appear in the morning and seems really happy to see me. He responds to the slightest touch. He…well…helped heal my sense of who I am and what I can be. My wife says she likes me again. Now when I get frustrated," he added, "I call Chet and come up here. There's nothing like rounding up cows from the back of a horse on a fine day to push away negative thoughts. I'm even happy back at my job as a mechanic. When things get difficult, I know I can come back here."

"What about you, Jeff?" Travis asked the other man.

"I'm not as far along as Austin," Jeff said. "I have a ways to go, but one of the best things about this program is being with other veterans. It's what I missed most when I came back. A civilian can't understand how close you get to other guys when you eat, sleep and fight together for years. You rely on them for your life. You get back, and you're alone."

He paused until Jenny nodded her head in encouragement.

"I'd never intended to be a soldier," he said. "I married my high school sweetheart, got a job and attended college part-time. I joined the Army Reserve to help with expenses. I never thought I would be sent off to a battle zone." He stood and walked nervously on the porch, his fingers clutching and unclutching.

"I came home to divorce papers. My wife had fallen in love with an officer on base but waited to tell me until I came home. My mother remarried after Dad died, and her husband was not a fan of the military. I was tolerated but no more than that.

"I was angry. I had PTSD and couldn't sleep without nightmares. My skills didn't fit many job descriptions and I admit my attitude wasn't the best. I couldn't find a good job and started drinking, then drifted into drugs." Jeff stopped pacing. "I probably would be dead today if a buddy from my ROTC unit hadn't become involved. He was in this program and mentioned how helpful it was, but they wouldn't take anyone with a drug problem. It was a lifeline. He helped me get clean and I finally was accepted."

He was silent for a moment. "I can't really tell you how much it has done for me. I've always liked animals but there's a connection between a horse and rider that's unique. You have to trust each other. Respect each other.

"Sometimes I ride out with the cattle, and then there's times I ride at sunset, just the horse and me, and I can feel peace again." He went red. "I didn't mean to be sappy or anything."

"You're not," Jenny said. "I know exactly what you mean."

He didn't look convinced.

"She does," Travis affirmed. "She was wounded in Syria while covering a volunteer medical unit for a news service."

The two vets looked at her with new respect. "That true, ma'am?" Jeff asked.

"I'm afraid so. I'm not so swift on ducking."

"I'm proud of meeting you," Jeff said.

"Do you know what you want to do now?" Jenny asked him.

"Well, ma'am, I'm thinking now about becoming a vet tech. Chet said he would help me." It was obvious Chet was a saint.

Travis was impressed. He wondered, though, if these two were typical or selected to put the program in a good light.

He looked at his watch. They were running late, but it had been worth the visit.

He thanked the two former soldiers, and they all walked together to the barn. There, Chet introduced them to the horses in the stalls and to additional program participants who were in various stages of unsaddling, cooling off and feeding their mounts.

There was laughter and good-natured grumbling about who did best during the day. Jenny was obviously the star as several competed for her attention. It wasn't easy to draw her away.

He thanked Chet. "I'll probably have more questions."

"Anytime," the rancher replied.

That was too sedate for Jenny. She reached up and hugged him. Chet looked chagrined, but he winked at Travis. "You can bring her anytime."

Travis grinned. "She's my secret weapon."

They left then. It was a long drive ahead.

IT WAS DARK when they reached the city limits of a small town west of Lubbock. They noted two motels and a barbecue restaurant just off the interstate.

"Your pick," Travis said.

It seemed forever since she traveled by road in the United States. She suspected the same of him. She selected the newest-looking motel. They registered separately, paid separately and were given adjoining rooms. Travis asked about restaurants and was told the barbecue restaurant was pretty much it. Breakfast was free at the motel, starting at 7:00 a.m.

Travis suggested they settle into their rooms and meet in thirty minutes to go to supper. She noticed he was walking with a more pronounced limp.

Everyone had been right about the aftermath

of yesterday's horseback riding, and she would have loved another long bath to soothe aching muscles. She made do with a hot shower. Then she ran a comb through her wet hair and applied a dash of lipstick. The barbecue place definitely looked casual. She put on her jeans and a clean T-shirt.

It wasn't a date, and yet she felt anticipation, as if it was one.

She knocked at the adjoining door, and it opened immediately.

He'd shaved and changed into a gray polo shirt, but she thought the jeans were the same. Her heart started racing. She'd been attracted to him from the first time she'd met him. She liked his face, the way the thin scar pulled up the side of his mouth in a half-smile and the fine lines around his eyes. She liked the way he smiled. And she liked the strength that radiated from him. He knew who and what he was. There was no pretense about him, just a quiet integrity.

She had seen several sides of him, and she liked them all. She warned herself there could be others she wouldn't like.

Don't like him too much, she told herself. As soon as her shoulder healed, she was returning to the Middle East. Somehow she had to find that medical group and discover what happened to the girl. Travis, on the other hand, had his own future to remake, and she was sure it would have something to do with settling down. She hadn't missed the look in his eyes when he watched Josh's son.

For the moment, though, she would enjoy being with him.

"Ready?" he asked. He had that slight smile on his face.

"Yes. I'm hungry again."

"How do you stay so slim?" he asked.

"I don't always eat like this," she said. "When I'm on a story, I basically subsist on air. And I was in the hospital and rehab center for a long time. They're not known for gourmet cuisine. As a result, when I'm presented with good food, I enjoy every bite."

She'd drifted into his room. Neither of them had brought much luggage, but his room looked as if no one had even been inside, while hers looked as if a hurricane had struck it. She was neat when she had to be, but when she didn't, she enjoyed leaving newspaper pages, books, papers, clothes and towels everywhere. She didn't dare examine why.

"Shall we, then?"

She nodded, and together they headed to the restaurant across the street. Travis was still limping, and she felt guilty. He'd walked several miles in Raton this morning, and then his leg had grown stiff in the car.

They caught the scent of smoke and grilled meat immediately. A good sign. Country music came from a sound system as they entered.

Jenny glanced around, absorbing every detail. Another good sign was the hatwear. She suspected the diners in worn Western hats were locals. Tourists, on the other hand, were identified by new Western hats, maps and guidebooks on their tables. The old hats dominated.

The interior walls were paneled and decorated by what seemed like a hundred black-and-white photos, some obviously dating back decades. They seemed to be the only effort toward warmth. The wooden tables looked none too sturdy.

A sign told them to seat themselves, so she led the way to a table next to the wall, where she could watch the room. She noticed his wry expression that once again she beat him to it.

Paper menus were on the table, along with salt and pepper shakers and a bottle of hot sauce. As they looked at the menus, a waitress appeared at the table with silverware and glasses of water. "Hey, how are you?" she asked in a Texas accent that was barely understandable. "What can I get y'all?"

It took Jenny a few seconds to translate. "What would you suggest?" Jenny asked.

"Beef tips," she said. "Smoked for a day. It's our bestseller with folks around town."

Jenny nodded. "Sounds good to me."

"Comes with two sides. Salad, baked beans, slaw, baked potatoes or fries?"

"Fries and salad."

"And you, sugar?" she asked Travis, her gaze lingering on him.

"I'll have the same," Travis replied.

"And drinks?"

"The local beer," Travis said.

"Me, too," Jenny said.

"I like Texas," Jenny said after the waitress left.

He gave her that slow smile that made her body respond in unwanted ways. "I can honestly say I have never met a woman so enthusiastic about food."

"What about your ex-fiancé?" It came out before she could stop it. But she'd been wondering about the woman since he had mentioned that she was a journalist.

"She barely ate at all," he said. "She was a television journalist and always said one pound looked like ten on television."

"That's another reason why I wasn't interested in television. Besides, have you ever seen a red-haired woman journalist on TV? Especially one with freckles?"

"Come to think of it, no," he said. His eyes smiled. Warmth curled in her stomach as their gazes locked, unwanted messages exchanged between two reluctant recipients.

No! She swallowed hard as she fought against the feeling. She couldn't get involved. Not with him. He was not a player. He was obviously a forever kind of guy. Panic filled her. She had her own goals, her own dreams, her own life, and they didn't include anything close to forever. She tried to keep her voice light as she replied, "Besides, I wouldn't like to stay anywhere long." It was a warning. To both of them.

He studied her for a moment. His face was unreadable. "I can understand that," he said in a neutral tone.

It was a step back for him, too, but she'd asked for it. Yet how could she explain her sudden panic after a perfectly sublime day?

Thankfully the beers came, and she didn't have to. The food followed shortly.

The beef tips fell off the bones, but her appetite had suddenly faded.

She worked at eating, though. She didn't like being vulnerable, and she felt vulnerable with him. She'd been physically attracted to guys before, and had been friends with many guys, but rarely had the two come together. There had never been the naturalness she felt with Travis.

The dining room was filling up when the waitress brought the bill. They hadn't talked about sharing costs, so she grabbed it. "You paid for lunch," she said. "I'll get this." Travis simply nodded.

She liked that. She had made an agreement with Josh Manning. Travis respected that.

She'd left her key in her own room, so she entered through his. As she walked over to the connecting door to her room, he followed her.

"Thanks," she said, turning and looking up at him.

"You paid for it."

"I mean for everything. For indulging me today in Raton, for letting me come with you, for being such a good...companion."

"You're not bad yourself," he said. "I can honestly say the drive wouldn't have been half as interesting without you."

The humor in his voice rustled something in her heart. She wished his eyes didn't crinkle with amusement and that he didn't have that droll sense of humor. She wished the air didn't catch fire. The beat of her heart quickened. She swallowed hard.

Step back.

She held her breath for a moment. She wanted him to kiss her. The last one had virtually shaken the earth, but she knew it would lead to something more, and neither one of them could afford that. She would be leaving Covenant Falls soon.

"I should go," she whispered.

"Yes, you should," he replied. Then he added ruefully, "Before we do something stupid."

So he felt it, too. She nodded, even while her body disagreed. She knew in her bones that something stupid could never be casual with him.

"Good night," she said softly as she stepped inside and turned around to face him.

"Good night," he replied and gave her that half smile that always challenged her. "What time do you want to leave in the morning?"

"You're the major," she said. "Any time is good for me."

"I'll meet you for breakfast at seven?"

She nodded, and he closed the door. She didn't want him to. She was full of need. She wanted to kiss him, to feel his hands on her. But she didn't want to start something she couldn't finish. The only way she could move on with her life was to visit that village in Syria…

Travis was too decent a guy for a one-night stand. As lightly as he'd mentioned an ex-fiancé, her rejection had obviously wounded him. It had been in his voice and perhaps had been responsible for his initial reluctance to bring her along. She didn't want to do anything that might make him regret letting her accompany him.

She took a deep breath and forced herself to move away from the door.

She went to the window and looked out. There was the interstate and hills. Above, clouds played hide and seek with the moon. Thoughts were furiously competing for her attention.

Don't think about Travis Hammond. It could lead to nothing but heartache.

Think about the story. A story. Any story.

She opened her tablet and started writing about Raton, the people there, its history, the historical theater that drew acts from San Francisco and the hat cemetery.

When she finished, she tapped Save on her device and closed it. She would read what she wrote tomorrow and decide whether it was worth trying to sell. It was entirely different from anything else she'd written in the past ten years.

But she was writing again, something she hadn't been able to do until now. Step one.

CHAPTER FIFTEEN

THE NEXT WEEK was going to be hell.

Travis knew he wasn't going to get much sleep tonight. Maybe not much for a week. How could he send Jenny back to Covenant Falls without admitting he couldn't handle being around her?

He took yet another icy shower. He suspected he had a number of them ahead. At this rate, he was going to be the cleanest man in the West, maybe in the country.

He'd obviously learned nothing from his previous experience with a journalist. Although Jenny wasn't anything like Dinah, they both had an obsession with their jobs. Jenny made no attempt to hide that her career was the most important thing in her life.

How could he fight that when he had absolutely no idea where his own future lay?

Still, he didn't know when he'd smiled as much or felt so lighthearted. She made every hour an adventure.

He heard the murmur of a television next door.

So Jenny Talbot couldn't sleep either. He barely resisted knocking on the door.

He located his book, a spy novel from his favorite author, put on a comfortable T-shirt and his skivvies and slid in bed.

He kept his eyes on the time, until the numbers on the motel clock turned 2:00 a.m. The murmur from next door had faded away. He put the book down and turned off the light, trying to think about the story he'd been reading. But he couldn't remember a damned thing.

He used to be able to grab sleep under the worst conditions, but two years in hospitals and rehab had robbed him of that ability. Now that he had time to sleep, it eluded him. It was a paradox.

He finally started to drift off when he was startled awake by a scream from Jenny's room. He was instantly awake and on his feet. He rushed to the adjoining door and opened it when he found it unlocked.

The room was dim. Light came through a half-opened bathroom door.

Her body, clothed in a T-shirt, was folded up tight, as if she were hiding. Her face was wet. "Help her. Have to help her," she cried over and over again. He remembered her telling him she had nightmares.

"Hey," he said gently. He knew only too well the perils of waking someone suddenly from a nightmare. "Hey there, Jenny," he crooned as his hand rested softly on her shoulder. "It's okay. Everyone is safe," he said, although it wasn't true. They weren't safe in the world she was in at the moment. He ran his hand down her arm as easily as he could. He wanted to wake her but not abruptly.

"Rick… Rick…" The cry was plaintive.

Travis felt a flash of jealousy. So there was someone in her life. Most likely someone without scars all over his body. He willed the thought away. "Jenny," he said a bit louder.

Her body jerked. Her eyes opened wide. Wet with tears. Confused. It took her several seconds before she realized where she was.

"Travis?" she said in a shaky voice. Then she sat up and leaned against him. His arms went around her.

"Last time I looked in the mirror," he said, suddenly aware that his army T-shirt and skivvies were precious little protection against an arousal that was starting to make itself known. He reluctantly dropped his arms and moved away. "Do you want me to turn on another light?"

"No." She sat up straighter, pushing a curl from her face. "I'm sorry I woke you." She tried to brush the tears away and looked upset with herself.

"You didn't. I was reading," he lied.

She tried to smile. "Another night owl."

"Sometimes it's hard to sleep." He didn't add that she was one of his reasons.

"I'll be okay now," she said. "It was just a nightmare."

"A pretty nasty one, I would guess. It's the one you told me about?"

She nodded.

"Is that why you sleep with a light on?" They had been honest with each other since they met. He didn't see a reason to hold back now.

She nodded again.

"Can I get you something? A glass of water? A coke from the machine in the lobby?" Damn, but he felt helpless. He hated the feeling.

She gave him a flicker of a smile. "No, but thank you." Her eyes were still luminous with the tears. For the first time since he'd met her, she looked vulnerable.

"Will you be all right?" he asked. It was a stupid question. He knew she wouldn't be all right. Not for a long time.

"It's gone now," she said. "I don't know what sparked it. There's never a reason."

"I have them, too," he confessed. "I think anyone who's seen the shit we have…" He hesitated, and then he added, "Can you tell me about it?" *And who in the hell was Rick?*

She shook her head. "I'm okay now," she said.

"Really, I am. Thanks for waking me, but you'd better get some sleep. You're driving." She tried to smile.

He hated to leave. She still looked vulnerable with those unruly red curls framing eyes that were just too damned green and still full of moisture. "Go then," she ordered.

"You're bossy, you know that?"

"I've been told that. But I need to take a shower."

He pictured her naked, standing under a hot shower.

He needed a cold one. Again. Damn but he wanted to help. He wanted to hold her, reassure her and wipe away the remnants of the nightmare. But he sensed it wouldn't be welcomed.

He left before his thoughts led to action.

AFTER TRAVIS LEFT for his own room, Jenny stood up. She was unsteady. Reliving those moments in Aleppo had sapped the strength from her. After several slow steps, she regained her balance and made her way into the bathroom.

Once there, she peered into the mirror. She looked terrible. Her hair was a mass of curls, and her eyes were bloodshot. Her T-shirt was wet with sweat. How could Travis help but be repulsed? She was grateful that he broke off the nightmare, but she was embarrassed about her weakness, about how she looked, about maybe delaying his trip again.

She'd always taken pride in being independent, not beholden to anyone, but now he'd seen her at her worst. She shouldn't care. This was a short interlude in her life. A pause before returning to what she did best. Be an observer, a recorder.

Suddenly, that didn't sound so great.

She took a hot shower. Then she washed the sweaty T-shirt. There wouldn't be time to dry it before leaving later that morning, and there was no hair dryer at this motel. She squeezed the shirt as dry as possible and then spread it out on the chair. Maybe she could do the same thing on the back seat of the car.

When she finished trying to tame her hair, she put on another large T-shirt for sleeping and went to look out the window. No mountains in sight here. These were the plains. The moon was at crescent. Wisps of clouds drifted across the midnight blue sky. No sign of dawn yet.

She didn't want to try to sleep for the few hours remaining before resuming the trip. She was too full of colliding emotions, thoughts and impressions.

She took up one of Travis's books on the healing power of horses and sat in the rather uncomfortable chair to read.

Travis hadn't set the clock nor his phone after he'd returned to his room. He'd relied on his internal clock. It seldom failed him.

It did this morning, however. He didn't wake until seven thirty. He didn't hear any sounds from Jenny's room and hoped she'd been able to sleep. He dressed and left to get coffee.

To his surprise, she was sitting in the breakfast room, engrossed in a newspaper. Her plate was filled with a waffle, some fruit and a bagel. There was no evidence of last night's trauma.

He found the paper plates and poured batter into a make-your-own-waffle machine. Then he collected some fruit. He got a cup of coffee while he waited for the waffle to finish.

When he approached Jenny's table, she looked up and gave him one of her blinding smiles, although he detected a nervousness about it. Even embarrassment. "I'm sorry about last night," she said.

"No need. I've had nightmares and flashbacks of my own. I've had two years to come to terms with them."

He knew better than to ask her how she was. Her eyes were tired, and he realized she probably hadn't gone back to sleep that morning.

"You haven't slept," he concluded.

"Do I look that bad?"

He shrugged. "I can honestly say no, you don't look bad at all, although your eyes look tired." He paused. "It doesn't seem to affect your appetite, though. What are you reading?"

"The Lubbock newspaper. I'm an addict," she added. "I have to grab any newspaper in sight wherever I go."

"You looked like you were devouring it."

"That's probably an apt description. I even read the obituaries. They tell stories of individual lives, even if it's just a short notice. Were they a veteran? Did they go to college? Marry? Have fifteen children? Eight dogs? I read one once that had been written by the deceased. It was full of wonderful humor and made me wish I'd met him."

He shook his head. She was the only person he'd met that actually read strangers' obituaries.

He took a big gulp of coffee and then a taste of the waffle.

She raised an eyebrow as he did and frowned. "It…lacks a certain something," he said.

"You forgot to put the good stuff on it, like butter and syrup."

"I didn't forget. I'm not much on anything sweet, except, maybe, those cinnamon rolls yesterday."

"Sugar is good for energy, and I need some this morning," Jenny replied. She hesitated and looked around. The room was empty, except for the two of them. "About last night…"

He shook his head. "You don't have to say anything."

"Yes, I do. It might happen again."

"I've had my share of night sweats," he repeated, closing the subject.

Twenty minutes later, they were back on the road, both with coffee to go. They zipped through Lubbock and headed east.

As usual, she remarked on the number the cattle they passed, or had to stop to read a historic sign. After a while, she was quiet. He glanced over and saw that she was asleep, with one of the equine therapy books in her lap. She didn't wake up until they were close to Abilene.

When she figured out where they were, she said, "I've been asleep that long?"

"I don't think a hurricane would have waked you."

"Certainly not one in the middle of Texas," she shot back.

He chuckled. "It's time for you to go back to work. You're navigator for the last leg. We're going off the interstate again."

"Is that a promotion or demotion from cruise director?"

"Let's call it a parallel adjustment."

"That sounds like military speak."

He smiled but didn't answer.

"Okay, what do you want me to do?"

"Look for the signs. We keep on this interstate until you see US 85. We turn south there."

She picked up her cell phone and started typing.

"No car museum in Abilene?" he asked.

"No, but there's an old army fort," she said with a little bit of a dare in her voice. She was reverting back to the usual cheeky Jenny.

"I think there will be a lot of forts along our way in the next week."

"I'll look forward to it."

She was silent for a moment, and then she said, "It suddenly seems odd that I have seen more of countries tens of thousands of miles away than in my own. Even when I was a travel writer, I always wrote about other countries. I love history, including American history, but for some reason, it seemed too familiar, and I wanted to see and experience places that were unfamiliar.

"I suspect that's why I loved Raton and the hat cemetery," she continued. "It's different and fun and yet, in an odd way, says so much about the country. Quirky and imaginative and determined. Building that pass was not easy. Traveling those trails from Missouri all the way to California took more courage than I have." She sighed.

"That's why I'll bug you all the way to stop at places that look interesting."

"And then go back to the Middle East?" he said with a raised eyebrow.

"Yes," she said simply.

He nodded. She feared that he was thinking she wasn't paying enough attention to the subject that brought them here. But she was a fast reader and had finished his binder.

She was silent for a few minutes as she looked at the map, and then she glanced back at him. "Thank you for interrupting the dream this morning," she said.

"Do you have them often?"

"Not too often. Usually when I'm tired, or emotional because of something I've seen on television... I keep thinking I might have been able to do something to help that little girl. Why didn't I charge out and pick her up?"

"I thought you were hit by shrapnel?"

"But there might have been time."

"Might?"

"Everything happened at once. I don't remember...maybe because I don't want to know." It sounded like she hadn't admitted that to anyone before.

"Somehow, in the short time I've known you, I don't think much frightens you."

She averted her eyes. "I'd better start paying attention to the turns."

"Might be a good idea," he agreed.

For the next fifty miles, Jenny concentrated on the map. There wasn't much to see except ranches and farms. According to her phone's GPS, they were in the central plains. They occasionally passed through a very small town. They stopped at a service station to get gas. In lieu of real food, they picked up some bags of snacks.

It was midafternoon when they entered Killeen, home to Fort Hood. They headed to a motel recommended by Dr. Payne, where Travis had already made reservations for two rooms.

It was nicer than the one in which they'd stayed earlier, and the parking lot was half-full. Dr. Payne had told him that motels were fully occupied with visitors to Fort Hood. It actually had a restaurant, business center and swimming pool.

This motel had given them adjoining rooms, too. It made communication easier, but it also increased the temptation level.

She went into her room and checked it out before returning to the car. She scooped up the T-shirt that had dried in the back seat and transferred Travis's binder, his books and her own carry-on into her room.

After unlocking her side of the connecting door, she channel surfed and caught up on the news for a few minutes. Then she turned to the horse therapy book she hadn't finished.

Her room phone rang, and she picked it up.

"Dr. Payne invited us to dinner tonight at the home of the dog trainer, the one who trained Andy's Joseph."

"That's terrific."

"Why don't you get some sleep? I'll call you an hour before six. That's the invite time."

"What about you? You must be dead tired after last night and then driving today."

"I never need much sleep," he answered.

"If you don't need sleep, we can always look around the city," she said. "I'm sure I can find some intriguing out-of-the-way places."

She heard him chuckle. "Damn, but you're incorrigible," he said. "Okay, I probably do need a few hours of sleep."

"Is that what I have to do to get you to do what you should do?"

"Now that's one heck of a convoluted sentence for a writer."

"Yes, it is," she said proudly. "I had to work on it."

The chuckle turned into a burst of laughter.

It was a lovely thing to hear, even on the phone. Then she panicked. She'd never felt this way before. Not for anyone. She didn't want to feel that way. Warm. Confused. Happy just to joust with him. Content with silence. Stimulated by conversation.

He made her lighthearted in a way she couldn't remember being before.

"I'll call you at five," he said. "I have directions to the dog trainer's home. Dr. Payne said it would take about thirty minutes." He hung up then. He was probably as disconcerted as she was over the growing intimacy between them.

She looked at the clock. It was a little after three, but her mind was too busy to sleep. She went into the bathroom and found a shiny, clean bathtub and a small bottle of bath oil on the counter.

She let the water run until it was deep and hot. The bath oil filled the air with a floral scent. She slipped into the water, leaned back and closed her eyes.

She tried to think of the future, of her shoulder getting better and of returning to the Middle East, but the prospect didn't hold its usual allure. Travis's half smile and intelligent hazel eyes kept interfering. He wasn't like other officers she'd met. He wasn't too bossy. He had a sense of humor, and he was tolerant. And he had a slow smile to die for.

He was also wary. It had been in his short comment about his former fiancé. It wasn't helpful that the woman was a journalist. She obviously had no depth if she didn't see what she was losing.

And it was probably the reason he'd been reserved in their first meetings and when he'd, on occasion, reverted from friend to stranger. *Why did she care?* In a couple of weeks, she would be gone. She had to concentrate on earning a living again. This trip had given her more than a few ideas to pursue if she couldn't get back overseas as soon as she hoped…

She woke to cool water and suddenly panicked. She had drifted off. *What time was it?*

She almost leaped out of the tub. She dashed into the room to check the time. It was nearly five.

She selected the one good blouse she had and the pair of black slacks. She ran a brush through her hair and used two large ornamental hairpins to keep it back from her face. She then added a touch of lipstick.

The phone rang, as she expected, exactly at five.

"Hi," Travis said. "Have a good afternoon?"

"A wet one." She hesitated. "I went to sleep in the bathtub."

He was silent for a moment. "Will you be ready in fifteen minutes?"

"Already am."

"You are one unusual woman."

"I'm usually the first to arrive at parties. You said it'll take us half an hour to get there?"

"Yeah, so we have some time. Do you want to get a glass of wine in the lounge?"

"Sure."

"We'll leave from there."

"Fine."

"You're being very agreeable."

"I like wine."

"Do you want to meet at the adjoining door or in the hallway?"

She knew what he was asking. The adjoining door in last night's motel heightened a temptation that was already moving like a forest fire. He was giving her a chance to stop before it became an inferno.

"The adjoining door," she said, ignoring the clamor of warning bells in her head.

"Okay. You unlock yours. I'll unlock mine."

She couldn't help laughing. "This is ridiculous," she said, because they were saying much more than their actual words. There was both unsaid trust and promise in their absence. She put down the phone and unlocked the door on her side. The one on his side opened.

He'd changed into a tan button-down shirt and darker tan khaki pants. He looked fine. Very masculine. Very intriguing.

"I do like that blouse," he said. "Ready to go?"

Jenny grabbed her purse and forced her gaze away from him. On their way out of his room, he put his hand on the small of her back. A courtesy, but she still felt on fire. They wandered down to a small bar area next to a larger dining area and found it empty, except for a waitress.

Jenny ordered a glass of chardonnay and he a beer.

"Is there anything I should know about where we're going?" she asked.

"I just know her name is Karen Conway. She's a dog trainer who specializes in matching rescue dogs to veterans with PTSD. She operates mostly on donations, although she does make money training dogs for the general public. Andy thinks she's one of the most terrific people in the world, although she adds that Karen can be gruff and demanding. She had to stay with her for several days before taking possession of Joseph. She had to be worthy of the dog."

"I think I'll like Ms. Conway."

"As far as I can tell, you like everyone."

"Not quite everyone," she said soberly. "I do have an I-would-like-to-punch-him-in-the-face list."

"Just a 'him'? No 'her'?"

"Maybe that…idiot who's a television reporter someplace."

Travis grinned. "What else does it take to get on that list? I want to know for my own safety."

"Telling me I can't do something," she said. "And people who betray other people."

"Anyone in mind?"

"My sister's ex-husband."

"You have a sister?"

"Two of them. Stacy is seven years older than me, and Lenore is five years older. And I have a niece who is too much like me for her own good."

"I don't know about that," he said. "I think she's pretty lucky."

Jenny didn't know how to answer that. Instead, she grabbed the glass of wine as it was delivered and took a quick gulp. "Maybe we should go on," she said to cover her confusion.

Travis looked amused. "Do you always get flustered at compliments?"

She took another sip of wine. She had no snappy reply this time.

CHAPTER SIXTEEN

TRAVIS TRIED TO keep his mind on the directions he'd written down as he drove to the address he'd been given.

It wasn't easy.

The scent of roses got in the way. So did thoughts he kept trying to brush aside.

Jenny Talbot was unlike any woman he'd ever met. She was instinctive, bossy, kind, intrusive, provocative and, dammit, irresistible. She lit up a room. He'd noticed it when she walked through the small Pueblo airport. There was an expectant quality, almost a dance, when she walked, as if she couldn't wait for the next adventure.

The traffic was light, and, as per instructions, he drove fifteen miles, until he reached a narrow dirt road, and then he turned onto it. He saw a group of buildings surrounding a small ranch house. A beat-up red truck and a newer sedan were parked in front. On one side of the house, there were fenced kennels, and on the other, there was a one-story building with a chimney. As they approached the house, the dogs in the kennel crowded the fence, apparently curious to see who was visiting. They started barking.

The door to the house opened, and a tall man in jeans and a pullover Texas Tech sweatshirt approached them. "I'm Richard Payne," he said as he shook hands with Travis and then Jenny. "You must be Ms. Talbot? Andy Stuart called and suggested you and Karen should meet."

Travis watched as Jenny spun her usual magic. "I fell in love with Joseph," Jenny explained. "I understand he was one of Ms. Conway's therapy dogs."

"You like dogs?" Dr. Payne asked.

"I like anything with four legs," she replied with that quick grin.

"Watch out, or you'll take a dog with you," he said.

"I'm not a veteran," she said.

"Maybe not officially," Dr. Payne said, "but I know you were over there with our soldiers. After Andy called, I looked up some of your stories. Impressive. It's obvious you care about the people you write about. They're not just stories to you."

"Thank you," Jenny said. "Andy's been singing your praises, as well. She said she didn't think she could have made it without you."

"It was Joseph who provided the magic," Dr. Payne demurred. He turned to Travis. "And Josh said good things about you, Major. He told me you were his superior officer. I'm interested in your continuing friendship. But come inside. I have to warn you, there's a few dogs in there."

"How many are a few?" Jenny asked.

"Four at the moment. They're learning good house manners. People all around here know Karen takes in strays and readies them for adoption. Only a few go into the intensive training to work as therapy dogs. They have to be smart and have a great temperament."

Dr. Payne led the way inside the ranch house. Three dogs, two large and one medium size, came to greet them. Another small dog, with white whiskers, in a face that resembled a monkey's, didn't move from a place next to an empty chair.

"That's Anna," said an attractive woman as she entered the room and realized everyone had been looking at the strange little dog. "And I'm Karen Conway."

Travis held out his hand. "Ms. Conway, thank you for taking time to see us."

She took it with a strong grip. "My pleasure. And call me Karen. Everyone does."

She looked as if she were in her fifties and wore jeans and a neat button-up shirt. "Anna was dropped off three weeks ago by someone who found her walking down a road. She was in pretty bad condition. She's a sweet girl but shy and a bit fearful. I've been searching for the owner but no luck."

"What is she?" Jenny asked.

"She looks like a purebred affenpinscher, and if you've never heard of one, you're not alone. It's a German breed, and the dogs are known for their little monkey faces. I think at one time she had a good home because she's house-trained, but I suspect the last few years have been pretty rough. She's not very trusting. It'll probably be difficult to find her a home because of that and because she's a senior. Most families want young dogs."

"Okay if I pet her?"

"Sure."

Jenny went over and knelt next to the dog. "Hey there," she said in a low, calm voice. She held out her hand first and let the dog sniff it. She then scratched behind Anna's ears, murmuring something that Travis couldn't hear. The little dog's tongue darted out to lick her hand.

"You have a way with dogs," Karen said.

"They probably know I like them."

"Do you have one?"

"I've never had a pet," she admitted. "My father wouldn't even consider it when I was growing up. Since college, I've been moving around, usually in other countries. I've been in the Middle East for five years."

"Well, let me know if you settle down. I always have good dogs who need a home. Anna's inside because she's still new, and I want her to feel safe and become accustomed to living in a house again."

"There's no hint as to what happened with her?" Jenny asked.

"No telling," Karen said. "She could have been abandoned when an owner died. She might have been lost. She's shy with strangers, but once she knows you, she wants to be held."

Karen introduced the other dogs. "They're potential therapy dogs. The large one is Shelby. I have high hopes for him. He's in the second month of training. We're looking for just the right owner for him." She scratched the dog's left ear, then in an authoritative voice said, "Shelby, get Richard a beer."

The dog barked and, wagging his tail, trotted through an open doorway that apparently led to the kitchen. Several seconds later, he returned with a can of beer in his mouth. He offered it to Dr. Payne.

"I'm impressed," Jenny said.

"He fetched it from the fridge. Problem is," Karen said, "I now have to get up and give Richard a glass, since dog germs are all over the can. Haven't figured out how to solve that problem yet. The other two dogs are Sam and April. They still have some learning to do. They know simple commands. April, shake hands."

April came over and offered a paw to Dr. Payne, and then to Jenny and finally to Travis.

"They are very polite dogs," Jenny observed with humor. "And the ones outside?"

"All rescues, up for adoption. We sort of rotate inside time."

Bemused, Travis watched the interaction between the three people. As usual, Jenny immediately fit into the group, including with the animals. It was as if she'd known them for months, rather than less than an hour.

He also saw the emotion in her face as she met the small black dog. He had a bad feeling about it.

"But enough with showing off," Karen said, interrupting his thoughts. "What can I get you for drinks? I have iced tea, wine and beer."

Travis and Jenny joined Dr. Payne in having beer. They were directed to the table, which was already set. Karen disappeared for a minute and returned with a platter of meat and bowls of slaw, beans and salad.

"One of Richard's best friends owns a barbecue restaurant," Karen confided. "In fact, it's one of the best in this part of Texas. Richard stopped there on the way and picked up some smoked beef brisket."

Travis was hungry. They had skipped lunch, and the brisket was even better than last night's.

He couldn't remember when he'd eaten more than in the past few days. His gaze met Jenny's, and they shared a smile.

As they ate, Dr. Payne turned to Jenny. "We invited you tonight because Andy Stuart wanted you to meet Karen and she's busy tomorrow. I also had a call from the veterinarian in Covenant Falls who suggested we meet. I know you two don't have much time and plan to leave tomorrow, after our meeting, so I suggested supper. I thought you could concentrate on the therapy dogs tonight, and we'll discuss the equine therapy project at our meeting tomorrow."

"Sounds good to me," Jenny said.

After dinner, the table was cleared, and the four of them settled in the small but comfortable living area. Anna immediately went over and sat by Jenny's feet.

"It was really thoughtful of both of you to invite us," Jenny said as one hand fondled the dog's ears. She turned to Karen. "I would like to start by asking how and why you started training therapy dogs."

Karen nodded.

"Do you mind if I record it?" Jenny asked.

"No. But if you print anything, I would appreciate some notice."

"Right now, this is strictly for the veterinarian in Covenant Falls," Jenny said. "But if I do a story, I'll certainly need more information and would check with you first."

Travis sat back while Jenny started the questions. There was little she missed, beginning with how Karen got involved in training therapy dogs.

"My husband and I were both dog trainers," Karen said. "We bought this place because it was a lot of land for the price. We trained cattle dogs, as well as other dogs for commercials and films. Our son joined the army and, because of his background, became a dog handler. He was wounded, and his dog was killed, during an engagement in Iraq. When he was shipped home, he wasn't the same boy.

"We saw it as soon as he got back, carrying all that pain. The VA diagnosed him with PTSD. They tried to help, but he never came out of it." She paused and looked down. Her voice grew faint as she continued. "He committed suicide."

Jenny reached out to take her hand. Karen looked up, her eyes filled with tears. "My husband died of a heart attack several months later."

Jenny held onto Karen's hand. Waited. Karen regained her composure and gave Jenny's hand a gratifying squeeze.

"The one thing that kept me going," Karen continued, "was wanting to help other young soldiers coming back. Animals are the best way to do it. They aren't judgmental. You can tell them secrets, and they're not going to go out and talk about it. They quietly sympathize, help when they can and demand nothing but a little affection. They seem to know when a flashback is coming or when sleep turns into a nightmare and try to wake or comfort their person.

"That's how I met Richard," she continued. "He heard what I was doing and thought I might be able to help one of his patients. He's sent me several since then, including Andy."

The interview went on, and Dr. Payne chimed in a couple of times. Travis sensed definite vibes between Karen and the psychologist. Although they weren't married, they interacted like a committed couple.

Karen detailed her training program for matching dogs and veterans. She insisted that the veteran stay at the ranch for anywhere between two to five days to determine whether they were a good fit. "I want to make sure they bond," she said.

"Would you use the same procedure for horses?" Travis asked. "Put them in close proximity for a period of time?"

"Equine therapy is different," she replied. "The relationship is different. Horses do develop close attachments to humans, but a lot of the therapy for humans is learning new skills, gaining confidence and doing it with others who have gone through similar trauma. Richard can help you more with that tomorrow."

Travis sat back and listened, impressed by Jenny's questions. He could almost see her mind shaping an article.

Anna raised a paw and put it on Jenny's ankle as if to say *please*.

"Is it okay if I pick her up?" Jenny asked her hostess.

"Sure," Karen said. "Once she trusts a person, that's where she's happiest."

Jenny lifted Anna into her lap. The little dog circled it once and then plopped down, with her tail wagging. She looked up and locked her big, expressive eyes on Jenny, as if Jenny were Anna's owner, handpicked by Anna herself.

"You seem to have a fan," Karen said. "Are you interested?"

"I thought you had a long procedure," Jenny said.

"No. She's not one of my therapy dogs. She's too old and shy to be one. She simply needs a home, and it will be difficult to find one. Senior dogs are the last to be adopted, and yet they're usually among the best behaved and most eager to please. Anna isn't unfriendly, but she's cautious of strangers, which is why I haven't put her out for adoption. It just takes the right person."

A little pink tongue reached out and licked

Jenny's hand again. The dog then closed her eyes in what looked like bliss.

It was nearing nine thirty before Jenny finished. Travis and Jenny thanked Karen and Dr. Payne and headed for the door. Anna followed and tried to leave with them.

Karen picked her up. "Sometimes dogs pick their own people instead of the other way around."

"I wish I could take her right now," Jenny said, "but I don't have a permanent home."

Travis heard the longing in her voice. He inwardly groaned.

Dr. Payne walked them out. "I'll see you tomorrow," he said.

Travis nodded. "Thanks for arranging this. Stephanie is going to be pleased. She wants to work with therapy dogs, too."

"Our pleasure," Dr. Payne said. "The more therapy dogs we can develop, the better. They've done wonders for some of my patients. We owe them."

JENNY WAS THOUGHTFUL on the drive back to their motel. It hurt, really hurt, leaving Anna, when the dog so clearly wanted to go with her. She knew, though, that she was in no position to have a dog. But those big, solemn eyes seemed to beg to go with her.

She'd never had a dog, and she shouldn't want this one now. She was in limbo. Anna was a senior and looked the worse for wear, but Jenny wanted her. Maybe because she needed to be needed. It was a new feeling for her and quite puzzling but there it was. She warned herself there was no way she could take care of a dog, even a small one with a sad, heartbreaking monkey face.

She tried to think of the job ahead, instead of the dog she couldn't have. How could she take Anna when she had no home? At least not a permanent one. Then she thought of her niece. Maybe she could share the dog with Charlie. She would call her sister as soon as they returned to the motel.

"Did you get everything you wanted?" Travis asked.

"Yes. I really like her. She would make a good story. It might help obtain a few more sponsors for her 'dogs for vets' program. I'll make copies of the interview for both you and Stephanie."

"I'm glad you were here," Travis said. "You asked questions I wouldn't have thought of. I would have asked the basic questions, but I wouldn't have dug as deep as you did. You added the human element."

"I'm happy I'm earning my keep." She paused. "I didn't see a wedding ring on Dr. Payne's finger," she said.

"I didn't notice."

"Women do," she said. "First thing," she added. "Do you think Dr. Payne is…?"

"Seeing Mrs. Conway? I do, and good for them."

They rode in unusual silence to the motel. Jenny kept thinking about Karen Conway. She wanted to write Karen's story. She might never submit it, but the story was already writing itself in her head.

Anna also kept popping into her head. She'd looked so forlorn being all alone, while the other dogs interacted. She'd seemed so content and hopeful when she'd settled down in Jenny's lap.

They reached their motel a few minutes before ten and went into Travis's room. Someone had been in the rooms and turned down the bed. She hesitated at the door. She wanted to talk to him now, to discuss the interview, but she wanted to call her sister first. She hoped Lenore liked dogs. It seemed strange that she didn't know.

"I should make a phone call," she said.

He had a question in his eyes, but he nodded. It was one of the many things she liked about him.

She went through the connecting door to her room and closed the door behind her. She took her cell from her purse and punched her sister's number. It was late, but she knew her sister often worked late on paperwork.

Lenore answered almost immediately. "Are you all right?" she asked with obvious concern.

"Yes, of course."

"I tried to call you several times," Lenore said.

"I'm sorry," she said. "I haven't checked my messages. Is anything wrong?"

"No, except our father is raising holy hell about you running around with a stranger and a bad shoulder. I thought I would warn you."

"I've been in war zones, for Pete's sake," Jenny replied. "I can certainly take care of myself here. Sorry to be out of touch. I'm not used to people worrying about me, especially my father. You, on the other hand, are welcome to worry. But I'm fine. Better than fine."

"You sound happy."

"I *am* happy. I'm onto several good stories. But the reason I called is, well, how do you feel about dogs?"

"I like them, why?"

"Can you have dogs at the condo?"

"Yes. Charlie always wanted…"

"I might know the perfect dog," Jenny said before Lenore could finish. "It's small, house-trained, not really active and very affectionate."

"What kind is he?" Lenore asked.

"An affenpinscher," she said. "You've probably never heard of them. I hadn't. She's black, with a face that looks a little like a monkey with white whiskers."

"What's the catch?"

"There isn't one, except she's not a puppy. More like middle-aged. But that's a good thing. As I said, she's house-trained. Very affectionate. Someone found her on a road in Texas, but the person who has her now is a professional dog trainer and vouches for her health and good manners." The words rushed out of her mouth, and she wasn't sure about the good manners, but she felt a little exaggeration was acceptable.

She sensed some hesitation on the other side of the line, but she was sure that once Charlie saw Anna, she would fall in love.

"How will you get her here?"

"I'm sure my driver will be happy to bring her." She crossed her fingers as she said the words.

"Who is this person?"

"Travis Hammond. He's an army major who is doing a study for the mayor of Covenant Falls and her husband." She was stretching the truth again, but the description made the trip sound official.

"Good-looking?"

"You could say that."

"Nice?"

"Patient," Jenny corrected.

"Sexy?"

And how. "Some might say so," she replied, trying to keep her voice analytical.

"Hmm," her sister said. "About the dog, I'm not making any promises. If it doesn't work out, she'll be your responsibility. *You* will have to find a new home."

"I'll do that," she assured her sister. "But don't say anything to Charlie. I have a few things to work out." She said good-night and hung up before Lenore changed her mind.

She stared at the phone. It had been a totally irresponsible thing to do. Maybe Covenant Falls and all its dogs and horses were getting to her. She had always steered away from anything that reeked of permanence. But flying away alone to a foreign shore no longer had the allure it did a year ago.

She should call back and say she'd simply had one too many glasses of wine and to forget it.

She couldn't do it.

What was happening to her?

She'd never let anything stand in the way of her career before.

Certainly not a silly little dog.

Or a major who didn't know what he would be doing next month.

Now where in the hell did that come from?

She turned toward the door. She'd shut Travis off to make the call. She should apologize. She knocked lightly on his door. Maybe he had gone to bed. It had been a long day.

He didn't answer immediately. She tried again, her knock louder, and he opened the door. His hair was wet. All of him was damp, and he smelled wonderful. His only covering was a towel wrapped around his middle.

His chest, upper arms and left leg were riddled with scars. But what she really saw was the pain he must have endured.

She looked up at him and smiled. "You're beautiful," she said.

The words escaped her before she could reclaim them. But, to her, he was. The scars on the lean, muscular body were hard-earned. Badges of honor and courage.

And he really was a fine specimen of manhood.

CHAPTER SEVENTEEN

TRAVIS STARED AT her in astonishment.

The towel started to fall. He grabbed it and clutched it around his middle. Heat clawed up his neck.

To his surprise, Jenny grinned, her eyes full of mischief. "I haven't seen you speechless before," she said, then added politely, "May I come in?"

He was too stupefied to answer immediately. His brain kept coming back to the word *beautiful*. After a few seconds of standing like a statue, he said, "I think you have," he said.

"Only if you move a few inches." Her eyes sparkled. "I just wanted to thank you. It was a nice evening. You were very tolerant of my butting in. It would be rude not to express my appreciation."

He detected amusement under the explanation for her late visit, and it did nothing for the sudden movement under the towel.

"I appreciate the thought," he said, just as formally, "but I didn't think you rude. Your curiosity comes naturally. However, your apology is accepted," he added.

"I think I'm going to withdraw it," she said with that engaging sense of humor that always startled him. "*You've* been rude standing there and not inviting me inside." Mischief practically danced in her eyes. Despite his discomfort at her seeing the scars he usually tried to cover, he couldn't help but chuckle. He never knew what was going to pop out of her mouth.

"Beautiful?" he finally got out. He hadn't been able to erase the word from his brain.

"Beauty is in the eyes of the beholder," she recited with dignity before she started laughing. "And yeah, beautiful. You have great muscles."

He raised an eyebrow. He had no idea how to respond to that, but he tried. "I don't usually entertain when I'm…not dressed."

"A pity," she said. "But you *did* open the door."

"I thought…there might be a problem," he defended himself. "You were knocking hard… maybe another nightmare."

"I wasn't knocking that hard," she retorted.

"Hard enough," he said, trying to keep himself a step ahead. She smiled, and he suddenly realized what he'd said. He suspected his face was even more flushed. Hell, he felt like a school boy.

"I thought you had gone to bed," he said.

"I had to call my sister before it got too late."

"Is there a problem?"

"No, I just had a few questions I wanted to ask her."

He should have known she wouldn't have just gone to bed. He shouldn't have dashed to the shower after she left. It was a trip that was becoming all too frequent. He should have grabbed some clothes before opening the door.

He clutched the towel closer to his body. "I have to put some clothes on," he said.

"You're fine, but if *you* would be more comfortable…"

He'd thought no woman could stomach what had happened to his body, the scars left by pieces of a rocket. But then Jenny had experienced combat herself, even if she'd been an observer rather than a participant. Maybe the wound *made* her a participant.

Still, he couldn't believe that any woman would actually be comfortable with the scars.

As if reading his thoughts, Jenny touched his chest and ran a finger down it, arousing all sorts of reactions. "I like your face a lot, too," she said seriously.

Damn, but she knew how to get inside his head. "Are you finished with your survey?"

"I'm getting there," she said. "I have a few scars of my own, you know. In a way, they're liberating. I don't have to try to be perfect anymore." She paused. "Not that I ever was. My hair is too red and uncontrollable, I have freckles and my body has always been like a stick. But as long as the majority of my body parts work, even if some not so well, I plan to make the most of it. If anyone is put off by it, then they're not worth knowing." The last comment came with emotion. For him, as well as for her.

She'd obviously remembered what he'd said about his ex-fiancé. *She would have made a damn good psychologist herself,* he thought while still hanging on to the towel.

He wanted to kiss the stubborn, honest, funny, passionate woman in front of him. He wanted it more than he could remember wanting anything.

But he also knew how foolish it would be. Despite all his attempts to do otherwise, his heart was already becoming involved. He looked into those emerald green eyes with so much passion in them. Passion for the moment, passion for life. Maybe even for him. But he reminded himself she had a greater passion beyond him.

She was a free spirit and took pride in it. She'd made it clear that her career meant everything to her, that the world fascinated her, and she wanted to be in the midst of action.

Small towns like Covenant Falls and Raton interested her for a day or two, but then her curiosity would take her to other places. He would be a fool to think the relationship could go beyond a kiss or a few nights, and he didn't want that with her. It wouldn't be enough.

She was looking up at him, and he realized he was still the next thing to naked and his anatomy was not being cooperative at the moment.

"Stay here," he ordered.

He went into the bathroom, gratified that he'd left his pants there in his haste to take a cold shower. He needed something more than the towel. Pants. Shirt. A space suit, if he had one. He looked in the mirror after he put on the pants, dashed cold water on his face and took a deep breath. Then, more in control—he thought—he returned to the room. She was sitting on the bed, looking at a book he'd brought with him.

"You like suspense novels," she observed. "So do I."

"I suspect you like everything."

His gaze was drawn to her face. She wasn't beautiful in a classic way, but she was so damned alive and…honest. He would never forget the way she'd blurted out that he was beautiful. It wasn't exactly true, but he knew that, at that moment, she thought so.

She looked irresistible propped up on stacked pillows. Hell, she'd been irresistible since he'd met her. Her humor. Her competence, mixed with whimsy. Her acceptance of everyone she met for who they were, not what she wanted or expected them to be.

He had known her only a few days, but he felt as if he'd known her far longer.

She looked up, those green eyes searching his, and he was a goner. The distance he'd been trying to keep between them had narrowed every hour since he'd met her. Now it was paper-thin. He leaned over and kissed her lightly. "I like you," he said. "A lot."

"I'm annoying," she stated. "I talk too much."

"You do talk a lot," he teased, "but I'm getting used to it."

"That's gracious of you," she said, the light words belying the quickly rising temperature in the room. He held out his good hand and pulled her to him. Her chin tilted up, until she was looking directly into his eyes.

Desire sparked between them. Despite an inner voice warning him not to get more involved with Jenny for a number of reasons, he ran his fingers over her face, exploring every curve. He then encircled her with his arms and did what he'd wanted to do since he met her. Ignoring all the warnings in his head, he leaned down, and his lips brushed hers. It was tentative. Searching. Tender yet sensuous. Every nerve in his body seem to come alive. He saw the same response in her face as she leaned into him.

Jenny's arms tightened around his neck as his kiss deepened and his good hand traced patterns along the back of her neck. She tried to breathe as she looked up at him. Sexual magnetism radiated between them. Her heart jolted at the strength of it. She tried to tame the dizzying currents racing through her body.

The need to touch him, feel him and make love with him was irresistible. The sparks that had glowed between them flared, enveloping them in a circle of heat. She lost herself in his touch, in the feel of his aroused body against hers. His hands moved along her neck as his mouth explored hers ever so slowly. She sensed he was only barely holding on to control.

So was she. She swallowed hard and told herself to pull away, to leave the room and close the door behind her. She was terrified of the feelings welling up inside her. She didn't want to be in love. Love was a trap. She kept trying to convince herself of that.

But she couldn't leave. Dammit, she wanted his touch, his kisses. She wanted to feel that tenderness in him wrap around her. For the first time she could remember, she wanted to feel real intimacy, the kind that came with caring. Not just sex, but something so much stronger.

She reached up on her toes so their bodies fit together. The kiss became frantic, exploding until they were so wrapped together she couldn't tell where one ended and the other began.

His hands moved up and down her back, soothing, enticing. Then his fingers started to unbutton her blouse, and he saw her scars, the puckered area around a long scar where the shrapnel tore into it, and cleaner ones that came from a surgeon's scalpel.

"You forgot to duck, too," he said with that crooked smile of his.

He touched it with such tenderness, she could barely breathe. Her body reacted to his touch, trembling slightly as he unhooked her bra and then caressed her breasts, until they were taut and swollen. He leaned down and kissed each breast, and then he reluctantly drew back.

He cradled her against his chest and kissed her again, slow and lingering. When their lips parted, he looked down at her, and their gazes locked on each other.

"I'm afraid I'm becoming addicted to you," he said softly.

She smiled gloriously. "Ditto," she said.

"I want you. Probably too much."

"Why too much?"

"Because after this week, we'll both be heading in different directions."

"True."

"What are we going to do?" he asked, leaving it up to her.

"I don't know," she said slowly, weighing each word. "I like everything about you. I like the way you help friends and take care of your young soldier. I like the way you're so serious and yet indulge my more quirky side. I like your face, especially when you smile. I like the way people instinctively trust you. I like the way you kiss. I like all those things and not necessarily in that order." She stopped. "Do you want me to go on?"

He stopped her there. His lips pressed against hers, his tongue playing with hers as the temperature in the room went from hot to steaming. His hands moved up and down her back, and her body trembled with the need he was creating.

A small *purr* came unbidden from her throat, and she drew him closer. Their bodies clung together, a deep need binding them.

Jenny had never been in love before, but she knew it was knocking on her door now, and it scared the wits out of her. Her career was her life. The fierce drive to be independent overrode everything else. She didn't want the confines of a marriage or even a committed relationship. There was nothing that terrified her more.

But when Travis kissed her, bells she didn't think existed rang long and loud. When he touched her, electicity ran through her body.

No! She wasn't going to let it happen.

She stiffened, and he went still.

"Second thoughts?" he asked as he searched her face.

Their gazes met, and she knew he saw the struggle in hers.

"Do you read minds, too?" she asked.

He kissed her lightly, although she saw the rigidity of his body as he backed off. "No, but you already told me you never stay anywhere long. You don't like ties."

She couldn't speak for a moment. He was right about that. But for the first time, she entertained the idea of staying in one place a little longer. But would she go crazy in a month? Maybe six months? She needed challenges like she needed air to live.

He stepped back and took her hand. He studied her steadily. "Sit down and talk to me," he said.

They sat on the bed. Desire was still pounding inside her. But she knew she could never have a one-night stand with him. Or even a few nights. It would be too hard to leave. She knew that, too.

She was falling in love with him, and it was moving too fast. She would only hurt him. And herself.

"You were right," she said and hated the trembling in her voice. "I will be gone. So will you."

They were on the bed, and she was in his arms,

but the sexual tension had relaxed. He shrugged. "Yeah. I've finally decided that I'm leaving the army. I'm tired of war, tired of sending kids out to face God knows what. It wouldn't matter whether I did it from the battlefield or a desk job in Georgia."

He was purposely making her relax, taking them back to where they were earlier in the day. Friends.

It wasn't entirely working with her, so she knew how hard it must be for him.

"Was it like this with…your ex-fiancé?" Her damn curiosity made the questions pop out. It was totally inappropriate, but she wanted to know.

"Which feelings are we talking about?" he asked.

"The lust part."

He laughed until he choked. "God help me, I never know what you're going to say next."

She started to chuckle. It *was* a totally inappropriate thing to ask, but it lowered the tension, although that wasn't her intent. She really had wanted to know. She realized she was jealous of that unknown woman, and she knew that her jealousy was ridiculous.

"No," he said. "I can honestly say it was not like this. It was more civilized."

"I'm not civilized?"

"Not entirely," he said, leaning down to kiss her lightly on her mouth. "But I like it." He paused. Then he said, "You've given me more than you know. In the past few days, I've discovered there's more than the army. There are other things I want to do, but I didn't know what direction to take. I've been thinking about what you said. About working with kids. I'm going to investigate the possibilities."

Her hand tightened around his. "That makes me happy," she said, and she meant it. "Isn't it what you wanted years ago? Before you joined the army." She paused and then added, "I watched you with Nick and Danny. You would make a great coach."

The conversation relaxed her. His hand took hers. "I meant what I said, Jenny. I like you. A lot. I'll not ask you to do something you're not comfortable doing."

She swallowed hard. "The problem is I *would* be comfortable, too comfortable. More than comfortable. But I'm afraid of hurting you...and me." She felt tears forming in the back of her eyes. She had to escape the room before they spilled out.

"I should go," she said. She grabbed her blouse and bra and walked to the door.

She closed it behind her. What a total idiot she was. What a mess.

She went into the bathroom and doused her

face with cold water. She thought she heard the shower next door, or maybe it was just in her head.

Her body was on fire. She stepped into the shower and ran it cold.

After drying herself while shivering, she crawled into bed. Her body still craved what had been denied it.

Why had she run as she had? She wasn't a virgin. She was an unattached grown-up. It was the fierceness of the desire that scared her. She'd never felt that before.

She'd been a coward. Plain and simple. She didn't like that image of herself.

Was it because she feared losing her freedom? Or was that only an excuse to avoid any kind of meaningful relationship? Was it something deeper? Was she afraid to love because she didn't trust it? Because she'd felt unloved by her family and didn't really believe anyone could love her? She'd read enough about psychology to know it was a possibility.

Whatever it was, she knew she'd just run away. Again. It was unbearably painful. And probably very stupid.

CHAPTER EIGHTEEN

AFTER JENNY LEFT the room, Travis stared at the door for a long time, wanting to knock and continue what had almost started. Then he backed away. Why pursue something that had damn little chance of finishing satisfactorily?

But he ached. It had taken every smidgen of will power to stop the natural course of things. To sit there with her when his body was on fire.

He'd seen the agony in her eyes, though, and knew she was right. They couldn't have a casual affair. And neither was ready for anything more.

He left the bed and sat in the uncomfortable motel chair and looked out over the parking lot.

Not a great view, but he was too tense to pick up the book she'd been looking at. He couldn't sleep right now, not on the bed where Jenny had sat. She had so obviously wrestled between want and rationality. Just as he had.

It was just as well that her cautious side won out. He didn't have protection—something he would remedy tomorrow. *Just in case.* It had been a long time since he'd needed it. He hadn't wanted to expose himself to the dismay he'd seen in his ex-fiancé's eyes.

Beautiful. He chuckled as Jenny's exclamation re-created itself in his mind. With that one word, she wiped away Dinah's initial reaction. He knew the scars hadn't bothered Jenny, hadn't turned her away. Maybe because she had one herself. But she was right. Her scar made no difference to him. If anything, they'd endeared her to him even more.

She'd obviously suffered a terrible wound, along with memories of that little girl. When she mentioned the nightmares in Covenant Falls, he'd thought it might be a ploy to go with him. Now he knew they were only too real. He also knew now that she detested revealing her vulnerabilities, and it had been a hard admission for her to make.

He should have known. There was damn little guile in her.

There was so much about her he didn't know. He knew little about her family other than they apparently disapproved of her choices and not much more about other parts of her past. Had she been engaged? In love? Was that why she was so leery of relationships? What made her keep wandering?

He just knew that she made him feel alive again. That in mentioning those few minutes of tossing the ball with Josh's stepson, Nick, she'd awakened something inside him. Excited him for the first time since his injuries. Reminded him of his adolescent goal to be a coach, to work with kids, to inspire kids as his high school coach had inspired him.

Maybe it took someone like Jenny to remind him of his old dream. He'd buried it for a long time, but now maybe he could revive it. Maybe it wasn't too late.

Was he too old now? He was in his late thirties, and he felt much older. What would the requirements be? He decided to check it out on his iPad. He tried to tamp down a growing enthusiasm. He'd had a close relationship with his coach, who knew the problems he had at home. There had been missed practices when his father had wanted him at the farm, doing chores or taking care of his younger brother. The coach had allowed him to work around the requirements.

He did a search for requirements for high school coaches in Colorado, although he had no idea where he would head next. Requirements were probably similar in most states.

A bachelor's degree. Apparently, any would do for coaching only. A teacher's certification would be required for any teaching duties.

Worth investigating. Maybe he would call Josh tomorrow and ask what he thought of the idea and if he knew of any possibilities in the area.

He got into bed. They would have a long day tomorrow. First the session with Dr. Payne, and then a long drive through Texas.

Hours in a closed space with Jenny. When they started the journey, he'd thought the hours together would cure him, that they would get on each other's nerves. They hadn't. The initial attraction had, instead, intensified.

He doubted he was going to get much sleep that night. He closed his eyes and tried counting horses jumping over fences. Sheep just weren't going to cut it tonight.

JENNY HAD EXPERIENCED a restless night. It had taken some time before her emotions settled down, even after doing her shoulder exercises with the darn rod.

She felt like a fool for running away.

She'd fled his room because her feelings for him were frightening in their intensity. Even now she could barely wait to see him, to watch those very sexy lips curve into that slow smile that could charm a dragon.

To keep her mind off him, she thought about Anna at the ranch and her big brown eyes. She remembered Karen's words that older dogs were difficult to place in homes. What if she never found one?

And Charlie of the tender heart would fall in

love with her. The thought relaxed her. She finally drifted off and woke up to rays of sunlight creeping into her room.

At 7:00 a.m., she sat on the edge of the bed and wondered if it was too early to call Karen. She didn't think so. With all those dogs to look after, she probably rose early.

Jenny had put Karen's number on her cell phone before leaving the night before and now she called her.

Karen answered after a few rings.

"Hello," Jenny said. "This is Jenny Talbot. I hope I didn't call you too early."

"No, not at all. I'm always up by six."

"I thought so." Jenny paused. "I was wondering if…maybe I could adopt Anna."

There was a long silence, and her heart dropped. "Don't you travel a lot?" Karen said.

"I'm staying with my sister, Lenore, and her daughter. My niece, Charlie, loves animals. She's always wanted a dog. I checked with Lenore last night, and she thinks it's a great idea." Jenny paused. "She's a real estate agent and is at home most of the time for Charlie." She hurried on. "Anna would have a wonderful home, even when I'm on the road."

Another hesitation. "How would you get her there?"

"She could go with Travis and me," she said,

crossing her fingers. "We can stop by after talking to Dr. Payne. Probably around 1:00 p.m. or so."

"You've had experience with dogs before?"

"Yes," Jenny lied. It was in a good cause. For Charlie, her sister and Anna.

"You'll have to sign papers, taking responsibility, and promise to return her if for some reason it doesn't work out. There's also an adoption fee. It helps take care of the shots and medical examination."

"Of course," Jenny said. "How much?"

"A hundred dollars."

"That's fine. I would like to donate, as well, to your dogs for vets program."

"I'll expect you after lunch," Karen said.

Jenny said goodbye and hung up before Karen asked more questions.

She sat down and wondered how she was going to broach the subject with Travis and convince him to add another passenger to the trip.

She washed up and put on some jeans and a T-shirt.

She knocked on the adjoining door. No one answered, so she grabbed her key and headed for the breakfast room. She was in sore need of a hefty cup of black coffee.

Travis was already sitting at a table, eating a waffle. She looked around. It was the same waffle machine that was at the other motel. "The dining room is only open from noon on," Travis explained. He was very matter-of-fact, as if nothing had happened last night. Had he felt the same thunderous feelings as she had?

"You should have knocked on my door," she said.

"I didn't want to wake you. I figured you would know I would be here."

"I didn't have the same thoughtfulness," she replied, miffed. "I pounded on your door." She went to the counter for coffee before sitting with him.

"You're quiet this morning," he observed after a few moments.

"I have a problem," she announced.

"Want to share it?"

"I want to adopt Anna."

It took him a minute to comprehend, and then he raised one of his eyebrows.

"Anna?" he said after a few seconds.

"The little black dog at Karen's house," she said.

"The one that liked your lap? At least she's smart." He stared at her. "But what is a roving reporter going to do with a dog?" he asked.

"I'm staying with my sister who has a condo in Denver. She said she would look after Anna when I'm traveling. She has a daughter—my niece—

who has always wanted a dog. She's serious and responsible and would take great care of her."

"Is that the call you made last night before you came to my room?"

She should have guessed he would have remembered that. He seemed to remember everything. "Yes," she admitted.

"You didn't say anything then." His eyes were cool, his voice flat.

"I wanted to talk to Karen first. I called her this morning. She agreed." Jenny couldn't hide the triumph in her voice.

"Have you ever had a dog?" he asked with that darn raised eyebrow again.

"No," she replied honestly. "But I know they require a lot of care."

"Why that dog?" he asked. "There's thousands out there that need a home."

"I don't know." But she did. Anna came to *her*. Anna had picked *her*. She didn't know why that was so important, but it was.

"What about our trip?" he said logically. "You can't leave her in the car, even for a few minutes, because of the heat. And I thought you wanted to learn about the programs. You can't do that while watching a dog."

She knew all that. She felt they could find a way, but it was his car. His trip. His mission. She was here on sufferance. If she was honest with herself, and she usually tried to be, she'd placed him in a difficult position.

"I thought about that. Alternatively, I *can* ask Karen if she can keep Anna for a few weeks until I can get back or make some kind of arrangements." Jenny knew it was iffy. She didn't know when she could drive again, and she'd heard too many horror stories of dogs being injured, lost or dying while transported by planes to consider that.

"If you don't mind," she asked gingerly, "can we drop by Karen's so I can talk to her about it, sign papers, pay the fee so she knows I'm serious?"

He nodded, his gaze not wavering from her face. "It's on our way out of town."

It was not the helpful, enthusiastic response she'd hoped for. She stood, not wanting to show her disappointment. She went to one of the tables and selected a few pieces of fruit and a bagel and returned to the table. The bagel was dry, the fruit overripe. She played around with it but couldn't eat.

Last night, the prospect of adopting Anna seemed so clear; now she saw the points she'd missed.

She didn't usually do that. The story had always been the most important objective in her life, and right now the story was the equine therapy programs. So why was she becoming so emotionally needy, first with Travis and then with the dog? She'd never been that way before. Maybe the shrapnel ripped away the shield she'd constructed around her heart.

"I'd best get back to the room," she said with her brightest smile. "I want to wash some clothes and dry them on your back seat if that's okay."

"They have a washer and dryer here," he said. "I have some clothes in there now. You have plenty of time. We don't need to leave until ten thirty."

"I'll do that then," she said. "Do I need change for the machine?"

"No, it's a freebie. Apparently many of their guests are service families here for ceremonies, to greet soldiers returning from, or leaving for, deployments. Their stays tend to be longer than a night or two." He paused and then added, "The dryer is down the corridor to the pool."

She nodded and turned toward the door so her face wouldn't show her disappointment.

When she reached her room, she walked in and leaned against the wall. The warmth she and Travis had shared last night had faded. Walls had gone up on both sides. He was right about Anna. It *was* impractical. She'd known it, but the last two days had been so magical, she'd thought nothing was impossible.

She was, though, going to get Anna. If she had to hire someone to drive the dog to Denver, she would.

Remember the story, she reminded herself. That was what was important.

TRAVIS WATCHED THE light fade from Jenny's face as he'd punched holes in her proposal. It simply wasn't workable.

It was September. The air was cooler now, but some days, particularly in West Texas, New Mexico and Arizona, could be extremely hot. No way could they leave a dog in the car, not even for a few minutes.

Dammit. For some reason, that dog had become important to Jenny. Was it because Anna had been alone in the corner before making a beeline for Jenny? He'd already recognized that she was drawn to underdogs, human or animal. It had been clear in some of the articles she'd written. Hell, he was no psychologist. He just knew some of the light went out in those eyes, and he felt responsible.

But a dog? Dammit, it wasn't practical. They would be stopping overnight at two of the ranches. Most ranchers had dogs of their own and may not welcome a canine interloper.

But, like Karen, he'd noticed the sudden attachment between Jenny and the dog, as well as Anna's determination to go with her.

He also thought of Jenny's years of wandering. Maybe she needed to be needed more than she knew. As strong and competent as she was, perhaps that was a part of her she'd refused to recognize.

He could call and ask the destination ranches whether it would be acceptable to bring a dog with them.

He looked at his watch. It was a few minutes before eight. He had three hours before their appointment at Fort Hood.

He picked up his laundry and headed for his room. He made calls to each of the ranches on his schedule. None objected to a tagalong dog. Two said their young children would be delighted.

It was after nine before he finished the last call. He stepped back into the hallway and knocked on her door.

The door opened. Jenny stood in front of him in bare feet. Wet curls framed her face. No makeup. She was in a well-worn shirt that reached past her hips. She looked…irresistible. "I've just washed some clothes and was about to take them to the dryer," she said.

"You can dry them in the car."

She gave him a quizzical look.

"We have some shopping to do before our meeting. We need to check out in thirty minutes."

"Shopping?"

"A leash, collar, dog bed, some dog food and whatever other stuff a dog needs," he said. "If you're sure you want that woebegone animal?"

Her startled look changed to pure joy. "You mean it?"

"Yeah I do, though I might regret it," he said. "I called the ranches on our schedule. They were fine with a visiting dog, especially a rescue one." He smiled. "You might want to close your mouth. You thought I didn't like dogs?"

She truly hadn't known. She reached up on tiptoes until her lips met his.

"We're in full view of the hall," Travis observed as he ended the kiss, "and you are practically naked. Not that I'm objecting, but you might step a few feet back."

She did so, and he followed her in, closing the door behind him. "We need to leave in thirty minutes," he warned her.

"I can be ready in ten."

"Then you're the first woman that could."

"You just haven't been going around with the right women."

"You could be right," he replied. Fireworks were flying between them as if it were the Fourth of July. The explosions were there, too, as he bent down and finished the kiss that had started at the door.

He forced himself to pull back before they were there a lot longer than ten or thirty minutes. "I have to get some notes together," he said as he took a few steps toward the door.

"Thank you," she said. "You didn't have to go to all the trouble."

"Yes, I did. It was important to you." His hand was on the door knob. "Twenty-nine minutes, now," he teased and slipped out before temptation overwhelmed his good sense.

Or had he completely lost it in the last week?

Once in the room, he looked at the notes sprawled out on the bed. He'd updated them early this morning, when he couldn't sleep. Specific questions he wanted to ask Dr. Payne. There were three big ones: Where was the greatest need? Who should they target? What length of a program was most beneficial? He had several hundred others, but those were the big ones, according to Jubal.

He took them and his personal items out to the car, paid the bill and told them he and Miss Talbot would be leaving within the next thirty minutes. He would leave his key in the room.

He turned on the news, but heard just a few minutes before a knock on the adjoining door. He tried not to think of the knock last night.

"Twenty minutes," she crowed when he opened it.

He looked at his watch. "And thirty seconds, but who's counting?"

"It took five minutes to check out," she countered righteously.

They must have just missed each other.

She wore black slacks and a sleeveless lime-colored blouse that had the effect of deepening the green in her eyes. She held a lightweight black jacket in her hands.

"Very businesslike," he said.

"And they wrap up into a small ball," she said. "I've become an expert in traveling light."

It reminded him of who she was and what she did and where she might be in a few more weeks.

"Let's go," he said.

CHAPTER NINETEEN

JENNY FELT LIKE she was walking out of the pet store with half of its inventory.

She didn't realize how expensive a dog could be. Of course, nothing but the best would do for Anna. That didn't mean cute clothes or a glittering collar. But it did mean a very soft dog bed, a retractable leash, matching food and water dishes, a car safety seat, toys, dog treats and the most highly recommended dog food.

The purchases took up most of the trunk. Travis looked at the pile of purchases with amazement, and then he worked on attaching the dog carrier to the seat.

They barely made the 11:00 a.m. appointment with Dr. Payne. The one hour appointment lasted two and a half. With Dr. Payne's permission, she taped the interview and also jotted down notes.

This time, Jenny was mostly silent while Travis asked the questions. It was his project. She was impressed with the methodical way he asked questions. Dr. Payne had worked with several of the equine therapy programs and had both comments and suggestions.

They reinforced much of what the soldiers had said two days ago.

"Combat today, and in the recent past, is different than in the past," he started as a prelude. "Veterans today see an average of 1,500 days of combat and go directly into combat when they land on the ground."

He looked at Travis. "You know all that. I wish more people did. Civilians can't begin to understand the intensity of their experiences, and when the vets return, they're suddenly without the strong personal relationships forged in war and with civilians who have absolutely no idea of what they've experienced."

"It also plays hell with families," Travis replied.

"That's why a network of therapeutic farms, horse rescuers, ranchers, professional horsemen and professional military members have come together to give veterans—and horses—a new lease on life."

He handed Travis a list of programs he'd compiled. "There are other mom-and-pop farms that we don't know about. They provide free horseback riding for veterans and their families, which is very helpful to both. It puts the vet together with children in a fun experience. On the opposite end, there's extensive rehab programs operating in conjunction with VA facilities. Those might range from a four-day weekend to others that last a month or more, with full-time therapists. Still, another group of them specialize in teaching vets horsemanship, with the aim of preparing them for jobs in the equine world.

"All," he added, "rely on the magic that develops between the horse and veteran, along with the camaraderie of other veterans."

"I hear some programs are using rescue horses and wild mustangs," Jenny inserted.

Dr. Payne smiled. "I'm especially fond of those. Both horses and vets need nurturing, and it seems that they recognize it in each other. Watching a vet making friends with a frightened mustang is really a wonder to behold. An emotional bond develops. It's a slow process, but it has great rewards. It gives the vet confidence and a kind of peace."

"But what's the greatest need?" Travis asked.

"They all play an important role, and they're all needed," Dr. Payne said. "It depends on your goals and financing."

Jenny had liked Dr. Payne at dinner and liked him even more as the morning wore on. Toward the end, she asked about Covenant Falls and why he thought it attracted so many veterans.

"Nothing magical about it," he said. "Josh was

the first of the nonresidents who landed there. He inherited the cabin now being used by Travis. When he got married, he called me and said he wanted it to be used by another veteran. I recommended Clint. Then Andy. I understand Jubal Pierce came because of a tie to Clint. So, in a way, it was a string of personal ties. But there's more. Covenant Falls is an accepting, patriotic community. The fact that there's a weekly poker game probably contributes to its appeal," he added with a smile. "Even before Josh, it produced an outsized number of veterans from every war. I plan to do a study of it one of these days."

Jenny knew most of that, but she'd wanted to hear it from his point of view. He continued, "The fact that the newcomers were drawn into the community by both the city leaders and former servicemen and women helped them adjust into civilian life. Apparently," he said with a smile, "they didn't just adjust but are becoming the heart of Covenant Falls."

He paused, then added, "I would love to see more communities like that in the country. Unfortunately, there's not many, and too many vets feel isolated and alone, even with their own families."

She had already noticed the strong camaraderie between the Covenant Falls veterans, both old and more recent. The partnership between

Jubal and Luke Daniels, a Vietnam vet, demonstrated that.

Travis started to get up. "We should be heading out," he said reluctantly. "We have a long drive ahead of us." He held out his hand. "Thank you. I'm sure I'll be calling you in the next few weeks."

Dr. Payne stood. "It was a pleasure meeting both of you," he said. "If I can help you in any way, just call."

She said *I will* at the same time as Travis. Dr. Payne looked from one to the other and smiled.

Blood rushed to Jenny's face. "Thank you for everything, including the dinner last night."

Dr. Payne accompanied them to the door of his office, shook hands with them and turned back into his office.

"Did you get what you need?" she asked.

"Not as definitive as I would have liked," Travis said. "A lot of options."

"Now you sound like a major."

"I hope not."

"You can copy the interview from my phone," she offered.

"I was counting on that."

"We make a good team," she said as they walked to his rental. She was trying to keep it professional, as if last night never happened. The problem was it *had* happened. The strong attraction between them lingered.

They were both trying to shove it aside, but it wasn't working all that well.

Only a few more days. Would they make it without doing something they both might regret? Odds were not good.

Maybe Anna would help. Maybe she could put some of those feelings into making Anna feel comfortable and loved.

Dammit, there was that *L*-word again.

She made it to the car before he did and helped herself into the passenger seat as he stepped inside the driver's side. They drove out of the parking lot.

Before leaving the base, he turned to her. "Maybe we should get something to eat before picking up the dog. I ate breakfast. You didn't."

Jenny noticed his tone was neutral. And he called Anna *the dog.*

He'd obviously decided they needed a little distance between them. It didn't bode well for a long and happy journey. It was her fault. She shouldn't have knocked on his door the night before. She should have anticipated what would happen when she saw him in the towel. Most of him, anyway.

"We're already late," she said. And her stomach was queasy. "Unless you want to stop."

"No," he said.

He turned on the main road, and she picked up the road map they had left on the dash. She knew he'd planned to stay in Stockton tonight, but they were running late and would be even later after stopping off for Anna.

Twenty minutes later, they arrived at the turn-off into Karen's property. As before, they were welcomed by a chorus of barking dogs.

Karen greeted them at the door. The noise from the kennel was more efficient than any doorbell ever invented. "Come in," she said. "Richard called and said you were running late."

She led the way to the living room. Anna was sitting in the same corner, but she sat up when she saw Jenny and walked over to her, her tail wagging madly.

"Are you sure you can take her?" Karen asked. "It's not too late to think she might not fit into your life."

Jenny picked Anna up. "I'm sure," she said. The dog immediately snuggled down in her arms.

"She definitely picked you," Karen said. "I have the papers ready. They include her vaccination record. Keep them with you. If you visit a groomer, a veterinarian or a boarding facility, you'll need them."

She hesitated just a moment. "I don't usually adopt out a dog without a fenced-in yard or more information, but instinct tells me you'll be good for each other. Anna deserves someone who will appreciate her." She then gave Jenny a paper to sign. In it, she promised to return Anna to Karen if, for some reason, she couldn't keep her.

Jenny put Anna down long enough to sign it.

"I have an extra leash and some supplies you can take with you," Karen said.

"We stopped at a pet store before meeting with Dr. Payne," Travis broke in. "Jenny depleted the inventory substantially. Food. Leash. Collar with Anna's name and address on it. Food. Treats. Bed."

Karen smiled. "You might go ahead and put the collar on now. You are now the owner of one affenpinscher. Any questions?"

"Not now, but I expect I'll be calling soon."

"A dog's main need is love," she said. "If I didn't think she'd get that, I wouldn't let her go with you. Please keep in touch and let me know how she does. Just a line or email once in a while. My email address, along with telephone and website, are on the copy of the paper you signed."

Jenny gave her a check for the dog and added another as a donation for Karen's dogs for vets program.

"Thank you," Karen said. "It will be used well."

"Would you approve of my writing a story

about what you're doing here?" she asked. "Andy told me what Joseph did for her."

"I would like to know what you would say."

"Not to worry. I know it's sensitive. And I would need a lot more of your time, maybe like staying through the whole process with a veteran."

"I'll call you if I have a candidate that's willing to do that," Karen said.

"Thank you," Jenny said. "And I think Travis and I had better get on the road. We have a long drive ahead."

"Have a good trip," Karen said. She put her hands on Anna's head and cupped her face. "You be happy, little one," she said and accompanied Travis and Jenny to the door.

Once in the car, Jenny insisted on holding Anna, rather than putting her in the dog car seat. "It's too soon," she said. "I want her to feel safe first, and she's lap size."

"Fine with me," Travis said. "She is an... interesting-looking dog."

"Thank you," she said. There was a ton of feeling in the two words.

He gave her that slow, sexy smile that sent her heart racing. "You're welcome."

THEY WERE BOTH exhausted when they reached Stockton, and it was nearly nine when Travis drove up to a motel that allowed pets. Jenny had been busy on her cell phone until she found one. They made reservations for two rooms, not necessarily connected. None of the rooms were connected, according to the response.

One worry off his mind. Adjoining rooms just didn't seem to work for them.

Or worked too well, Travis thought.

He'd had damn little sleep last night. It had been one of aching misery. The morning had been difficult, too. But at least he'd had a new experience.

He'd never been in a pet store before, and when he thought about it, it seemed rather sad. He knew he was going loco when he hesitated in front of a counter stocked with dog raincoats.

The point was, though, that now he required undisturbed sleep tonight, or he would run the three of them off the road. Only his many years as a soldier kept him alert, but he was reaching his limit. It was hell getting old. Or older, he corrected himself.

As they checked in and were told breakfast was included, he bet himself a ten spot that it included the same infernal waffle appliance. Jenny had to pay an extra deposit for the dog.

They'd stopped at a fast-food restaurant at 3:00 p.m., with Jenny giving several small bites to Anna, who'd gobbled it down like she'd been starved.

But now it was nine, and he was hungry for something more than a burger and cold fries.

He asked the manager whether any restaurants had takeout. He wasn't sure about leaving Anna in a room by herself. The manager recommended a place called the Gray Mule Saloon. It was a winery, he said, but they served a great cheese and fruit plate, and, eyeing Anna, he added that dogs were welcomed on the patio.

Travis saw Jenny's eyes light up, but she didn't say anything. It was that discretion that led Travis to suggest they go.

Besides, wine might help him forget that Jenny would be somewhere in the same motel with him.

They were, thankfully, on different halls. They agreed to meet in ten minutes in the lobby. Anna would chaperone.

He'd thought she would soon discover that some of her vaunted freedom was limited by a dog. The motel clerk's recommendation disabused him of that idea.

He washed his face. He had some stubble beginning to appear, as he hadn't shaved that morning. He decided not to worry about it tonight, nor change his shirt. His ankle and leg hurt from driving so long. A bourbon would be good.

Wine, not so good, but what the hell. A couple of glasses, and he would probably sleep like the dead.

She was waiting in the lobby with Anna on the leash—or a lead, as the pet store owner called it. Anna greeted him with a wag of the tail, but it was obvious that the person she adored was Jenny. Anna tolerated him.

He got walking directions, and they started out. She had about five brochures in her hand and recited Stockton's history as a fort. As usual, she told it in such a way that he could almost see the cavalry riding down a dusty street.

They arrived at the saloon and were seated on the patio with other dogs accompanied by their people. It was a gentle night. The moon was huge, and the stars seemed to be in the millions now that they weren't competing with the city lights. One look at Jenny, and he couldn't help but smile at the pleasure in her face. It was far more intoxicating than a glass of bourbon.

Several different wines were offered for a tasting. To his surprise, he and Jenny selected the same one, and he ordered a bottle along with a cheese plate.

They didn't have to talk. They were perfectly comfortable with each other. He'd never been around a woman with whom words weren't necessary.

It was after ten when they arrived back at the motel, and he walked her to her room.

She unlocked it and then looked up at him. "It was a good day."

"Yes, it was. Meet you at seven in the morning?"

"For waffles?"

"Unfortunately likely," he said. "I would like to be on the road by eight at the latest."

"Anna and I will be ready."

"Tell her I said good-night."

She stooped down and, in a loud whisper, said to Anna, "Travis says good-night."

"I'm sure it means a lot to her," he replied.

"Of course it does. She likes you, too." She straightened and touched his face. "You didn't shave. I like it. I hope you keep not doing it."

"Unfortunately we have appointments for the next few days. But then…"

"But then what?" she asked.

The words pointed to a future, but he knew there was none for them beyond a week or two. How much did he want to hurt when she left?

"Good night," he said abruptly. He turned and went down the hall. When he glanced back, her door was closed.

CHAPTER TWENTY

JENNY WOKE TO light streaming through the windows and a tongue licking her hand. Sometime during the night, Anna had left her dog bed and managed to get onto the bed with Jenny. She now stared into Jenny's eyes with adoration.

Anna may not have been a trained therapy dog, but her presence had a healing effect. No nightmares last night. Jenny rubbed the dog's head, and Anna's soft moan of contentment relaxed Jenny, even as she realized she had a responsibility now.

The phone rang, and she looked at the clock. It was a little after seven. She rarely slept that late. Her internal clock usually made sure she was up by six.

Dang it. She knew Travis wanted an early start. They had a long drive ahead to the next ranch.

"Good morning," he said when she answered the phone. "Ready?"

"Not quite, but I can be in fifteen minutes, if you take Anna for a walk while I take a shower."

"Done. How did she do last night?"

"Perfect."

"I'll be right there." He hung up.

Jenny jumped out of bed and rushed into the bathroom to run the brush through her hair. She'd managed one swipe before she heard a knock on the door.

She opened the door. He looked wide-awake and ready to go. He'd shaved and smelled woodsy.

"I overslept," she admitted. She knew her eyes were probably encrusted from sleep and her hair a jumbled mess. She grabbed Anna and the leash and thrust them into his arms.

"I'd rather have you there," he said with a grin.

"Sorry about that. I'll be ready shortly. Really shortly."

"I'll try to find us some coffee. Come on, dog," he said as he put Anna down on the ground and led an obviously reluctant dog away.

She took the world's quickest shower, threw on a pair of jeans and a clean T-shirt, brushed her hair and skipped the lipstick. She gathered up her belongings and was out the door and in the lobby when he returned.

"Anna?"

"In the car and ready to go." He held two cups of coffee and gave one to her, grabbed her carry-on and headed to the door. "I've already paid. We can settle up later," he said, anticipating her protest.

Jenny nodded as she settled Anna in the new dog carrier that Travis had strapped in the back seat. She wasn't happy but Jenny knew it was safer for the dog. She was just as anxious now as Travis. The ranch they would visit today incorporated wild mustangs in the program. She sipped the coffee as Travis headed for the highway.

THEY ARRIVED AT the ranch seven hours later and were met by Bill and Louise Stacy. They had been invited to stay the night. Travis had checked ahead about Anna and had been assured that dogs were welcome.

"Had anything to eat?" Bill asked.

"We did. Sandwiches on the way."

"Good," the rancher said. He looked at Anna. "So this is the dog. She seems very quiet."

"She is. And shy."

"Then she can stay with you. Otherwise she could go inside the house." He changed the subject. "I understand you and a group of vets in Colorado want to start an equine program for vets. We sure can use a bunch more. Breaks our hearts to turn people down."

He walked them over to the barn. "I know you've read all the details, so I'll take you over to the corral. Each veteran is assigned a mustang after an indoctrination program. Many of the horses have never seen a human until rounded up, and they're terrified. It's up to the vet to gentle his or her horse, and in doing so, magic seems to happen."

"How many vets at a time?"

"We usually have ten to fifteen each month. Some are pretty advanced and can ride out with our ranch cowhands. Others have never been on a horse before they come here."

Jenny watched as several vets worked with their horses. One was feeding his horse carrots and whispering to it. Another was saddling a thin pinto. Still another was in a corral riding a chestnut horse around a ring, leaning over and rubbing his hand down the animal's neck as he did.

She and Travis spent the rest of the afternoon talking to the vets, and she learned the individual stories that brought them here. Nightmares. Flashbacks. Divorces. Alcohol. Inability to adjust to civilian life. She saw a newfound confidence in those who were finishing their stay and the uncertainty in the ones who were beginning.

They opened up to her after learning she'd been injured in Syria. She was one of them. As usual, she used her phone to store their stories.

One, in particular, touched her. He'd come home to learn his girlfriend had married someone else. His father, a police officer, couldn't understand why he wouldn't take a job on the police force that the father had arranged for him. The soldier couldn't explain that he didn't trust himself with a gun any longer.

But watching him later with his mustang, rubbing its head against his shoulder, she thought he would be okay. She felt tears welling up in her eyes. She looked away.

Anna was a hit. She adored being petted and gave everyone a moist kiss. Jenny's shy little girl was turning into a social butterfly, or maybe she just identified with the vets. She, too, had gone through a rough patch.

They were joined by Bill's wife, Louise, at the bunkhouse, where several of the vets had taken over kitchen duty. Louise had provided a huge bowl of potato salad and a platter of hamburgers that were being grilled outside.

One of the vets picked up a guitar and sang a couple of cowboy songs, while the others kidded each other.

Jenny leaned back in a chair. The sky was clear, the stars endless, and the moon rode high in the sky. She understood why this was so therapeutic.

Word had gotten around that she'd been in the Middle East. Before long, they were all gathered around, telling their own stories.

"We sure appreciate you telling people about Mr. Bill and this program," one said toward the end of the session. "He saved my life. I was drowning. Didn't think anyone cared. Now I know different."

Bill broke it up then. "I think we'd better let our guests get to bed." He led them to the house and then turned around. "Do you ride?" he asked them.

"Yes," she said. Then she saw Travis's raised eyebrow.

"A little," she amended.

"Travis?" Bill asked.

"A little," he echoed.

"Want to go out to see the cattle tomorrow with some of the vets? There's nothing prettier or more peaceful than a herd of cattle grazing at sunrise. I have two well-behaved horses you can ride."

"I would love it," she said. "Can we leave Anna here?"

"Sure. My wife loves dogs. Is 6:00 a.m. too early? I'll have you back at ten."

It was dawn when a knock on the door woke Jenny. She came to life immediately. *A ride at sunrise.* She was ready several minutes later and met Travis in the hall. Coffee, eggs, bacon and rolls were waiting for them downstairs.

"It's going to be a great day," Bill said at the breakfast table. "Johnny, one of my instructors, is bringing the horses."

Jenny ate quickly, then followed Bill out the door. She suddenly remembered her shoulder and had a moment of doubt. Could she mount a horse on her own? Jubal had helped her in Covenant Falls.

It was still dark outside, but the first glimmer of light was visible over the horizon and a parchment looking moon provided enough light to see men saddling horses. A lean man in his fifties was holding three horses.

"This is Gypsy, ma'am," he said as he handed her the reins to a small bay mare. "She's real gentle," he added. "Want a boost?"

"Yes, thanks."

He easily propelled her into the saddle. Then Travis mounted. His eyes smiled at her, or maybe she imagined it. Bill rode over to them.

"Both your horses have an easy gait and are steady and well-behaved. Can you trot?"

She'd tried it during her first lesson. "I think so."

They joined a group of riders waiting at a gate leading outside the corrals. She and Travis joined them.

Gypsy did have a smooth gait. Jenny found herself moving easily with the horse as they rode away from the house. The sky was gold now, and a breeze rippled through her hair.

They crested a hill and Jenny saw the cattle

below as the sky turned into a kaleidoscope of colors.

She turned to Bill. "It's gorgeous," she said.

"My guys are going to move them to another pasture where there's more grass."

Jenny watched as the riders with them rode ahead and turned the cattle east. "Are they all vets?"

"Most of them," he said. They watched as the cowhands darted in and out of the cattle, turning them toward an open gate into another pasture. Jenny was captivated.

Bill looked at his watch. "I know you have to go, but I wanted you to feel what these guys feel. There's something liberating about the open skies and a good horse that can chase away demons."

"Thank you for bringing us here," she said. He was right. She saw the camaraderie of the riders, the high spirits and the joy of being alive.

After grateful goodbyes, they were on the road again. Anna, apparently fearful she was being left again, demanded Jenny's lap.

They stayed in a motel that night and made their last stop the next day at a ranch that offered five-day weekend stays.

It didn't have the mustangs, mainly because their participants didn't have the time to develop relationships with horses. It put more emphasis on camaraderie and professional therapy sessions in the evenings.

Jenny spent some more time with the participants in the program, while Travis concentrated on the business aspects of the programs. Three of the ranches depended on ranch income, donations and grants while the fourth received referrals from the VA, as well as donations. Bill's ranch raised some revenue by selling the trained mustangs.

It was noon when they left the last ranch. Travis headed north.

"HAVE YOU BEEN in Arizona before?" Travis asked after an hour on the road. Jenny had been poring over the map.

"Phoenix," she replied.

"Not Sedona? Grand Canyon?"

She was embarrassed. An American landmark, and she had not seen it. Paris, yes. Istanbul, yes. And most of the capitals in Europe. But America's most photographed treasure? "No."

"We can start back to Covenant Falls. Finish up tomorrow or..." He left the word dangling.

"Or?" she asked.

"We can drive to Sedona. We can reach it about midafternoon and stay there tonight. The sunsets and sunrises are spectacular," he said, adding, "You like small towns. Sedona isn't that small anymore but it's still rather quirky, and you seem to like quirky. We can spend the morning there, then drive to the Grand Canyon and stay Sunday night. Drive back to Covenant Falls Monday. It will be a long drive."

She tried not to smile while her heart did a happy dance. "Sounds great," she said. "If you don't have to be back sooner?"

"I think Monday will be fine. It seems wrong to be this close to the Grand Canyon and not visit, especially if you've never been there." He turned to her. "How can you never have visited the Grand Canyon with all that curiosity of yours?"

"That is a very good question," she said. "I've been in the northwest because I worked for a newspaper there, and in most of the big cities. Denver. New York. Dallas. Washington. But all of those were short stops. And then I've been mostly out of the country for the last seven years."

"No family vacations when you were a kid?"

"Usually to fancy places in California, associated in some way with my father's business," she said. "I stopped going when I went to college."

Her voice was suddenly stilted. "And when I graduated, I had that job in the northwest, until I decided to skip the country and write about faraway places. I'm beginning to see the error of my ways."

He nodded his understanding. "Why don't you use that phone of yours to research motel rooms in Sedona? Look for one that says it has a great view, although merely by being in the area, you have one."

"Yes, sir," she said. "You've been there then. When?"

"A long time ago," he said. "A buddy of mine from Ranger School was from Sedona and I went there with him when we had a few days of leave. He talked me into hiking up to the Devil's Bridge in Sedona and down into Grand Canyon on steaming August days. We were in good shape then," he added somewhat philosophically.

She mentally weighed those sentences. He didn't go home after the months of grueling military training. He'd said very little about family. For the same reasons she didn't talk about hers? A difficult relationship or something more?

She also wondered what happened to his friend, but she kept the question in check. She didn't want anything to ruin his mood. Or hers. It was enough he suggested this side trip, and that he did so without prompting from her.

She did as he suggested. She started searching for motels in Sedona.

TRAVIS DIDN'T KNOW why in the hell he'd suggested Sedona.

Except he was becoming addicted to her exuberant interest in just about everything. They'd finished their job now and spent a lot of time in the car. Sedona wasn't far from their route home, and it would be good for both of them to relax the next day.

He'd already shot down her suggestions to stop at historical places along the way, including a side trip to the ghost town of Lincoln, New Mexico, said to be the hometown of Billy the Kid.

She'd been a good sport. She'd never complained, was a good companion and very perceptive. Her individual interviews with participants in the different programs were invaluable. They'd talked to her a lot easier than they would have to an army major. One of the things he wanted to do in the next few days was match his interviews with the providers to her observations with the participants.

And Anna had been the perfect dog. She slept through most of the driving, and at the ranches, she'd broken the ice with some of the vets they'd met. The dog's shyness seemed to bring out the protector in them.

If only he didn't have an ongoing compulsion to grab Anna's owner, kiss her and carry her off to the proverbial cave, it would have been a perfect partnership.

He glanced over at her. She was tapping on

her cell at an extraordinary rate of speed. "Price range?" she asked.

"Doesn't matter. Some splurging might be in order, but be sure they'll accept Anna."

Anna, who was resting on Jenny's lap, raised her head at that directive, as if she knew what it meant.

He took his hand off the steering wheel and scratched Anna's head. She responded by licking it.

"Okay," Jenny said. "Be careful, Major, or I'll get jealous." Then she went back to work.

Fifteen minutes later, she said, "I have a possibility. A family-owned lodge with high approval ratings from guests. It overlooks one of the most scenic vistas of Sedona, or so it says. It's reasonable. It has vacancies for tonight. Permits dogs and even mentions a dog park."

"Sounds good. Go ahead and book two rooms for tonight in Sedona and see what you can find in the Grand Canyon."

"Yessir. I'll use my bank card to safeguard it."

She made the reservation and nodded to him. "Thanks for offering it."

"You deserve it after all the help you've been."

"Along with being a pain in the neck," she said mischievously.

"Along with that, too," he admitted.

"That wasn't much of a denial about being a pain in the neck."

"No," he said agreeably.

"My feelings should be hurt."

"I don't think so. I get the distinct impression you like being a pain in the neck."

"Maybe," she suggested, "I can massage it later and make it better."

He chuckled. "Something to look forward to." He changed the subject. "Now that we have lodging in Sedona, try the Grand Canyon."

She lowered her head. After ten minutes, she lifted her eyes from the phone. "I found one," she said. "A lodge near the rim. Dog-friendly. Problem is they only have one room." She waited for several seconds while he digested that.

"Two queen-size beds," she added. "It sounds great. Rustic. I like rustic. Rustic has character."

Travis nearly choked. One bedroom. He, who had been doing his best not to do anything that could complicate both their lives, was sorely tempted. He wanted her to see the Grand Canyon, particularly the sunset and sunrise from the rim, and he wasn't surprised that there were few rooms available on a day's notice.

Maybe he could sleep in the car. He looked at her expectant face. He was always charmed by her enthusiasm. She would find something to like in the worst hovel. It was probably why she had survived as long as she had in the world's trouble spots.

Enthusiasm had been in short supply in his life. And a rustic lodge and one room sounded great. To hell with being a Boy Scout. They were consenting adults. Sharing a room didn't mean sharing a bed.

Except with the sexual tension radiating between them, it undoubtedly would, which is why he'd mandated two rooms. It wasn't morality that made him pause. It was the fact he was falling in love with her and he couldn't see a future together. He'd already had one painful experience, and he knew this one could be far worse.

But just the thought of sharing a bed changed the contour of his jeans. And this time, he did have protection.

He tried to quench some of the blaze by remaining silent.

"It would be financially responsible to share," she pointed out in a perfectly reasonable tone. "We could cancel the extra room tonight and save even more money."

She had no shame.

He liked that.

"We need some sleep tonight," he said gently. "Tomorrow will be a long day."

"Why don't we just compromise," she said.

"Two rooms tonight and one tomorrow in a wonderful rustic lodge."

He wasn't going to fight it any longer. Not when every ounce of his 180 pounds were urging him to agree. "Sounds reasonable," he said, though it was a perfectly unreasonable situation.

"I'll make the reservation," she said cheerfully.

"And tonight, we'll work," he said. "I want to coordinate your discussions with the participants with my notes on the theories behind the programs. I talked to some of the participants, but I imagine they talked to you more frankly."

"They all said how grateful they were. They felt they were getting their lives together. They're having goals again. Especially valuable was knowing they weren't alone. Several said it probably saved their lives. Just knowing people cared meant a lot."

That, he knew, was why she was a good reporter. She listened. She cared. She remembered what people said and even the inflections in their voices as they said it.

He also realized, however, that as good an observer as she was, she very rarely spoke about her family or personal life. Nor had she spoken much about her life overseas.

She soaked up everyone else's story but was extremely stingy with her own.

It was a little before six when they arrived at

the Sedona motel, just in time to see the setting sun glow against the red rocks, turning them gold. He glanced at her and saw the awe on her face.

They registered and discovered they had rooms next door to each other but not connected. He helped carry in Anna's dog bed, food and dishes. Then they watched the rest of the sunset from her balcony. She'd brought her camera and took a number of shots.

When the moon replaced the sun, he left her room and asked the desk clerk about restaurants and where to get a bottle of wine. The clerk suggested a Mexican restaurant about a mile away that allowed dogs on the patio. Like their last stop, Sedona was a dog-friendly town.

Travis washed and shaved, while Jenny changed clothes. He was slowly unwinding. It had been difficult rushing from one program to another, especially with the ongoing sexual tension between them. His leg was stiff and hurting from being cramped for so long. He was tired physically and mentally.

He was ready when she knocked at his door. He opened it, and his exhaustion fled. His world always brightened when he saw her. There was usually a smile on her lips and a dare in her eyes.

He'd thought at the beginning of the trip that familiarity would dim the attraction he'd felt from the first minutes they'd met. Instead, it was the opposite. She was tireless, smart, funny and liked by everyone she met. He couldn't remember when he'd smiled so often. Anna barked a welcome, too. It was a first.

"Hi," he said, taking in the casual green shirt that highlighted her eyes. "I do like a prompt woman."

"What about a very hungry one."

"I've never met a woman with such a big appetite."

"Should I remind you we had a bag of potato chips for lunch?"

"Only so you could get here for the sunset," Travis defended himself. "No one has really lived until they've seen a Sedona sunset."

"You're right," she said. "You did good. Let's go."

She turned and headed for the door. He was laughing as he followed.

JENNY WAS FALLING in love. She knew it. It was a first for her, and she couldn't seem to stop it from happening.

She liked every aspect of Travis. He was serious and dedicated, and yet his sense of humor emerged at the most unexpected times. He was a great questioner, thorough and thoughtful. He not only tolerated Anna but was probably more sappy about the dog than she. She knew that, although he'd been a major and Josh a noncom, they were close friends, equals in every way. She suspected there were depths and depths of him yet to be discovered.

He drove to a colorful Mexican restaurant. Anna was welcome, and they found seats on the patio. To the sound of Mexican music, they ate a huge meal, helped along by margaritas. She couldn't remember the last time she'd had one, but they were good. Wonderful, in fact. She had a second one, and the world grew even grander.

For the first time in a week, they didn't have to worry about being alert in the morning. A cool breeze tempered the day's heat, and the dark blue sky was decorated with a million stars and a rising moon.

Candles were lit as they ate their desserts, *tres leches* for him and *sopapillas* for her. They tasted each other's and debated which was best.

They finally left and dropped by a local wine-tasting room, which offered samples. Jenny stayed outside with Anna, while Travis bought a case of six bottles, two of which, he said, were for Josh and Eve, in appreciation of dinner at their house, and two for Jubal. The final two were for them.

Travis drove back to the motel and carried the wine to her room. He opened one of the bottles and poured them each a glass, and they sat on her balcony. The moon provided enough light to see the rock formations.

Warmth filled her, and a sense of well-being. She was with someone who accepted her for what and who she was, not what he wanted her to be. She didn't realize until then how much she'd needed that. One reason she'd always fled from any lasting relationship was the fear that the other person would discover her wanting in some major way. Did it go back to her father, who was always disappointed in her?

The stubborn, redheaded child who always disappointed. She'd made her own world in which she would never let anyone in. They couldn't disapprove then. Or be disappointed.

He took her hand in his. "You're thinking deep thoughts."

"Too deep," she said wryly.

"Sedona does that," Travis said. "A lot of people come here because they feel it's a place of meditation, that it's a special spot where energy is entering the earth."

Jenny was fascinated. She never would have expected him to have an interest in the spiritual. But then he was full of surprises.

"It's one reason Sedona has become so popular, and you'll see a lot of shops displaying spiritual music, books, jewelry and related items," he said as he put his arm around her. "You can add it to your list of interesting places."

"What about your friend? Did he believe the spiritual part?"

Travis shrugged. "I don't know. I looked most of it up when I left. It was interesting." He hesitated, and then he added thoughtfully, "I do know the beauty of this area helps whatever ails you. I needed it after the last few years. I thought you might, too."

Another side of him that surprised her. He was so damned perceptive. She *had* needed it, only she hadn't realized how much.

She leaned over and kissed him. "I like you," she said. "I like you very much."

"Ditto," he said, using the word she had days ago.

He stood and offered his hand. She took it and they went inside, closing the balcony door. Then he kissed her long and hard, fierce and gentle, until her knees were weak. Her arms went around him and played with the back of his neck.

She leaned against him, welcoming the warmth of his body against hers. It felt so natural, as if it was made just for her. She looked up at him. A hank of hair had fallen on his forehead, and his hazel eyes seemed darker, the amber in them more evident.

Emotions swirled, each one different but growing in strength. Tenderness, wonder, need, want. They kept tumbling into each other like a snowball going downhill. Her chest tightened, and her breathing became more difficult. She wanted to lie in bed with him and feel him everywhere. She wanted him to feel her everywhere.

He gave her a crooked smile. "Are we both done with being cautious?"

"Yes," she said simply as she started to unbutton his shirt.

"I do have protection this time," he said.

"Good thinking."

He unbuttoned her blouse and then unhooked her bra. He fondled each breast until the nipples hardened.

"My turn," she said, anxious now to hurry the process. Her body ached. She pulled his shirt over his head and caressed his scars. She then stood on tiptoes to kiss him.

It was gentle at first, but then his lips moved passionately on hers. Eddies of desire enveloped her.

She unzipped his jeans and pulled them down, but then discovered a problem. She couldn't slip them down over his shoes, and he couldn't move with them like they were. Perplexed, she looked up at him. "I didn't think about that," she said.

He burst out laughing.

"I love that look," he finally managed to say

when he finished laughing. He leaned down and pulled his pants back up. Then he went over to the bed and took off his shoes. "*Now* you can take them off," he said as he stood.

"The moment is over," she declared indignantly.

"No, it isn't," he said as he discarded his pants and skivvies and pulled her down on the bed.

She fell on top of him. "Now how are you going to take off *my* clothes?"

"Easily," he said, turning her onto her back. He then unzipped her pants and slid off her panties.

"Damn, but you're delectable," he said as his hands caressed her body and his tongue explored her mouth. She was consumed with wanting. His lips left her mouth and nibbled her ear, sending shivers of pleasure through her. He kissed the pulse at her throat, and she felt tenderness in each caress.

Tremors ran through her body as his hands continued to stroke it, sparking blazes wherever they touched. She savored each new jolt of sensation.

He bent his head and his mouth touched her breasts, teasing and nibbling until her nipples hardened and ached. Sizzling fires danced up and down her spine. He left her for a second, and then he returned and kissed her again.

His lips touched her cheeks with such tenderness that her heart hurt. Then his mouth recaptured hers in a kiss that rocked her to the core. Her body strained against his, and he entered her slowly, deliberately, igniting ripples of warm, expectant sensations. Her body moved with his as his rhythm increased, until bursts of exquisite pleasure rushed through her and his body fell on hers.

They lay there together, Travis holding Jenny in his arms as aftershocks continued. And, for the first time in her life, Jenny felt truly content.

CHAPTER TWENTY-ONE

JENNY WOKE UP to Travis's gentle nudging.

"Hmm," she murmured. She was in his arms, and she didn't want to move. "What time is it?"

"A little after six."

She yawned and snuggled deeper into his arms. "My internal clock is off."

"Good for your internal clock. I like feeling you next to me." He kissed her long and hard.

She responded with enthusiasm, even as a worrying little voice in the back of her head had questions. "What have we done?" she asked when his lips relinquished hers.

"I think they call it making love," he said lazily.

"And it was splendid but…"

"You want more than splendid?" he asked. "Greedy little devil, aren't you?"

"Practice makes perfect," she said suggestively.

"I think it's already perfect, but I'm up for more practice," he retorted.

She ran her tongue over his chest, and his body reacted immediately.

"Dammit, woman, you're playing with fire," he said. "And I woke you for a reason."

"What better reason could there be?"

"The most spectacular sunrise you've probably ever seen."

"Even better than yesterday?"

"Yep."

"That's a big promise."

"And I have a surprise."

She broke into a huge smile. "I love surprises." Still, she couldn't decide between his arms or the sunrise, but then her curiosity won. They were leaving in a few hours. She might never again have a chance to decide whether a Sedona sunrise would be the most spectacular she'd ever seen.

He knew she could never resist a challenge. She rose and peered out the balcony door and was instantly beguiled. She couldn't remember seeing anything quite as beautiful. The sun's rays bounced off the spectacular red rocks, spreading an artist's palette of gold and bronze and every possible shade of red.

Travis joined her, wearing his blue jeans. He held her long T-shirt, reminding her she was utterly naked. Before she could slip it on, he kissed the back of her neck, sending tremors down her back. "That was not fair," she said, "but nice."

He disappeared again and, in several minutes, showed up with coffee he'd brewed in the room's coffee machine. She gratefully took a sip and, now at least partially clothed, opened the balcony door and stepped out. The view was wider outside, even more spectacular. She knew now what he meant.

The colors, the rock formations and the pure deep blue of the sky made her soul sing. She doubted whether the energy of the place had anything to do with it. But Travis certainly did. He knew her. Despite the short time they'd been together, he knew her better than anyone ever had.

And he still liked her. Maybe even more than liked.

"We have so little time here," he broke into her thoughts, "and there's so much to see, I thought maybe you would like to take a Jeep trip up into the hills. It goes off-road and it's about two and a half hours. The drivers are great, really knowledgeable about the history of the area, wildlife and flora. You can learn a lot about the area in the shortest possible time. I checked, and we can get one at nine thirty."

"What about Anna?"

"Since we're the only passengers, we can take her."

"How did you arrange that?"

"I have my ways," he said.

She eyed him suspiciously. This was probably a very expensive Jeep ride, but it sounded wonderful. Just the kind of adventure she loved.

She stood on tiptoes and kissed him roundly.

"Do we have time for anything else?" she asked suggestively.

He grinned. "I can always make time," he said. And he did.

JENNY COULDN'T STOP talking about the Jeep trip during the two-hour drive to the Grand Canyon. It had been a wild off-road trek over rocks and through trails with a humorous guide who was a retired banker. It had been scary, educational and fascinating.

"How did you know about the Jeeps?" she asked, petting Anna in her lap.

"That Ranger buddy of mine took me on one years ago. As a teenager, he used to help in their office and filled in as a guide when necessary. Each guide does his own thing, although there are some central musts."

"They seemed to enjoy scaring the wits out of passengers," she said of the hair-raising ride up and down giant rocks without roads, but she got a close glimpse of the trees and plants, and even some wildlife. She loved every moment of it. Anna, on the other hand, slept all the way through the experience.

"That's part of the attraction, I think," he said. "You should come back sometime and take the hot air balloon tour. It's always early in the morning, when there's usually less wind."

"You've done that, too?"

"Yeah. I have good memories of Sedona, although it's changed a lot since I've last been here. It's a lot larger, and the traffic is a hell of a lot worse."

She'd wondered how he'd arranged the Jeep trip for just the two of them on the spur of the moment, but suspected a lot of money was responsible. She would insist on paying half. It was worth every cent.

She stopped talking then and concentrated on the drive up to the Grand Canyon.

It was a two-and-a-half-hour drive. They stopped for a quick lunch in Flagstaff, at a restaurant with a dog-friendly patio, and then they were off again.

She was in awe of it all. The drive was spectacular, and Travis pointed out the golden aspen, the giant pines and the majesty of the ponderosa giant oaks.

She'd been in the Alps and the German Black Forest and the Scottish Highlands, and all had their individual beauty, but there was something about the majesty of these red mountains that took her breath away.

Was this what she'd been looking for? She'd found so many stories on this trip. Stories that weren't about death and destruction and starvation and the murder of children.

But then who would tell those stories?

"You're very quiet," Travis said as he pulled into an overlook.

"I'm just soaking it all in," she said. "It's breathtaking, and I don't use the word often." She petted Anna, who repositioned herself on her lap. Anna's whiskers signaled approval.

"I like that dog," Travis said. "She has good taste."

"I knew you would," she said with satisfaction.

She started to ask a question, when her cell phone rang. Except for using it to record conversations, she hadn't used it much. She hadn't expected anyone to call, but saw it was Lenore. "Hey there," she answered, surprised at the call.

"Where are you?" Lenore asked.

"Nearing the Grand Canyon."

"I thought you were on a business trip."

"I am. We're on the way back, and since I've never seen the Grand Canyon, we're making a stop. I'll be back in Covenant Falls by Monday night."

"Someone called for you. A David Brent. He wants you to call him."

"He didn't say anything else?"

"No. He called Mother because that was the

only number he had. Your old number apparently isn't active. He wants you to call him." She hesitated. "I didn't give him your number. I thought you might want some warning first."

David Brent was the executive editor of the largest news service she'd submitted articles to. He'd called her when she was in the hospital, and she'd told him she would contact him when she was ready to return to work. It wasn't a matter of if; it was a matter of when.

She didn't think it was a social call now. David didn't do social.

She didn't have to write the number down. She knew it well.

"How's Charlie?" She didn't want to think about the implications of David's call yet.

"Fine. She likes the new school and is already in accelerated classes. She'd dying to meet Anna. The photos were great. So you will be back in Covenant Falls Monday night?"

"That's the plan."

"Are you going to stay in Covenant Falls longer?"

"Yes. I'm not sure how long."

"Charlie has a school holiday coming up in two weeks. Teacher Training or something. She's dying to go down there. If you're still going to be there, I thought we could drive down on Friday morning and stay the weekend if you're not too busy."

She didn't know whether she would be or not, but she knew Charlie would love Covenant Falls. Jenny wanted her niece to visit Jubal's ranch and learn to ride. "Of course not," she said. "I'll make reservations for you at the inn. You'll love it. It's loaded with personality."

"Great," her sister said. "I'm looking forward to it." She paused, and then she added, "And don't forget about Mr. Brent. He seemed anxious."

"I won't," she promised and hung up before Lenore could ask another question. She didn't want to talk about the future in front of Travis. She didn't want to talk about it at all now.

Wasn't that what she wanted? Her shoulder was getting better, or at least she thought so. The pain wasn't quite as sharp when she did her exercises. Was it well enough to return to the Middle East? Did she *want* to go back? She'd always been so sure before. Always known every step she would take.

"Charlie's your niece, right?" Travis asked.

"Right."

He didn't ask any more questions. Of course he wouldn't. He didn't pry. She was relieved he didn't because she didn't have any answers. A month ago, she would have returned David's call immediately. Now…she wasn't sure. She didn't want to spoil this weekend. She didn't want to think about next week, or next month.

They saw signs indicating the approach to the Grand Canyon entrance gate. Travis paid the entrance fee and obtained directions for the lodge. The roads were crowded, but she suspected not as much as they were yesterday. She'd discovered that Sunday night was usually less crowded in popular attractions. Still, traffic had slowed to a crawl.

He found the lodge, and they checked into their room. Then he grabbed her hand in his good one, and with Anna in tow, they took off for the rim.

It was about a mile away. A shuttle existed, but it didn't take dogs. That was all right. They were both stiff from the car, and there was a clear sky and cool breeze. And she was a people watcher. There were certainly a lot of people to see. Many were foreigners who had come long distances to see what had been in her backyard.

As they neared the main rim area, she saw more and more of the canyon. The afternoon sun painted the cliffs in gold. They took her breath away.

They reached the outlook and glanced down. A long, steep trail led downward, and she would have been on it a year ago. Now she wouldn't trust her shoulder to catch her if she slipped.

She looked at Travis's face. It was so damn

strong, but she saw the same wistfulness she felt. She remembered him saying he walked down into the canyon with his friend. His leg probably wouldn't allow it now. Her hand tightened around his, and she leaned into him.

She knew she wanted to come back, maybe ride a donkey down into the canyon or raft down the river, or just bask in the wonder of the sheer majesty of the place.

"Thank you for bringing me here," she said simply as her heart seemed to overflow with so many emotions, she didn't really know how to contain them. Wonder. Joy. Warmth. Possibilities.

AN IDEA HAD started to form in her mind from the seed that had been planted in Raton. It had grown throughout the week as they visited ranches owned by people who cared enough about veterans to spend all their resources in helping them. There were the small-town restaurants with good-hearted waitresses, the quirky museums and Karen who trained dogs for veterans with PTSD.

She envisioned a series of articles about the sublime to ridiculous that could then be made into a book. She wanted to share her own amazement and joy and appreciation of a country she barely knew. She even had a tentative title: "Exploring America through Fresh Eyes" or something similar, with the subtitle, "The Beautiful and the Wacky." She might have to work on that a little bit.

She wondered if she could sell David on it. That reminded her of his call. She couldn't believe she had forgotten it, that she hadn't called him back.

She realized then she didn't want to go back to war. It had slowly been killing her soul. She hadn't really felt joy in a very long time. There had been satisfaction in writing a good story. Writing was her life's blood, but writing about tragedy had also been draining her.

She took her eyes away from the canyon and looked up at Travis. He raised one eyebrow, recognizing that something had happened, had changed, and his arm went around her.

He smiled, and her heart cracked. It was that crooked smile caused by the scar, but she had come to like that face very much. Despite his career as a warrior, he was compassionate, with a desire to make the world better.

His ex-fiancé had to be one of the world's greatest fools.

Her fingers tightened around his. Anna barked as if she sensed a change of some kind.

They walked around the rim, getting different views and stopping at one of the big telescopes to get a better look. "How does it look from down there," she asked wistfully.

"Even more awesome than from here," he said. "Maybe someday we can raft the Colorado through here."

Someday. We. Implying a future.

But he didn't know what he would do or where he would go next, and neither did she.

He broke the spell, as if uncomfortable himself with what he'd said. "I'll treat you to an ice cream cone."

They bought ice cream cones with chocolate fudge toppings and found a place to sit where they could watch the canyon walls change color as the sun headed west. Anna happily settled down under the bench where she could safely watch people go past, some of whom stopped to tell her what a charming dog she was and asked what breed. No one had ever heard of an affenpinscher before. The usually shy Anna seemed to bask in the praise.

Travis and Jenny stayed there until the sun went down in glorious colors, and they oohed and aahed with everyone else. Jenny started conversations with any number of the tourists, including a seven-year-old boy who wanted to take Anna home with him.

They bought two hot dogs for supper and watched the moonrise. She thought it amazing they could be silent and still so comfortable. She found herself leaning into him. His arm went around her, and she felt safe and happy and wanted. It was nearly ten before they left, Anna trotting happily alongside them. Jenny could barely believe she was the withdrawn dog of a week ago. She obviously felt comfortable. Safe. It suddenly hit her that she hadn't had a flashback or nightmare since that first night. Because of Anna? Or Travis? Or both?

When they reached the room, he poured them both a glass of wine and they sat on a lumpy sofa, his arm around her, and Anna at her feet. "I don't want to leave," she said.

"I don't either," he said. "But we should be on the road by six in the morning. It's going to be a long drive."

"I think my shoulder is better," she said. "Maybe I can relieve you in the long stretches without much traffic."

He nodded and said, "We had better go to bed. It's nearly eleven. I'll take Anna out for a last walk."

After he left, she eyed the two queen beds and tried one, and then the other. They didn't compare with those at the Camel Trail Inn. She picked one, turned it down and went into the shower.

The water was perfect by the time he joined her. They soaped each other and then fell into each other's arms, oblivious of the hot water. She'd never wanted someone so much.

She didn't know who turned off the water, but they stumbled from the shower, grabbing towels and drying each other before falling on the bed. The first time they made love, he'd been a gentle lover, but now he was as hungry as she. He thrust again and again, sweeping them both into pure sensation that climaxed in one magnificent, blazing explosion. He fell on her, and together, they rolled to the side.

He wrapped his arms around her, and they went to sleep.

THEY WOKE AS the sun filtered into the room.

Travis looked at the clock. They were well behind the hour he'd expected to leave.

He didn't regret a minute of it. Yesterday and last night ranked as the best in his life.

Jenny was still sleeping. She looked peaceful and had a smile on her lips, as if she'd experienced a wonderful dream. He leaned down and kissed her. Her eyes opened, and the smile widened.

"Good morning," she said slowly.

"It is that, but we should leave. It's after seven."

"Oops," she said. "I'll be ready in twenty minutes." She practically jumped out of bed and headed for the bathroom.

Nineteen minutes later, she met him in the car. And ten minutes after that, they left the park. She looked longingly back but knew that yesterday would always be vivid in her heart. It was the best day of her life.

CHAPTER TWENTY-TWO

TRAVIS WARNED HER it was a long drive with few places to stop.

He was right.

The traffic going in and out of the park Monday morning was not nearly as bad as it had been coming in. Travis drove for an hour, and then he stopped at a gas station, where he filled up the gas tank and ordered two large coffees to go. Food choices were limited.

Neither had eaten breakfast. Hunger made them choose overcooked hot dogs—one each for the humans and one for Anna—and they were back on the road.

Jenny was sleepy and had to force herself to stay awake. Travis turned on the radio, but there were only a few channels available, mostly country and talk. While Jenny liked country once in a while, a steady diet grew old fast.

But the noise kept them alert. She'd put Anna in the dog car carrier so she could follow the map while she sought to discover more about Travis.

Particularly his family, because he'd said so little about them.

"Eve said you played baseball in college," she said. "Where did you go?"

"The state university. Baseball isn't nearly as big as football, but it had a good overall sports program."

"And you were a pitcher?"

"Yeah. Not good enough for the majors, and I knew it. But I liked sports, and it was a field that interested me. I wasn't cut out to be a businessman, or engineer or manager who is in an office every day."

"And yet you turned out to be some of all three, unless I'm wrong about the role of a Ranger officer."

He looked sheepish. "I guess you're right."

She plunged and asked the big one. "What about family?"

He didn't answer for a long time. She thought he wouldn't, that she shouldn't have pried, but then they'd seemed to be beyond that now. She wanted to know what made him who he was today.

He shrugged. "I told you my father had a farm. It had been in the family for nearly a hundred years. Farming was his life, and his goal in life was to ensure that the farm remained in the Hammond family. After I was born, my mother had two stillbirths, but my father demanded she keep trying. He wanted sons in the plural—mainly, I think, because he recognized that I wasn't at all interested in farming." Jenny saw his fingers tighten around the steering wheel as he continued.

"Mom became pregnant again. She was older then, in her forties, and she died in childbirth. But she gave my father what he wanted, my brother, Adam.

"My father and I fought from the time I was little, but it became worse after my mother died. I don't think I ever forgave him for my mother. I blamed her death on him. I thought he was sacrificing us for a way of life that was dying. It was work dawn to dusk, with barely enough money to pay the bills. The land was worn out. He couldn't let himself see it."

His voice turned hollow as he continued. "As much as I hated the farm, I loved sports. Dad thought I should work the farm and wouldn't sign the necessary papers for me to play high school baseball. I made a bargain with him. I would work early in the morning and late in the evening, but the afternoons were mine. That's when I practiced baseball.

"It worked for a while, but Dad was increasingly demanding. He was losing control, and he knew it."

Jenny interrupted. "You don't have to..."

"Yes I do," he replied. "I've never talked about it before. Maybe it's time." Still, he hesitated before continuing. "Adam was getting old enough to work on the farm. He was ten when I was eighteen and he loved working with the animals and growing things. He would offer to do some of my work for me, and I took advantage of it. He was a good kid."

The tone of his voice changed. "I did get two scholarship offers, one in my home state and one at a university two states away. I took the one two states away. The farther I could get from the farm, the happier I was.

"I had a lot of reasons not to go home. In addition to academics and baseball, I volunteered with an inner city Little League team and had a part-time job with a youth center. It meant I didn't go home which was okay. I wasn't welcome there."

He glanced at her, and she nodded for him to continue.

"I finished with a bachelor's degree in sports management, but I needed a master's. I wanted to go into the athletic management on the college level. Then Nine-Eleven happened and I went into the Officers Candidate School, then Ranger training.

"Adam and I had kept in touch through letters mailed to a friend of his. Two days after his high school graduation, he enlisted. He hadn't asked me about enlisting, or talked to me about it, maybe because he feared I would argue him out of it. He applied to Ranger School, made it through and was sent to Iraq. He was killed in his fourth month there. I heard it happened when he was trying to help some Iraqi kids.

"My father blamed me. He basically disowned me. I tried to call after Adam's death, but he always hung up on me. One time I visited, and he wouldn't open the door.

"He died three years later of a heart attack, after losing the farm to the bank. He never told me he was in financial trouble. If he had, I would have helped him."

There was such sadness in the last sentences, she almost cried. It was obvious he blamed himself for both deaths.

She reached over and touched his hand on the wheel. "Adam must have been one heck of a kid."

"He was."

"Is that why you're looking after Danny?"

He looked startled for a moment, and then he nodded. "I wasn't aware of it, but yeah, maybe."

They lapsed into silence then. He turned the radio up.

It explained a lot about him. About why he hadn't mentioned his family, why he'd been so good with Nick and other kids he'd spoken with on the trip, why he'd basically adopted Danny. Had Josh known about his family, or had he just recognized someone who cared about other people? Was that why he'd enlisted him in this project?

She rested a hand on his leg. She wanted to do more, to let him know she understood.

It was time, she thought, to share her own insecurities. She wanted him to know why she'd felt such a need for independence. They were at a point now, she knew, to either break apart clean or explore a future that could forever change their lives. Were either of them ready for that?

She only knew she'd never been happier. She would be a fool to throw it away because of fear. But could she merge a life with Travis and her instinct to run to the nearest story?

She was jumping ahead of herself. He'd never said anything about a life beyond this week. Sure, the past week had been terrific. But would it be enough for her? Or Travis?

She decided to be honest. "We have something in common," she said. "A difficult father. Mine also wanted me to be something I wasn't, never could be. Women, in his world, were obedient wives and daughters. From the day I was born, he resented me. My sisters—both of them—were tall and blond and obedient, at least until lately. They were popular, ran with the right crowd and married men in the same class, and of the same stripe, as my father. I was a skinny redhead, rebellious and fought with him until I left after high school. I put myself through college with scholarships and part-time jobs."

"Your mother?"

"A pretty woman who drinks too much and is afraid to say no to him. He's often away, and I'm sure—and I think Mother is, too—that he's having affairs. He expects her to entertain grandly, and when everything in't perfect, he doesn't take it well.

"The house was never happy, although I think my older sisters were oblivious. They were cheerleaders, popular among the affluent community. I've heard daughters often marry men like their fathers. They did. Successful, charming men who didn't want partners but a useful wife who stayed at home and didn't complain when they had affairs.

"But I was always different," she continue. "I escaped into books, and I had this intense curiosity that drove my father nuts. I was always disappearing into the local library."

Travis was silent but his right hand left the steering wheel and covered hers for a moment before returning to the wheel.

She put her hand on his leg. "After I was released from the hospital, I was pretty helpless.

My mother insisted I stay with them. My father was gone most of the time—he had an apartment in San Francisco where the corporate headquarters is located. He's head of the firm's central region. He could be very charming when he wanted something."

She hesitated.

"Go on," he urged her.

"I stayed there because Mother wanted it, but as soon as I was well enough to do things on my own, I moved in with my sister, Lenore, and her daughter, Charlie, whom I adore."

"And now?"

"I don't know. The call that came while we were on the way to the Grand Canyon? It was from the executive editor of one of the news services I worked with."

"And?"

"And I haven't called back."

He smiled. "That doesn't sound like you."

"It's not," she said. "But he wouldn't call to fire me, since I'm not an employee. I'm an independent contractor."

"You think he wants you to go back?"

"Maybe. Part of me wants to return. I want to know what happened in Aleppo the day I was injured, but in the past few days, I've learned there are other important stories to tell."

She paused, and then she added, "I thought

telling war stories was important. I'm learning it's just as important—no, more important—to tell the stories of people who make a difference. I've seen so much in the past few days I want to write about. Not only the places, but the people. People like Karen and Dr. Payne and the ranchers who are pouring their hearts and souls into programs to help veterans.

"Then there's Covenant Falls and the woman doctor who chose to work in a small town, and Stephanie, who goes out in the worse possible weather with search and rescue dogs to find lost people. I haven't met her yet, but I want to. People like Jubal and Eve and the others we met this past week. I'd forgotten how generous people could be."

She was afraid she sounded like she was on a soapbox, but ideas were running rampant in her mind, had been for the past week. "People need to read about those stories, as well as the bad," she continued slowly, trying to find the right words. "I didn't realize how writing about conflicts and the resulting damage was eating into my soul, until I saw the Grand Canyon.

"Even sadder," she added, "I can't remember when I last laughed before meeting you. I can't stop smiling now, and I want my words to bring smiles, not tears."

She took a long breath.

"Don't stop now," he said. "I like the direction you're taking."

"I just know I want to watch hundreds of sunrises with you, and I want to dance with you in the rain, even if awkwardly. I want to watch you on the athletic field with kids who think you're wonderful."

"Wow. All of that," he said with that lopsided smile. "That's kind of a big order."

"You think it's too much?" she said worriedly.

He burst out laughing. "It's one hell of a list. But after watching you in action this past week, I don't think anything is impossible."

She looked at him, wondering if he was understanding what she was saying.

They were on a straight slice of road, and he reached out for her hand and put his over it. "I think it's a terrific list."

The car started to wander to the left, and he grabbed the wheel with both hands again.

Jenny's breath caught. The bottom fell out of her stomach, but she tried to make light of it. "Just think?" she asked.

"Pretty sure," he added, "but I'm not sure this is the place to discuss it."

"I'll wait," she said and put her hand on his leg. "When is the next stop?"

"You're very forward, aren't you?" he teased.

"It's better than not being forward enough," she replied.

"Point taken."

They reached Durango and grabbed a quick lunch. While he was getting gas, she called David.

His hearty voice greeted her. "Your sister said you're doing better. Well enough to go back?"

She didn't answer immediately.

"I have an offer for you," he said. "Full-time war correspondent. I keep getting calls from newspapers wanting your stuff."

It had been what she wanted these past years. What she had worked for. She looked back at Travis. He was replacing the gas cap. The sun glinted on his hair, turning it to gold. She thought about those warm hazel eyes that smiled. She hesitated.

"I have other news," David said. "Rick returned to Syria, found a doctor from the medical unit present when you were injured. He told me how affected you were about a child…that you kept asking about her. Well, apparently, she survived. She's in a refugee camp in Jordan." He paused. "Now what about that job?"

"Did he get the name?" she asked, ignoring his question. "Does she have any family left?"

"Apparently she does. You'll have to contact Rick for more information. Now about that job…"

She swallowed hard. "I'm not going back," she

said. "But I have an idea…several actually. I'll send them to you." She hung up before he could say anything.

The girl was safe. That was what was important. She couldn't wait to tell Travis. But she would wait. Until tonight.

IT WAS 9:00 P.M. before they finally drove up to Josh's cabin. They'd stopped twice more, each time staying no longer than fifteen minutes. They had been in the car twelve straight hours and hadn't killed each other. It was a good sign.

He'd asked whether she wanted to go to the inn, and she looked at him as if he'd just turned green. "No," she said. "I texted that I wouldn't arrive tonight."

He raised an eyebrow. "Taking things for granted, are you?"

"I think Susan would be happy if I changed my mind." She teased.

"No way, woman."

He unlocked the door, walked Anna inside, sprawled wearily on the huge sofa and patted the seat next to him. Before she could take it, Anna jumped up and settled next to him.

"That's my place," Jenny said to Anna as she set the dog on the floor. "You have to wait your turn."

"It's nice to be fought over," Travis said. "What about joint custody?" he shot back.

It took her a minute to realize what he meant. Or did he mean what she thought it meant? For a moment, she panicked.

"Joint custody?" she finally asked.

"We share her," he said patiently. "But you'll have to move to Covenant Falls."

"What about you?"

"I called Josh a few nights ago and asked if he knew of any available jobs in the area. I want to see Jubal's program through."

"And?" she asked, holding her breath.

"Damn if he wasn't way ahead of me." He held out his hand and pulled her down next to him. "There's a vacancy coming up at the high school. A coaching job. The current coach had a good offer at a larger school but hadn't wanted to leave until the season is over. Josh mentioned I might be available, and he said there was instant enthusiasm. Apparently I'm qualified to be a coach now on a provisional basis, and I can teach once I get a teacher's certificate. I can do most of that online."

"You're a shoo-in," she said. "What school wouldn't want a former Ranger heading their athletics? Talk about keeping kids in line. And isn't it what you always wanted to do?"

"It's not a certainty," he warned.

"Ha!" she said. "I've known Josh Manning long enough to know he wouldn't have brought it up if it wasn't a done deal. His wife is mayor after all."

"A lot depends on you," he said. "And that list of yours, especially the part about watching sunrises and dancing in the rain even if I am a bit clumsy. Would you consider making Covenant Falls your base?"

"My base?"

"I wouldn't expect to tame that roaming spirit of yours, nor would I want to. It's who you are, but maybe you can make this your home base. I've seen enough people send their spouses off. I know how to make it work." He paused, and then he added, "Now that I've found you, I don't want to lose you."

"*Spouse.* That's a scary word."

"I didn't think anything scared you."

"You might just have found the one thing that would," she said. "But I think losing you is even scarier. And I certainly don't want to get into a custody battle over Anna."

She held onto his hand. "I talked to the editor of the news service I've been working with," she said suddenly. "While you were getting gas."

He stilled. "And?"

"He wanted to give me a full-time job overseas. I said no. I want to stay here in the States and tell happier stories. Because of you. You made me see them and how important they are."

"Another thing…" she added.

He raised an eyebrow in question.

"The girl I told you about. She's alive. She's in a refugee camp. Maybe…"

He nodded. He knew exactly what she was thinking. Maybe he always had… He kissed the tip of her nose. "Have I told you that you have a big heart." His hand caressed her cheek before adding, "Along with a very nice nose, fantastic eyes and a thoroughly kissable mouth?"

"Nope. Not yet," she replied. "Has anyone told *you* that you are a superb kisser, an extremely nice man…"

"Ouch," he said. "That's the kiss of death."

"Be quiet, I didn't finish," she scolded. "You're also the sexiest man and…"

"Have I…?"

"Be quiet," she said and leaned over and gave him a kiss that told him everything he wanted to know.

EPILOGUE

Seven months later

It was a beautiful April morning, and to her amazement, Jenny Talbot was getting married.

"Are you ready?" Travis asked with so much love in his voice that her heart sang. No reservations?

"A few quivers, maybe," she said, her smile belying the words.

As usual he could read her. He knew she was nervous. She was doing something she'd vowed never to do.

According to wedding etiquette, he shouldn't be here, but she'd never paid attention to protocol and tradition before, and this was not the time to start.

The simple fact was she needed him with her to quash any doubts that lingered.

It wasn't that she wasn't sure she loved him. She did. With all her heart and soul, but the old doubts kept cropping up. Could she let go of that lifelong struggle for independence and compulsion to wander the world? She knew Travis understood that was a part of her. He'd made it clear he would support any stories she wanted to cover, wherever they may take her.

Her lust for dangerous places and taking chances, though, was fading away. She had found something else. In addition to Travis, she had Anna now and a veteran-trained mustang, thanks to Jubal. She'd become closer to Lenore and Charlie, and the entire Covenant Falls veteran family had taken her into their ranks.

"I should go," Travis said as he leaned down and gave her one last kiss before they officially wed. "I have some shaving and dressing to do, and your mother, sisters and Charlie will be here soon. I don't want them scandalized. By the way, I think Charlie's turning into another you."

"Scary, isn't it?" she said after kissing him and reluctantly shooing him toward the door.

"For some lucky guy, yes," he replied as he opened the door. "See you at our wedding. I love you."

He left, and she contemplated the closed door. She hadn't wanted him to leave, even if he was just walking four houses down to Josh's cabin. She hadn't seen much of him in the past few days. He was working long days as the new coach at Covenant High School, and they were now in the midst of baseball season. He was finally doing what he'd always wanted to do, and he loved it. He loved his kids, and the baseball team was winning for the first time in years. Football hadn't gone that well, but he vowed it would next year.

She'd stayed at the inn for several months after their return. It had been free because she'd continually worked with Josh, Jubal and Travis in developing the equine program. She also wrote quirky ads and news releases for the inn which was steadily becoming more popular.

Then a cottage on the lake came for sale and Travis bought it. He stayed in Josh's cabin while she moved into the cottage. It wasn't exactly perfect because his new job required a certain amount of discretion. She didn't think anyone was fooled, though.

Tonight, it would be official.

They'd planned a small wedding at the waterfall at noon, the best time for the rainbow.

It was where she had first started to fall in love with Travis although she hadn't known it then. Because the park wasn't suitable for a large gathering, they'd limited the wedding to the group of veterans—and their families. Jubal was planning a much larger reception and barbecue at his ranch at four.

She thought back to the day she'd met them. So much had happened since then.

Jubal had followed Travis's recommendations

to develop a program much like Bill's. It joined the emotional benefit of interaction with horses with building useful skills. The first group of twelve veterans had finished the month-long program and a new group had just arrived. Three members of the first group left with service dogs that Stephanie and her husband, Clint, trained with the long-distance help of Karen.

There was a waiting list now, and the ranch was receiving referrals from the VA. Donations were coming in, thanks to an article written by Jennifer Talbot.

The doorbell rang, Anna barked, and Jenny opened the door to receive a hug from her mother who'd arrived yesterday with Lenore and Charlie, who was clutching a small black poodle puppy Jenny had given her in lieu of Anna. Then Stacy stepped out from behind them. "Hello, sis," she said.

Jenny thought her heart would explode. She hugged her older sister. "I'm so happy you came."

"I wouldn't miss it. We wanted it to be a surprise."

"Father?"

Stacy shook her head. "Business," she said.

"Where are you staying?" Jenny asked. "I thought the inn was full. You could have stayed with me."

"We didn't want to complicate things for you,"

Lenore said. "Mom and I had reserved separate rooms at the inn. Stacy is staying with me and Charlie is staying with Mom along with the puppy. They're getting along just fine. By the way, Charlie and I think Travis is terrific."

"They've been singing his praises," Stacy said as they walked inside the living room. "I've brought along a few items..."

Lenore handed her a box of cinnamon rolls sent by Susan Hall. "I love the inn," she said. Then she noticed Travis's jacket on a chair and two coffee cups on a table.

"You didn't?"

"I did." Jenny grinned as she took a bite of cinnamon roll.

"Well, let's get you ready," Lenore said. She'd helped Jenny select the classic moss green dress that fit her slim body well, along with matching shoes. "I'll start on the makeup. Stacy will do your hair..." An hour later, Jenny barely recognized herself. Miracles had happened. Or maybe it was just the glow she felt as, for the first time, she felt like a loved and accepted member of the family.

EVE PICKED THEM up and drove them to the waterfall site.

To Jenny's astonishment, the parking lot was full, including two school buses. They were met by Josh and an equally puzzled Travis, who spread out his arms as if to say he didn't know what in the heck was going on.

Josh gave her a kiss on the cheek. "Sorry about this," he said, "Apparently the news got out. The football and baseball teams threatened to crash the wedding if they weren't invited. It sort of grew from there."

Jenny looked around. Probably a hundred or more chairs had been placed in front of an arch entwined with roses. A group of high school musicians tuned their instruments. The park's picnic tables were covered with white tablecloths, and Maude was guarding several large refrigerated chests of food. The owner of the Rusty Nail stood by with more refrigerated chests.

Big high school football players bashfully approached them to offer their congratulations. The leaner baseball players sauntered over and saluted.

"You did good, Coach," the spokesman said, and the others hoorayed.

It seemed the entire community had wrapped their collective arms around them.

Tears came to her eyes. Gratitude swelled through her as she clutched Travis's hand. For someone who had been the ultimate observer, she was moved beyond any expression. Her hand tightened around his. He squeezed it as ranchers and townspeople surrounded them.

The sun seemed even brighter as everyone took their seats. A young woman started singing "One Hand, One Heart" from *West Side Story* as Travis tightened his hold on her hand and they walked down the aisle to face the minister.

The one thing she'd insisted on was approaching the altar together. She didn't want him waiting for her, or her waiting for him.

"Ever the rebel," Travis had teased.

When they reached the arch of roses, she turned to him. His gaze was so full of love, it made her ache down to her toes. "I love you," he whispered.

"Me, too," she whispered back.

And then Pastor John started. She'd heard the words a hundred times in films but now every word had a special meaning. Together, they meant forever. For a moment, fear overtook her, and then his touch chased it away.

When they finished exchanging vows, and Pastor John said they could kiss, Travis's lips touched hers with so much tenderness, she thought she would melt.

She started to hear laughter as the kiss continued, and he reluctantly released her, but kept his hand on hers as they turned. Everyone was standing up, laughing, applauding and rejoicing with them.

One of his football players yelled out, "Way to go, Coach."

She knew then that her observer days were over.

Both she and Travis had found the place where they belonged. They had come home.

* * * * *

If you enjoyed
THE SOLDIER'S HOMECOMING,
you'll love the other books in
Patricia Potter's
HOME TO COVENANT FALLS *miniseries!*

THE SOLDIER'S PROMISE
TEMPTED BY THE SOLDIER
A SOLDIER'S JOURNEY
THE SEAL'S RETURN

All available now from
Harlequin Superromance.

We hope you enjoyed this story from
Harlequin® Superromance.

Harlequin® Superromance is coming to an end soon,
but heartfelt tales of family, friendship, community
and love are around the corner with
Harlequin® Special Edition
and **Harlequin® Heartwarming**!

Romance is for life, and these stories show that
every chapter in a relationship has its challenges
and delights and that love can be
renewed with each turn of the page!

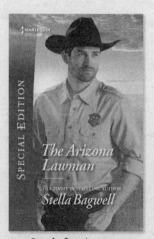

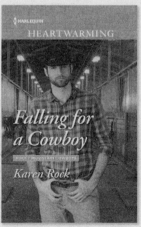

Look for six new
romances every month!

Look for four new
romances every month!

Get 2 Free Books,

Plus 2 Free Gifts -

just for trying the *Reader Service!*

Get 2 Free Books,
Plus 2 Free Gifts —
just for trying the Reader Service!

Get 2 Free Books,

Plus 2 Free Gifts—

just for trying the Reader Service!

YES! Please send me 2 FREE Harlequin® Special Edition novels and my 2 FREE gifts (gifts are worth about $10 retail). After receiving them, if I don't wish to receive any more books, I can return the shipping statement marked "cancel." If I don't cancel, I will receive 6 brand-new novels every month and be billed just $4.99 per book in the U.S. or $5.74 per book in Canada. That's a savings of at least 12% off the cover price! It's quite a bargain! Shipping and handling is just 50¢ per book in the U.S. and 75¢ per book in Canada*. I understand that accepting the 2 free books and gifts places me under no obligation to buy anything. I can always return a shipment and cancel at any time. The free books and gifts are mine to keep no matter what I decide.

235/335 HDN GMWS

Name _____ (PLEASE PRINT)

Address _____ Apt. #

City _____ State/Province _____ Zip/Postal Code

Signature (if under 18, a parent or guardian must sign)

Mail to the **Reader Service:**
IN U.S.A.: P.O. Box 1341, Buffalo, NY 14240-8531
IN CANADA: P.O. Box 603, Fort Erie, Ontario L2A 5X3

Want to try two free books from another line?
Call 1-800-873-8635 or visit www.ReaderService.com.

*Terms and prices subject to change without notice. Prices do not include applicable taxes. Sales tax applicable in N.Y. Canadian residents will be charged applicable taxes. Offer not valid in Quebec. This offer is limited to one order per household. Books received may not be as shown. Not valid for current subscribers to Harlequin® Special Edition books. All orders subject to approval. Credit or debit balances in a customer's account(s) may be offset by any other outstanding balance owed by or to the customer. Please allow 4 to 6 weeks for delivery. Offer available while quantities last.

Your Privacy—The Reader Service is committed to protecting your privacy. Our Privacy Policy is available online at www.ReaderService.com or upon request from the Reader Service.

We make a portion of our mailing list available to reputable third parties that offer products we believe may interest you. If you prefer that we not exchange your name with third parties, or if you wish to clarify or modify your communication preferences, please visit us at www.ReaderService.com/consumerschoice or write to us at Reader Service Preference Service, P.O. Box 9062, Buffalo, NY 14240-9062. Include your complete name and address.

HSE17R3

Get 2 Free Books,
Plus 2 Free Gifts—
just for trying the Reader Service!

H HARLEQUIN *Desire*

READERSERVICE.COM

Manage your account online!

- Review your order history
- Manage your payments
- Update your address

*We've designed the
Reader Service website
just for you.*

Enjoy all the features!

- Discover new series available to you, and read excerpts from any series.
- Respond to mailings and special monthly offers.
- Browse the Bonus Bucks catalog and online-only exculsives.
- Share your feedback.

Visit us at:

ReaderService.com